Assigned to Murder

Assigned to Murder

a Philippa Barnes mystery

Trish McCormack

Glacier Press

First published in 2009 by Poutini Press
This edition published in 2016 by Glacier Press

Published by
Glacier Press
Wellington
New Zealand
glacierpress@gmail.com
2016
Cover photographs by Stephen Lowe
Cover design by Jared Davidson garage.collective@gmail.com

ISBN: 978-0-473-35784-9

Typesetting services by BOOKOW.COM

To my parents Elizabeth and Peter McCormack who always believed I could do this - but never thought I would finish it!

Acknowledgments

This book has become a reality with the help of many people. I would especially like to thank Di Hooper who rang me out of the blue one day and asked me if she could read my manuscript. Since then we have met many times over a glass of wine in Wellington to discuss the Coast and my novel. Di was my first publisher, her company Poutini Press transformed my novel into a real book. I would also like to thank Dr Anne Hall for her belief in my writing – and for telling Di about it. Di's fellow publishers Bruce Watson and Bruce Hamilton have been immensely supportive. Cecilia Edwards read my first efforts back in the days when we both lived in Hokitika – then years later in Wellington read Assigned to Murder and made some great suggestions. Ann and the late Francie Bradley added fantastic colour to life below the lake surface with their stories of eels. Thanks also to Mike Bradstock for his meticulous editing – and for more facts on eels. Kate McKenzie gave valuable feedback on the manuscript– and came up with the perfect title. My cousin Stephen Lowe took atmospheric photos of Lake Kaniere in its many moods which have been used by Jared Davidson to create an evocative cover to fit the crime. And in this digital world we live in, the continuance of the bricks-and-mortar bookshop is a thing for us all to celebrate. My thanks to Claudia Landis and Bruce Watson for promoting authors such as myself in their wonderful Hokitika book shop. And to Caro Lankow and Cat Connor for doing the same in their unique indie bookshop Writers Plot Readers Read in Upper Hutt. Bookshops like these are gold.

Chapter 1

I've come back, though I said I never would.

The lake is black. The waters reflect the mountains and hide death. I walked to the shore last night and waited for the ghosts to come creeping out to meet me. They didn't. There's no atmosphere at all, just stillness and peace. No accusation. No sense of terror.

Nothing lasts. Not love, not cruelty, and not fear.

Some years I go to the Anzac service just to hear those lines about the soldiers who never grow old - the ones who died. It's soothing. But it's not enough. I want to confess, but too many people would be hurt if I tried to ease my conscience, and it can make no difference now to the person who really matters.

Today I walked beside the lake, stopped outside the bach and tried to remember just what it was that made us go so far. I looked down the ragged line of trees and counted the broken palings on the fence. I walked up the driveway, a tunnel of foliage, brushing aside spiky coprosma and tree fern fronds, and smelling the rank, decaying leaves under my feet.

The key was still under the rock at the bottom of the garden. The bach was the same colour of bush green, though the paint had peeled back to bare boards in places. The trees had edged closer to the building, the long rimu fronds rasping against the windows.

The door gasped as I pushed it open, and the familiar sound brought back the memories. Frozen for a second, then fleeing to the edges of my mind.

I turned and ran, escaping through the tunnel of trees to the lakeshore, where I glanced at the clear blue sky before bending to dip my hands in the cool water.

I had to go back there. Inside.

Dust prickled my nostrils. The scratch of the rimu fronds was louder in this dark room which hadn't been opened in years. I looked at the brown armchairs, and picked at the stuffing exposed by the rotted fabric. I touched the stains on the floor with the tip of my foot. I saw an old dwelling place which no one loved.

It was gone. There was nothing to reproach me here. Encouraged, I walked through the hall towards the stairs.

White stars in the darkness. I screamed and jumped backwards.

A small body was lying on the floor, naked, broken and covered with tiny white flowers.

It's a doll, I told myself, it's only a doll.

And this time there's no blood.

...

If my sister hadn't wanted to see Prince William I'd never have got involved in a murder.

I should have settled in for another year of glacier guiding. That way, I'd have kept my life under control even if I had nothing interesting to put in my Christmas cards.

'Why, Kate?' I'd asked. 'You've never been interested in the Royal Family.'

'They've never been here before,' my sister had said.

They had, but not in her lifetime. Next day we stood in a downpour waiting for Wills to make a dash through a rainforest which was more than living up to its name. The West Coast was renowned for its rain, so it wasn't as if the prince hadn't been warned. He had spent the last few days out of the media spotlight enjoying life on a high country station but now he was back at work, checking out a rainforest and smiling at the cameras. The story I had heard was that his father, Prince Charles, was trying to get him interested in conservation. I couldn't see it working. Wills was an action guy and now his New Zealand fun was over, I was pretty sure he would prefer to jet back home to his Kate.

Security staff searched the bush and prowled the edges of Lake Kaniere. It would have been a good place for an assassination attempt, there was plenty of cover. Cloud blotted out the mountains and tangled itself among the crowns of the lanky kahikatea trees. The lake was as opaque as woodsmoke, small waves scratching the gravel on its shore.

Miserable faces peered from the windows of a tour bus. The paparazzi weren't having much of an outing and their discontent was obvious as they straggled out into the rain. A weka burst out of the trees. The paparazzi ignored it. West Coast ambience wasn't on their mind.

'Darling, what I'd give for a Bloody Mary,' one woman said.

'What's that?' Kate asked me.

'A drink. Tomato juice and vodka.'

'Yuk.'

The media looked as if they shared the sentiment. Lake Kaniere wasn't their scene. They were surrounded by nature and out of cell phone range, a paparazzo's idea of hell.

A huddle of locals watched the road for signs of Wills' arrival, while the West Coast media splashed around in gumboots, holding umbrellas over their cameras. They looked a lot more interested in their Royal-watching assignment than the jaded overseas journalists who got to do it all the time.

A woman appeared from the bush, head bent as she adjusted her camera, and I stared at her in disbelief. Kirsten Browne was an investigative journalist, and she'd been in the headlines almost daily a couple of months ago as she uncovered a paedophile ring. Chasing nature-loving princes wasn't her kind of work at all.

Kirsten and I had shared a flat with three others when we were at university. The rest of us had fitted study around our lives, our energies focused on having a good time. I was free of my family, loving it, falling easily into late afternoon barbecues, lazy days at the beach, learning how to windsurf, checking in on lectures and assignments only when I had to. All the others were the same, but not Kirsten. She gave all she had to her journalism class, moving around the flat in her own news zone, plugged in to her iPod, or bundled up in front of her laptop in her cold bedroom. We could have disliked her refusal to run with our crowd but somehow it didn't matter. Occasionally she'd appear unplugged and would drink wine and talk to us. She was edgy but fun. Her humour was dark, sharp, different. She had fascinated me though I really never felt that I knew her. We had lost touch after university, she heading for a journalism career and me for the wilderness.

What was she doing here? And what was wrong with her? Her face was white and taut and she jumped as someone moved behind her. This was the woman I'd once seen toss a death threat into the rubbish bin, munching on a chocolate brownie as if nothing had happened. The Kirsten I'd known didn't have a problem with nerves.

Her eyes widened as she saw me.

'Philippa!' What are you doing here?'

'I was wondering the same thing about you.'

'It's called variety.'

'Yeah, I've been following your stories. Some country air might be good for you.'

'Not too much. I'd die of boredom.' Kirsten took a handful of blonde hair and squeezed. Water dripped onto her shoulders and she glanced around, relaxing as she turned back to Kate and me.

I introduced my sister.

'You're alike.' Kirsten looked embarrassed. 'Look Philippa, I'm sorry I didn't get in touch when your parents were killed. You must have been through hell.'

'It hasn't been easy.' I glanced at Kate. Her face was closed, as it always was when anyone talked of Susan and Liam.

'So you're looking after your sister. That's quite a responsibility to be landed with.'

'Kate's all the family I have left. We're fine together.' Good old Kirsten. She hadn't learnt anything in the way of tact - while I couldn't seem to cure myself of touchiness.

'No. I didn't mean that.' Kirsten hesitated. 'Look, Philippa, it's a cheek after all these years but I'd like to talk to you about something. What are you doing once this circus is over?'

'Going home.'

Home was near the Franz Josef Glacier under the same mountain range that enclosed this lake. It was hard to believe that somewhere up in that grey cloud were the Southern Alps, the land uplifted high which cut the island in half. On Kirsten's side were plains, cities and culture, on mine was wilderness.

'Right. I'm travelling in the media bus anyway so there probably won't be much time. Perhaps... well, can I get your phone number?' Kirsten wrestled a notebook out of her coat pocket and flipped through trying to find an empty page. There weren't any. She tried unsuccessfully to write on the damp cardboard cover while I fished in my pocket and came up with my shopping list, tearing a bit of paper off the bottom and scribbling down my name and number.

'Thanks' Kirsten slipped it into her jeans pocket. She glanced at something in her notebook.

'It looks like you've got a ton of stories to write up,' I said.

'What?' Kirsten jumped as another weka burst out from under a fern. 'This place is giving me the creeps. Stories? More like a journey into hell.'

Kate looked interested, and Kirsten noticed and shut up. Then a look of anger crept over her face and I glanced in the direction she was looking, just in time to see someone turn sharply and head away up the road.

'Shit,' Kirsten muttered. 'This is difficult enough without ... Why can't people stay out of things they don't understand, Philippa?'

'You're asking me? I never do that.'

She laughed. 'Nor do I, come to think of it. Natural curiosity – I guess that's one of the things you and Mark Nolan have in common.'

Mark, my journalist lover, had left me for someone else a few months previously and I still didn't feel like talking about it. It had thrown up some emotions I'd thought I was immune to. There's nothing so depressing as realising you're pretty ordinary after all.

'Philippa and Mark split up ages ago,' Kate said.

Kirsten looked surprised. 'Really? I was talking to him last week and your name came up. He didn't tell me you'd parted company.'

'No reason why he should. I'm old news as far as he's concerned. I haven't seen him since last year.'

'Mark was always crazy about you, Philippa.'

'It's lucky you're a journalist, not a psychologist. Relationships were never your thing as I recall!' Kirsten's love life could have kept a counsellor permanently employed back in the days when I'd flatted with her. She had amazing resilience but it was strange that someone as clever and worldly as her could get it wrong every time when it came to men.

She smiled. 'Things have changed a bit since then. You know something? I think I've finally got that side of my life sorted out - even if it has caused a whole new set of problems. That's partly why I want to talk to you.'

'Well you've come to a real expert. I can't even stay the distance with someone as easy-going as Mark.' As I spoke a hiss of car tyres announced the arrival of the royal party. The paparazzi surged closer to the track entrance.

Kirsten grimaced. 'Running with the rat pack. Never thought I'd be on this kind of job. See you a bit later.' She pushed her way forward like an expert and vanished into a forest of cameras.

Wills was dressed casually and did not look fazed by the weather. He glanced at his coterie of media, grinned, made a remark to his aide, then waved at the bedraggled group of spectators. Kate waved enthusiastically back at him. He disappeared into the bush flanked by his party and staff from the conservation department. The media crowded behind him.

'Is that all?' Kate looked disappointed.

'You'll see him come out of the bush and get in his car. But that's about it.'

It seemed like forever before Wills appeared at other end of the circular track. He stood under a canopy of tree ferns, blinking raindrops from his eyes and looking relaxed and ordinary.

'Do you really think it's been worth standing here in the rain?' he asked Kate.

'No,' my sister said, 'but if I hadn't come I'd be scared I'd've missed something.'

Wills smiled, chatted to a few more people, and disappeared into his car. The journalists scrambled aboard their bus and the locals didn't hang around either.

Five minutes before, the small bay had been crowded with humanity from all over the world. Now Kate and I were almost the only ones left.

What had happened to Kirsten? I'd been standing right by the track exit and had seen all the journalists troop past but she hadn't been with them. There was a chance she hadn't completed the short walk and had come out the way she had gone in, but if so why hadn't she come and talked to me? I recalled her tense face and felt uneasy.

'I wonder if Kirsten's still on the track. We'd better go in for a look.'

'She won't be. What's there to see now Wills is gone?' Kate splashed through a puddle. 'I'm starving.'

'I'll just go in a little way.'

Kate trailed behind me, looking mutinous. The light was dim in the bush and I paused under the branches of a kahikatea tree peering into the green darkness and straining to hear any sound of Kirsten above the sound of the rain. Saturated moss, threaded among the branches, dripped water onto my hair. The leaves, glazed with rain, reflected light onto the grey stones of the track.

I walked round a corner, jumping as a wood pigeon swooped from the trees to land somewhere close to my head. The ragged kahikatea crowns tossed in the breeze, the noise of their creaking branches combining with the splashes of a nearby creek.

'Kirsten!' I yelled. There was no reply.

Where the hell was she? There was no way she'd left on the media bus, so she must still be here somewhere. I thought of her recent anger, and the turning figure on
the road. Whoever it was had walked away and Kirsten had not followed. But the person could have come back.

Being on a dark wet bush track probably wasn't helping my perspective but the more I thought, the more sure I was that something was wrong. The Kirsten I knew had been fun to be with no matter what pace her life was running at. She'd never been nervous and upset, and I'd seen her well tested a few times.

I called again, my vision blocked in a hundred places by tree trunks. Anyone could have hidden here and taken a shot at Prince William. But they hadn't. There's no one here, idiot, I told myself. Kate was the nervous one in our family yet here she was with nothing more pressing than lunch on her mind, while I was lurking in the bush worrying about terrorists and being scared off by wood pigeons.

'Philippa! What are you doing?' Kate's voice cut across the sounds of the bush and I jumped again. It was time to get out of here.

I shut my eyes and stood still for a moment. A lot of people hated the West Coast bush, finding it claustrophobic and threatening. I'd never understood that reaction before. Now I did.

Later I hated myself for not going on. I might have stopped it, that's the painful truth I have to live with. If I hadn't given in to paranoia and my sister's stomach, Kirsten might still be alive.

Chapter 2

I ignored it.

It was a warning that came from nowhere, echoing in my head.

No!

It was a winter morning. I was standing near the lake watching the light striking the dark waves. Sunshine lit the fresh snow on the mountains; a cool wind burned my face. I can remember the feel of the day as if it was yesterday.

'It's so quiet here.'

I jumped. The voice had come out of nowhere. R was standing right beside me. The most important meeting of my life and I never saw it coming.

The warning slammed through me: Don't say anything. Turn your back and walk away.

I didn't, of course. I recognised someone unusual and interesting. A person who did not belong here.

We talked. About not much. Weather and sandflies, mainly.

The warning receded to the back of my mind but it never went away. I could have listened to it any time over the following months but I didn't, and in the end there was no escape for R, for me, for anyone.

I had spent my life keeping well back from the chasm. I knew it was dangerous to feel, and that love ended in disaster.

The chasm. I had nightmares about it when I was a child. Of a grey, sensible life transformed into colour and fun. Laughter, closeness, warmth. Then a free-fall into a black pit, losing everything that mattered, while the world laughed on without me.

I knew where it led, yet I stepped towards the chasm that day.
'My name's Robin.'
It's the wrong name, I wanted to say. It doesn't suit you.
Robin. Harmless, earthy, androgynous, and safe.
R describes the person better. It's a hard letter. Uncompromising and lacking kindness.
I have to write about it.
Because I can't tell anyone, and when I die there are people who should know.

...

The police can get to you anywhere, even on a glacier.

I was back at work, and had just led my tourist group off the Franz Josef Glacier when I saw or local cop Stu Adams standing, arms folded, waiting as if he wanted to talk to me. It could have waited until I got home, but perhaps he thought it would have seemed too close to the day almost a year ago when he knocked on the door to tell me my parents were dead. So he found me in the glacier valley instead, much to the interest my tourist party.

I'd been thinking about Kirsten, wondering where she had vanished to the day before. But I wasn't worried about her, not really, and she wasn't on my mind when Stu interrupted my glacier walk. I'd been enjoying the day. I never tired of the glacier. Today it was cleaned by the recent rain and lit by the sun. Blue, silver and white light shone off the pinnacles and ice ridges. I could understand why people ignored the warning signs and risked being squashed in an ice avalanche just to touch it. The glacier is magical. It doesn't matter if you've seen it a thousand times or just once. The effect is the same.

There were other problems on my mind that day, and it had been a relief to slip into my role as guide, explaining the process of glaciation to strangers. It's so much easier to think about climate change and glaciation than it is to acknowledge emotions of which you are ashamed.

I was irritated. It's amazing how willing people are to tackle your problems, especially problems you didn't know you had. Small communities are especially good at this. The woman in the local store had started it, but others were quick to take up the call.

'A perfect solution for you, Philippa. She needs somewhere quiet to live and you could do with a bit of cash. She'd help out with babysitting too.'

'Kate's not a baby,' I'd said, 'and I don't need extra complications in my life right now.'

They'd been talking about Jane Sherman, a recent arrival in the village. She was in her forties, and had apparently decided one day that a demanding career no longer appealed. She'd come to Franz Josef because she loved the outdoors, and taken a job as a kitchen hand in one of the hotels. She was living in staff accommodation and it was driving her mad. Her flatmates were young and in constant party mode. I could see why she was unhappy. My hectare in the country was important to my sanity and I couldn't have lived with a never-ending party in my home.

Jane had come up on the glacier with me today. She often joined the guided walk as she loved getting onto the ice but didn't have the confidence to tackle it on her own.

The tourists had climbed over the steep terminal face of the glacier onto a flat section of ice where, situated high above the river valley, they could spread out and take photographs. I hoped Jane wouldn't come and talk to me and glanced at her as she stepped over a small ice slot, crouched and peered down at the blue walls of the crevasse. She was tall, with stooped shoulders and a face that looked warily on the world. I had the feeling there were things wrong in her life, that she needed someone to talk to, and I was determined that person was not going to be me.

Jane stood up and stretched, her face lit with a slight smile as she looked around her. She really loves it here, I thought. But when she turned to me the smile was gone. She raked long brown fingers through her crop of grey hair as she looked at me, and before I could turn away she was beside me.

'I saw you at Lake Kaniere yesterday,' she said. 'Bad luck that they had such awful weather, wasn't it?'

'I didn't see you there.'

'No. I was going to come over but I saw you talking to that blonde journalist and I didn't want to interrupt. Is she a friend of yours?'

'Why?'

Jane looked startled. 'Oh. No reason.'

I swallowed irritation, much of which was directed towards myself. I'd taken an irrational dislike to this woman. She could have been an interesting friend if I hadn't been too bloody-minded to allow it. From what I'd heard she had made none of the traditional choices in life. She had worked all over the country with special-needs children, living in remote country places few other professionals would have been willing to go. Then she'd thrown it all in and become a kitchen hand.

Jane got on with just about everyone in the village, which was no mean achievement. But every time I saw her my defences went up. It probably had something to do with having her forced on me as a housemate, but there was more to it than that. I had a gut feeling there was something about Jane that wasn't on the level, but this was probably way off beam.

Jane seemed as if she was about to turn away, then shrugged and said: 'It's just that I saw the woman journalist the night before at the lake. She was out on the jetty having a heavy discussion with someone. I guess I'm being curious and I'm sorry. It's none of my business.'

'She's under pressure. She always is. It's her job.'

We stepped off the glacier as we spoke. Jane looked at me for a moment, and then walked away. I had the vague feeling that there was something important to be learned here, but I was distracted by the appearance of Stu Adams. His police uniform looked wildly out of place in the glacier valley.

'Philippa. We need to talk,' he said.

...

'It's nothing to do with your family, Philippa, don't worry.'

'There's not a lot of it left. You're not arresting me, are you?'

'Of course not.'

'Perhaps you should tell my tourist party. I'm sure they'll go home telling everyone their glacier guide was taken off to jail. It'd beat the hell out of boring their relations with holiday pictures.'

Stu smiled, but it didn't reach his eyes. 'It's a bit urgent. I'm sorry I didn't wait till you'd got back to the village.'

'Well I'll have to drive them back. I can't leave them stranded here.'

'Are you the only guide today?' Stu looked hassled.

'Yes,' I said. 'Look, can we meet at the cafe when I get rid of them? It'll only take half an hour.'

'Okay – I'll buy you lunch.'

'Now you're talking. See you back in the village.' I herded my tourist party onto the bus. They all looked interested and I can't say I blamed them.

'So what's happening?' I asked as I joined Stu in a café the tourists never frequented. The locals knew better. It looked uninspiring but served the best food in town. I looked at Stu's scar. It looked as if someone had taken a blunt knife to his face. Stu had come here to escape urban crime, and in his first week found himself embroiled in a fight on the banks of one of the rivers, the appropriately named Mad Mile, caught by flying glass as whitebaiters defended their patches.

'You knew Kirsten Browne?'

I stared at him. 'Yes. Why?'

'There's no easy way to tell you. She's dead. Murdered.'

'What? Where?'

'Her body was found this morning on the Kahikatea Track at Lake Kaniere.

I stared down at the table as my thoughts returned to the wet bush and the uncanny fear I'd felt in an environment I'd always been comfortable in.

'So there was something. I knew there was something wrong but I talked myself out of it. Went and had fish and chips with Kate.'

'Wrong? What do you mean?'

'Kirsten was all over the place. Nervous. That's unusual for her. And she was supposed to meet me but she didn't.' I told Stu about my search at the start of the track.

'It's just as well you didn't go on. We could have ended up with two bodies on our hands.'

I swallowed. 'How was she killed?'

'A hammer or something like it. She wasn't a nice sight, poor woman.'

'How did you know I knew her?'

'She had your name and address in her jeans pocket.'

I remembered how Kirsten had tried to write my address on the cover of her damp notebook, the closely written pages and my comment about the ton of stories she must have in there to write up.

'More like a record of a journey to hell,' I murmured to myself, remembering Kirsten's tense face. 'What was in the notebook, Stu?'

'What notebook?'

I told him about it.

'There was no notebook on her body,' he said. 'The paper with your name on it and her press card were the only things we found.'

'It should have been in her raincoat pocket. I saw her put it there just minutes before everyone arrived.'

'Well it wasn't there when her body was found. I wonder why.'

'Who found her?'

'A local woman. Ali McKee. An artist.'

'Ali McKee lives at Lake Kaniere?' I had one of her paintings. Many artists had tried to capture the glacier but she was the only one who had come anywhere near to it. It was as if there was some secret ingredient she'd added to the watercolour, something that had turned a shape on a canvas into living ice. Looking at the painting you could almost see the glacier breathe and grow. It was confined by rock walls and flanked by rainforest, yet sliding away like quicksilver. Its own entity. Ali had caught the turbulence in the mountains too - the scarred faces of rock cut by weather, with cloud swirling behind to darken the bush and intensify the glow of the ice. A stormy valley. I'd seen the painting at an exhibition and bought it. Kate and I then had to live on less than fifty dollars until my next payday, which had not made me popular. I'd had the painting for nearly six months, but it could still stop me dead. If I lived to be a hundred I'd never take it for granted.

'She's pretty upset,' Stu was saying. 'Apparently she walks that track every day before she starts painting. She won't want to go back there in a hurry after this. It's going to be a hell of a case to crack. The place was swarming with sightseers and the world's paparazzi. Not to mention the fact it was pouring with rain. We'll get nothing useful from forensics.'

'Why would anyone want to kill Kirsten?'

'We're spoiled for choice, apparently. She was one hell of a controversial journalist, secretive to the point of paranoia with her sources, and rumour has it that she was working on something really big.'

'Maybe that's why she was killed. And that's why the notebook was stolen. It must have been full of stories after all.'

'The weird thing is,' Stu hesitated and looked at me, 'I shouldn't really be telling you this, so don't spread it around. It doesn't look like a professional hit. It looks like a sex killing.'

Chapter 3

There have been times when I've thought we must have been mad to do the thing we did, but I'm not so sure now. It would be a relief if it were true. It wouldn't be justified, but we wouldn't be responsible.

Your judgement can get bent when you live in isolation without anything else to focus on. Perhaps that's what happened. I don't know. I'm not trying to excuse myself, I'm well past the need for that now, but before I die, I want to understand.

People say Lake Kaniere's isolated now. They should have seen it then. There were no telephones and only a few holiday baches. Hardly anyone lived there permanently and there was no way of keeping in touch with the outside world when you got there.

I didn't come here to escape people. You can do that in a city with the right attitude. But R came here for that reason.

Neither of us knew where our friendship would lead. If I'd left R alone, if I'd never become involved, it wouldn't have happened.

'You're staying in that place?' R had been horrified. 'It's a ruin. Why don't you come and stay with me. The bach I'm in is huge - more like a house really. We can have a storey each.'

I thought R owned the place and had I known the truth I'd have been more cautious. As it was, I made the mistake of thinking there was no one out there who cared about R but me. But I'm getting ahead of myself. That day all I wanted was respite from mosquitoes. I was staying in a decrepit bach owned by the national park service. It had holes in the walls and the mosquitoes poured in at night.

'It sounds as if the door gets a fright every time you open it,' R said, and it did seem as if the timbers gasped as they moved. I've already

written about the bach and it's amazing how little it has changed in thirty years. The rimu fronds weren't scratching the windows back then, but inside things were much the same as they are now. It was a place that was always going to feel old.

Dozens of tiny white daisies, dry and as brittle as paper, lay scattered on a table in the hallway.

White stars in the darkness.

R saw me looking at them and smiled, scooping a handful and letting them float back down to the table like thistledown.

'I don't know what they're doing here. They look like remnants from a funeral long ago.'

I shivered.

...

'I want to come too.'

'Well you can't. You've got school today.'

Kate glared at me. 'And you've got work. Doesn't stop you buggering off when you feel like it.'

'I don't exactly feel like it. I've got to go and talk to the police. And anyway Tim hasn't got any work for me today. I'm part-time after the summer. You know that.' I was ignoring Kate's swearing, hoping it would go away. It wasn't as if I never let fly with anything myself but it sounded so much worse coming from my young sister. She was small and seemed weighed down by her long dark hair, her face so sharply chiselled that it never really looked childlike. She looked like a troubled young saint but often sounded more like the foreman on a building site.

'And what about Spree? He hates being on his own,' she said.

It was a low blow. Spree, our giant schnauzer dog, was the gregarious type and inclined to go looking for trouble if he felt ignored. He loved travelling in the car, his long hairy nose protruding from the window, but I didn't think anything today would be helped by his exuberant presence.

Kate had seen the advertisement in the paper a year ago: 'For sale, giant schnauzer pup, or swap for Canadian canoe.' Our father had tried to start a canoe safari business years before and when the subsequent entanglements with bureaucracy proved too infuriating for him, he had abandoned the idea and consigned the canoes to the woodshed. I'd been cursing them every winter so I could hardly turn round and tell Kate I wanted to keep them after all.

I rang, but the pup, it seemed, was in demand. The deal must have fallen through because late that night the owner had rung back, full of enthusiasm for the pup and our canoe. Before I knew what had hit me he'd been and gone, a canoe on his roof rack, and Esprit the pup was busily engaged on his first major project, reducing the garden to scorched earth.

Esprit soon became Spree. He was hard to scold. He'd glance over the top of an azalea bush he'd just uprooted, hairy black head on one side and dark eyes sparkling. He was a dog with attitude. But he was a dog who was going to have to stay home today.

I turned away from my sister, poured a mug of coffee from the plunger pot, and retreated to the conservatory. The mountains were not enough for me. For most of my life they'd been like a charm against the hassles of life. Just looking at them could usually get me back on track but this wasn't working any more.

I stared at the sculptured Matterhorn-like shape of Mt Elie de Beaumont, and the other high mountains of the Southern Alps. Kirsten Browne had died at the foot of this range of mountains, a couple of hundred kilometres north of Franz Josef. I imagined the crime scene tape, obscene litter tangled among the slender trunks of the kahikatea trees.

My parents, Susan and Liam, had died in the mountains. Theirs had been an instant death, following a plunge from one of the mountains at the head of Franz Josef's neighbouring Fox Glacier. They'd disappeared into the mountains like a pair of irresponsible children, happy to be together in an environment they loved, unconcerned about the risk.

Fourteen months later I was still coping with the fallout. My grief was not as sharp as it had been, but their deaths had scarred Kate, possibly forever. It's tough to have to learn, when you're ten years old, that you can't rely on your parents, that they'll never be there for you again. Susan and Liam had treated us like people, never as children to control, but they never felt bound by us either. There was always a downside.

I wished I could get past the anger, but it had outlasted the worst of my grief. I'd never wanted commitments like marriage and children, and as a result I'd lost an important relationship with a man who wanted both. And I had commitments now anyway: a sister who challenged me every step of the way. There was not much that was warm and cosy about the way Kate and I were coping with our bereavement.

I'd laughed my way through problems in the past, but then I'd never had real problems before. Tom, my brother, was overseas, the free spirit I'd always wanted to be, while I was stuck in Franz Josef, a place I'd loved until I had to stay here.

The door slammed and I watched Kate drag her bike from the shed and depart for school without a glance in my direction. I turned by back on an indignant Spree, stormed around the house searching for the car key, then set off at a fast crawl in my elderly car. I stopped for petrol, glancing past the petrol pumps on the main street to the mountains that looked down on the village. It was unusually quiet here today. During the summer the combination of sandwich-board advertising signs, the noise of skiplanes and helicopters, and crowds of humanity made you wish nature tourism had never been invented. I thought of Jane Sherman stuck in her party-wracked house and felt guilty. There could be no peace for her there.

If Jane had seen her at the lake the night before Prince William's visit, Kirsten couldn't have been travelling on the media bus after all. So why had she lied about it? It seemed strange and unnecessary. It wasn't as if I'd been involved in her life. I was just an old flatmate from her distant past.

What had she wanted to talk to me about? I hadn't told Stu about that, sensing it could lead to all kinds of trouble, and now I would have to tell some detective who I didn't know.

The car shuddered and I looked at the clock, startled to realise I was travelling at over a hundred kilometres an hour. Rimu trees bordered each side of the road, their straight trunks patterned with moss and lichen. Gradually the forest gave way to farmland. Hereford and Aberdeen Angus cattle grazed in paddocks among billboards advertising adventure tourism. There weren't enough farms to go around so the local people needed a new gospel, and for now, tourism was it.

Kirsten had some kind of family problems back in the days when I knew her. Or maybe 'problems' was too strong a word. She had rarely spoken of them, but she had interesting parents. Her mother, Loraine Latimer, was a judge and her father, Alex Browne, had been a well-known youth worker. He'd often come to Franz Josef, bringing groups of troubled teenagers and taking them tramping and climbing. I'd recently seen a documentary on his work with at-risk teenagers and he'd come across as a sincere person, skilled at fusing vision with practicality. A few weeks after the documentary had screened he'd dropped dead from a heart attack. He was only in his fifties and seemed fit and healthy. I'd sent Kirsten a card but had never heard back from her.

I almost missed the Lake Kaniere turnoff, slammed on the brakes and slid round the corner on a couple of wheels. It gave me a fright and for the rest of the journey I took more notice of the road.

There was little sign of life at the lake. Two days ago it had been teeming with rain and people but now the sun was shining and I could have been the only person on Earth. I walked to the lakeshore, bent and ran my fingers through the cool water. The hills framing the lake were purple, blending to dark blue and grey on the slopes of the mountains. Snow reflected in the dark water and I enjoyed the feel of the breeze on my face as small waves rasped against the shore. I peered up the road and saw a police van parked on the verge by a bach. As I got closer I saw more police vehicles lined up in its driveway. This must be the Operation Lake base. I hesitated for a moment, then walked up and knocked on the door.

Detective-Inspector Barney O'Callaghan looked tired. He and his team were perched incongrously in the rustic bach. Their laptops and whiteboards looked wildly out of place, and the light was abysmal. He took in my glance around the crowded room. 'We'll be pulling out of here soon. We're almost finished talking to the locals.' He glanced past me and hailed a policewoman who had edged her way behind a computer terminal. 'Can you help me with this statement, Gina?'

She joined us in the corner, set up a tape recorder and got ready for the interview while O'Callaghan talked to me. He was a big man with thick dark hair and looked like he spent too much time in the police canteen given the state of his belly. His eyes were slightly bloodshot, but his expression was intelligent. And focused. My impression was confirmed as he took me through my meeting with Kirsten. He seemed to know just how much to say to draw out everything I knew.

'So you don't know what this life-changing thing was?'

I hesitated. 'No.'

'Sure?'

I sighed. 'I've thought of nothing else. But no. There's nothing.'

...

I walked away from the Operation Lake base feeling drained. O'Callaghan had told me it was all right if I wanted to walk round the track. Forensics had finished with it. Kirsten. I stared at the place I'd seen her that morning. None of the things that had happened seemed real. The remnants of crime-scene tape still clung to the bushes, but the track was deserted.

I felt uneasy as I stepped away from the sunshine into the filtered green light on the track. The kahikateas, the swamp trees that could grow out of water, were even noisier than the rimus, cracking and creaking in the wind.

Don't be so paranoid, I told myself. There's no bush psychopath lurking here. There was nothing to show where Kirsten had died, but I looked at several parts of the track, wondering if the dark stains on the stones were from decaying vegetation or human blood.

A twig snapped right beside me and I whirled round. Fronds of tree fern moved and I found myself face to face with a woman who looked as terrified as I felt.

'You just about gave me a heart attack,' she said, clutching a jade pendant around her neck with both hands.

My heart was hammering and I couldn't speak for a moment, but I managed a faint laugh. 'You scared me too.'

She stepped back onto the track, picking leaves out of her hair, and I looked at her, wondering where I'd seen her before. She had long tangled black hair well sprinkled with coarse grey strands, and a lined and alert face. She wore Levis and a red shirt tucked in loosely at the waist and torn at both wrists. As she pulled leaves from her hair, silver and turquoise bangles clashed on her left hand.

'I'm Ali McKee,' she said.

'The artist? I thought I recognised you. I was at your exhibition last year. I bought one of your paintings.'

'Oh? Which one?'

'The Franz Josef Glacier. A watercolour.'

'The storm study. Yes, that was my best. It took me ages to get the glacier right. I'm trying to do the lake at the moment and it's so bloody difficult. I'm not leaving here till I have it perfect.'

'I didn't realise you lived here.'

'I came back. Not that I exactly lived here before. Anyway, it's that kind of place - part of my past that's grabbed hold again. What about you?'

'I'm from Franz. I'm Philippa Barnes. I came up here to talk to the police team.'

'What did you need to talk to them about?' Ali's voice was sharp.

I stared at her for a moment before replying, then told her I'd talked to Kirsten the morning she died.

Ali lifted a hand. 'Sorry to snap at you. I'm a bit strung out about all this.' We walked out of the bush.

'Would you like to come home for coffee?' Ali asked.

'Actually, that would be great.'

Ali looked upset. 'I found her, you know.'

'Yes, I'd heard.'

'How? They didn't mention me on the news did they?'

'Not that I know of. The police contacted me the day after Kirsten was killed. She had my address in her pocket.' As I spoke I felt sadness wash through me. Kirsten, who'd been so alive, so vibrant, didn't exist any more. Somehow it hadn't seemed real before. Now it did. She'd stepped into the bush and been murdered. This was real.

'I'm sorry.' Ali put a hand on my arm. 'You were close?'

'We were friends. But not close. I don't think anyone ever got close to Kirsten. She was private.'

We walked in silence for a minute, then Ali pointed towards a tree-lined driveway. 'That's where I live.'

The house was built into the hillside, a green weatherboard structure which sprawled over several storeys with wide decks on each level. The windows were open and the curtains moved in the breeze. They looked like bright abstract paintings but inside the lemon-washed walls were bare, which was surprising for an artist's house. The bay windows were full of hand-woven cushions and untidy stacks of books, and there were so many pot plants hanging from the roof that their leaves were entangled. Ali threw open the French windows and we walked out onto the deck, leaned on the railings and looked up the lake. The dark blue waves were cut with white-caps and the bush reached down to the shore and blackened the edge of the water.

'It changes. Always a different colour and mood. The challenge is to paint something that expresses that,' Ali said. 'I'll leave you to enjoy it for a minute while I make coffee.'

If it hadn't been for the sandflies, I could have stayed out there for hours. As it was, I retreated back inside scratching my arms and hands.

'They're little bastards,' Ali said. 'People say you get immune to them but you don't.'

I settled back into a battered grey Chesterfield, balanced my mug on a table littered with papers, and glanced at a silver-framed studio photograph on a bookshelf.

'My brother Michael,' Ali said and I looked up surprised by the sudden intensity in her voice. The photograph was old, but the young man who stared out of the frame looked like he would never age. He had one of those faces which never seems to change. It was as if the lines and character in his face must have been stamped there from childhood. He was very like Ali, with the same thin face and springy black hair. He looked humorous, yet there was something untouchable about him which seemed to match the hardness of his grey eyes.

'He's special,' Ali said. 'I was spoiled having a brother like that. No other man matched up.'

I felt uneasy for some reason, possibly because I couldn't quite understand the feeling. It wasn't the way I felt about my brother. 'What does he do?' I asked.

'He's a doctor. A healer.' Ali's voice was taut, and she noticed my surprise and laughed. 'Sorry, Philippa. It's just that I keep thinking of that poor girl, your friend. I'm old and tough, but what I saw yesterday morning will be with me until I die.'

'I can understand that. It's bad enough just imagining. The police said it was a pretty ghastly crime scene.' I couldn't say that Kirsten must have looked ghastly. I felt a rush of sympathy for Ali.

'Put it this way: they won't be getting her family to identify her. It'd be too traumatic. But the worst thing wasn't her body, the mess and blood. It was these.' She got up and pulled a sprig of flowers from an arrangement on the bookshelf. 'Everlasting daisies. They grow all round the place here and if you pick them, they dry and keep for years. Someone had sprinkled them all over her body. That's really sick.'

My stomach lurched. 'So it did look like she was sexually assaulted?'

'The police weren't saying, but I guess that's the implication. Her jeans were pulled down. I saw that.'

'It was a strange time and place for a sex attack. It was pouring with rain and half the world was there with cameras,' I said.

'Who knows what people will do? Some of them are so bloody sick, they have dark voids where their souls should be.'

'The police told me she was about to break some big story and she was killed for that reason, that the killer might have tried to make it look like a sex attack when it wasn't.'

'In a way, I hope that's true. It'd be less … I don't know … less invasive, somehow. How did you know her, anyway? I somehow didn't have the feeling she spent a lot of time in country places like Franz Josef.'

'She didn't. I met her while I was at university. We flatted together. I hadn't seen her for years, but it was obvious there was something badly wrong with her that day. It was as if she was in the middle of a personal journey through hell.'

'That's a pretty heavy thing to say.'

'Yes, but I think it's true. She practically told me that.' I was irritated, but could hardly blame Ali for not believing me. It sounded a bit over the top.

'She didn't tell you why?'

'No. She wanted to talk to me but she never got the chance.'

'It was a pretty bold crime, when you think about it,' Ali said. 'The place was crawling with police and security staff, all on the lookout for trouble.'

'They were protecting Prince William, not the paparazzi.'

'Sure, but they were there, for God's sake. It takes … what … ten minutes to walk that track? The place was crawling with people and someone managed to distract Kirsten, keep her back from the royal party, and whack her over the head with a hammer, then dress her body up to make her look like she's been killed by some pervert. Then he walks away knowing the police haven't a snowball's chance in hell of interviewing everyone who was there. It must have taken some timing, but it's the perfect crime when you think about it.'

I shivered. 'Perhaps she was killed after everyone had gone.'

'I doubt it. That was the whole point, surely - to do it when everyone was still there.'

'I could have found her myself. I knew she hadn't left in the media bus and I went part-way down the track looking.'

'I'm pleased you didn't find her. It was no sight for a friend.'

A door downstairs slammed and we both jumped at the sound of running footsteps on the stairs. Seconds later a man burst into the room. He looked like a shopworn angel. Age had corroded his face and greyed his blonde hair, but there was an innocence and beauty in his expression that I'd never seen in a man of his age. He looked scared and, ignoring me, touched Ali on the shoulder then pulled his hand away.

'I thought you were talking to yourself. I thought there was something wrong.'

'Don't worry, I'm not mad yet. This is Philippa Barnes. She's a friend of Kirsten's. Philippa, this is my husband, Simon.'

We talked for a few more minutes, then I got up to leave.

'Call again if you're up this way,' Ali said. She glanced at her husband, but he had turned away and was riffling through bank statements on the table, an untidy figure in faded jeans and a sweatshirt that should have been thrown out years before.

I looked out the window and watched a woman pulling a canoe up onto the beach. She stood on the shore, stretched, and looked up at Ali's house for a moment before turning away and pulling off her lifejacket. 'Who's that?' I asked.

Ali and Simon looked at one another and it was a while before either said anything.

'She's a scientist. Working here on bird population studies,' Ali said.

'She's not the kiwi survey woman?'

'Sam Acheson. Yes, that's right. Not that she'll be finding many kiwis here. She's only just got back today. She's been away for a couple of weeks.'

Why was Ali telling me that?

'She's a bit of a loner. Like a lot of us here. She would've hated being caught up in all the hoopla with the royal visit.'

'I wonder if she knows about Kirsten,' Simon said.

'Why the hell should she? It doesn't affect her. Are you suggesting we go down and tell her, because if so -'

'Ali.' He lifted a hand. 'I'm not suggesting anything. I'm sorry.'

There was an awkward pause and I rushed into it with an ill-considered question. 'Did either of you see Kirsten the night before she died?'

'She wasn't here the night before.' Ali's voice was sharp. 'She came on the bus with the other journalists.'

'She told me that too. But she was lying for some reason. She was seen here the night before.'

'By whom?' Ali frowned.

'A woman from Franz. She was up here camping. Jane Sherman.'

There was a crash as Simon knocked over a stool. He retrieved it, saying nothing.

'What did she see?' Ali asked.

'I'm not exactly sure. We were interrupted before she could tell me. But she was certain it was her.'

'Why did she come here? She was an investigative journalist, not a royal watcher. Was she meeting some overseas media contact, do you think?' Ali crossed over to the window and peered out, looking as if she wasn't that interested in a reply.

'I wondered that too,' I said, 'but if so, why did she come here the night before? And why did she lie about it?'

Ali turned back to me, a vague look on her face as if she was struggling to remember something. If she did, she didn't tell me what it was.

'I'd better get moving,' I said.

'Al, I think you should lie down,' Simon looked worried.

'I'm fine. Sure, I found that poor girl's body but I'm not about to die of it.'

Ali walked down to my car with me. 'Sorry about the tensions, Philippa. Simon's all over the place about this, and I'm not exactly cheerful either. Did we embarrass you?'

I laughed. 'I used to have public slanging matches with my ex. I never considered what it was like for the observers. It is a little uncomfortable.'

'Sorry. But I bloody hate being patronised. After all these years you'd think he'd know I'm strong enough to cope with things. If I was in tears and needy, he could feel adequate for once in his life.'

'He's probably just worried about you.'

'It's years too late for that. Are you married?'

'No. I'm not into commitment.'

'Who says you need that for marriage? Get out when it's gone, that's what people should do. I didn't, of course. I was idealistic once and believed in protecting the people I love, but you can be tried too hard.'

...

Later it was the image of Sam Acheson, the woman in the canoe, which remained the most vivid impression of the day. It was strange, because I'd only seen her for a minute. I recalled the way Ali had tensed beside me as we watched Sam dragging her canoe up onto the shore. Maybe she just didn't like her. Or was there something about her that she didn't want me to know?

Chapter 4

I thought I was strong, but it was an illusion.

It's hard to remember just how it happened. Like a marriage falling apart, it's gradual: you don't see it happening, then one day you wake up and think: I don't believe that any more. I'm not going to do the things I once did.

When the final collapse comes you might be hurt and glad and terrified, but you can never say exactly what made it happen.

These days we are taught to be assertive and positive, never to see ourselves as failures. It's a dangerous attitude. Seductive and wrong.

I thought R was complicated and interesting. I didn't understand how someone living in such a well of sadness could generate such fun. Life became exciting. We laughed a lot. There was always a kind of unreality about our relationship, nurtured as it was away from any other person. Nothing intruded.

It wasn't about sex. I never wanted to sleep with R and I never did until that terrible night when we huddled in the same bed trying to get warm after our nightmare trip out on the lake.

R slept. I lay there wanting to die. To be gone. The problem was, I was scared of hell. If I could have been sure that death means oblivion, I'd have done it years ago, swum out through that black lake water until I could go no further. Drowning is supposed to be peaceful and easy, but I don't know because I'm too scared to try. Even now.

We used to row out on the lake in an old wooden boat we found in the boatshed. We'd laugh at the echoes or sit in silence, rocking in the current and listening to the creak of the oars in the water.

Even now, I can remember the things we talked about as if it only happened yesterday. R would shock, amaze and dazzle me. Truths I'd believed absolute changed shape. I was drunk with new ideas, my mind full of possibilities I'd never imagined before.

It was a subtle kind of dependence. I didn't recognise it until I was completely addicted.

R moved on but I'm still trapped by emotions that are no longer wanted by anyone on this earth. Perhaps that's my punishment.

When I die that might be the end of it. If only I could be sure there was oblivion out there, not another watch in hell.

...

It was six o'clock. I ran for the remote control, pressed the button and came up with a television screen full of snow. By the time I'd got the channels sorted out and tripped over a stack of books the headlines were over, but the murder at Lake Kaniere was the first item.

Kate trailed into the room, half-heartedly nibbling on a honey sandwich, and this was grabbed by Spree who treated it with much more enthusiasm. They clambered onto the couch with me as a reporter gave a brief resume of Kirsten's career and details on the paedophile ring she had uncovered.

'Kirsten Browne was said to be working on another major story. Can you confirm that?' the reporter asked Detective-Inspector Barney O'Callaghan.

'We're looking at the possibility,' he answered. He looked even more tired than when I talked to him. He stared at the camera for a second, then said 'There are several possible scenarios with this murder. It was a particularly brutal crime and, though it could have been a sex killing, we're keeping an open mind about that.'

Then Justice Loraine Latimer was on the screen. I recalled what I knew of Kirsten's mother, who incidentally didn't look a day older than she had when she'd visited our flat years before. She was well known, one of New Zealand's first female judges, who had presided over some of the country's most controversial trials.

'Being a woman makes no difference,' she had said in a magazine profile, and it was true that anyone hoping from a more lenient sentence from a woman judge was quickly disillusioned. Loraine Latimer extended the non-parole period as far as it would go when she sentenced murderers, and this had led to calls for changes in the judicial system.

She looked composed and her voice was calm as she spoke of her daughter. Her short dark hair looked as if it had just been styled, and the skin was stretched tightly across her cheekbones, accentuating her well-shaped face. Her arched eyebrows gave her a permanent expression of disbelief. She spoke in a low voice, and though her personality was understated, its force glowed from the screen. She had captivated Kate. I watched my sister lean forward, her fingers tightly laced on her lap.

'Someone might have seen something or spoken to my daughter. Please contact the police with any information, no matter how unimportant it may seem.' Loraine paused and her lips trembled with just a suggestion of grief. She didn't need tears or emotion to get across a sense of loss.

I shivered. She was a powerful woman. But nothing was going to bring her daughter back.

...

'How long will it take Kirsten to rot?' Kate asked as I turned off the television.

I shut my eyes hoping she'd be gone when I opened them. She wasn't. It had started soon after our parents were killed, this relentless need to know everything that happened to bodies after they disappeared into the ground. I wasn't exactly an expert on the subject and found it hard to cope with some of the images she conjured up. Her friend Sally Stuart had wound her up with dubious stories of souls leaving bodies and suspending themselves somewhere above the glacier before disappearing to heaven. The girls had spent a night watching for this to happen after someone in the village died, and when they saw nothing Kate had become hysterical at the thought of our parents' souls trapped in their rotting bodies. I'd fobbed her off with the suggestion that souls could be invisible, but I wasn't really satisfied. Having little theological knowledge, I was in no position to take things further, and had copped out by leaving Sally to continue my sister's religious instruction. A mistake.

'Sally said bodies are covered in white mould after they're buried,' Kate said.

'How does she know?'

'Her cousin died last year.'

'So she dug up the grave and had a look, did she?'

'You're a bloody bitch, Philippa. It's not funny.'

It certainly wasn't.

'Look,' I took a deep breath, 'unless you're a pathologist or undertaker, I don't see how you can really know. I certainly don't know what happens. Why would I hold out on you, Kate? I've never seen a body after it's been buried.' As I spoke, I recalled a graphic description of an exhumation in a Patricia Cornwell novel. Should I let my sister read it?

'Wonder if it's like cattle?' she said. 'They kind of collapse inside. The skin looks okay long after the rest's stinking like hell.'

'It's probably a bit different for a body that has been buried in a coffin. I remember reading once that people who die violently don't rot.'

'Really?'

'Yeah. It's an old Norse legend. Some modern-day pathologist was commenting on it. Said it was true in a lot of murder cases.'

If Kate started spreading this kind of stuff round the village, the aunts would be after me again. Susan's sisters lacked her free spirit, and if it wouldn't have curtailed their own lives, they'd have done all they could to get Kate away from my bad influence. They compromised with unsolicited advice, usually just as I sat down to watch television. 'Philippa, I don't like to mention this, but… ' was as familiar as the Coronation Street theme tune, the prelude to many a scrap with the relations. Kate disliked them as much as I did. It was one of the few things the two of us agreed on.

As I went through to the kitchen I heard her on the phone to Sally, relaying my snippet of information. Usually Sally was the one with the gore, and Kate was always on the lookout for something to shock her friend. It wasn't easy.

There was nothing in the fridge worth eating. I peered into the pantry and found things equally uninspiring, but managed to scratch together enough for a vegetarian pasta dish. I liked that kind of food but my sister didn't.

I tried to concentrate on my cooking but I could not stop thinking about rotting bodies.

...

If I had known how complicated the day was going to be, I'd have stayed in bed. It had been a fortnight since Kirsten's death, and although I hadn't forgotten her, she was no longer the main subject of my thoughts. That was about to change. Along with my life and sanity. It's just as well we can't see into the future.

The phone was ringing as I came back in from feeding the chooks. I gave it an unfriendly look.

'Philippa? It's me, Mark.'

I felt a jolt of shock and cursed myself. I'd always known I would hear that voice again one day, and I'd worked out exactly what I was going to do about it. But the plot had left me. I said nothing.

'Philippa? Are you there?'

There was uncertainty in his voice now, but not too much.

'Mark,' I said.

'Look, I hope you don't mind me getting in touch but I need to talk to you. I thought I'd come over tomorrow if that's okay with you.'

'Why?'

'What? Oh, there are a few things - us - and Kirsten Browne.'

'There's no 'us', Mark. Hasn't been for nearly a year now. And what about Kirsten?'

Mark bypassed the murky water of our relationship, which was a wise choice. 'I talked to Kirsten a few days before she was killed and she said a few things. I've been wondering about something she said, and I thought of you. You knew her. I just - I want to talk to you. The phone's hopeless.'

'You'd be better to talk to the police.'

'I have, but there's nothing concrete to tell them.'

'Well, okay, come over if you want to. But I don't see what I can do.'

Mark ignored my lack of enthusiasm. 'Great. See you tomorrow.'

'You could come for dinner, I suppose.' I'd issued more hospitable invitations but Mark didn't seem to notice my reluctance.

'Great,' he said again. 'How's Kate?'

'Bloody.'

'Runs in the family.' He laughed. I didn't. You don't need to have the truth pointed out to you by ex-lovers.

'Philippa? Be careful, won't you.'

'Of what?' I asked, but he had gone.

The next phone call was easier to deal with. It was my boss, Tim Wallace, wanting to know if I could take a party of tourists on the glacier that morning. I was pleased to have the distraction, and to be talking to a man who wasn't interested in turning my personality into a more conventional shape.

'There are about twenty people,' he said, 'all young and fit looking so you shouldn't have any hassles. Oh, and there's a guy here who wants to see you.'

'Who is he?'

'I didn't ask his name. He's about our age, tall with fair hair. He's going on the glacier walk. Asked about you as he bought his ticket.'

I was puzzled. He didn't sound familiar. My easy day turned into one big rush as I flew around the house shutting windows and tripping over Spree at every turn. Our house had changed radically since the days when it was an ordinary and uninspiring farmhouse. My parents had spent thousands of dollars redesigning, utility giving way to aestheticism in the process. There were bay windows to read in, floor-to-ceiling glass everywhere there was a mountain view and a huge conservatory cluttered with an untidy collections of plants. Susan and Liam had knocked out walls to create rooms that were airy and interesting to live in during the summer but freezing in the winter. Luckily they left the kitchen alone so we had somewhere warm to go when the frost started biting. I loved our home, though it was far too big for Kate and me. There was plenty of room for a lodger like Jane Sherman, but I wasn't going to think about that.

I tugged and a sash window came skidding down, missing my fingers by millimetres. I swore. Security was something we'd never had to worry about until recently. People went out without locking their doors and left their car keys in the ignition, but Franz Josef had now entered the real world. There had been a spate of burglaries in the village over the summer, and a year ago a prowler had targeted Kate and me. It made you more careful, though resentful of the need to be so. Spree was no watchdog. Once he was asleep you could shine a torch in his face and he would snore on regardless.

I scrabbled around for car keys, cursing my lack of organisation. They were in an especially obscure place, so by the time I got up to the village Tim had loaded the tourist party into the bus. I wasn't sorry to have missed the hassle of issuing everyone with hobnailed boots for their walk on the ice. A lot of tourists didn't speak English, and the boot sizes were different to shoe sizes so there was always a lot of confusion involved.

Tim looked relieved to see me. He'd probably been wondering if I was going to make it. 'Sorry about the short notice,' he said, 'but I've got a heap of business stuff to catch up on - more than I realised - and if I don't do it today I'll miss my GST deadline.'

Tim was a great boss. He expected his guides to work hard, but freely admitted his obsession with his business was something he could not expect his staff to share. It was not all about money, either. Tim loved the glacier and understood it, which was more than he did people. He was too inclined to be positive, which might not sound like a bad thing, but when you were as cynical as I was, it could be a touch irritating.

'Sorry I'm late,' I said, 'but I've had a crazy morning. Mark's just rung to announce he's coming over tomorrow.'

'Philippa, that's great! I was sorry you two split up. You were a great couple.'

'There's no such thing.'

Tim laughed. 'You should try being on your own for as long as I have.'

'There's no need for you to be.' Tim seemed unaware of his dark good looks and I'd seen him miss plenty of signals from women over the years. He was never rude, just oblivious. I did not think he was gay, though I guessed I wouldn't have a clue really.

'Any woman who took me on would be getting a glacier too,' he said.

'There are worse extras. Not good enough Tim. You're keen to inflict

relationships on the rest of us, but you won't touch them yourself.'

He laughed. 'Your mystery man's sitting at the back of the bus. Looking our way.'

I glanced at him. I'd never seen him before.

Tim gave me a brief rundown on the route onto the glacier and I forgot about the stranger in the bus. Glacier guiding is never easy: it's not like taking people on the same bush walk every day. Ice changes all the time, especially when it's advancing. The result is spectacular but unpredictable. We'd lashed aluminium ladders and ropes onto the terminal face at one stage, and the resulting glacier walk gave tourists an adventure to remember. Things were relatively easy at present, with a steep ice staircase onto the terminal, but this could change at any time.

I climbed into the driver's seat of the bus, turned to introduce myself, and drove up the valley, stopping at various vantage points to explain features of glaciation. The bus roared like a superannuated tractor and whiffs of sulphur came in the open windows as we drove high above the smoke-coloured Waiho River.

'Is this thing about to explode?' someone asked.

'I hope not,' I said. 'The sulphur smell is coming from the valley not the bus. The Waiho River is so cold it would kill you if you fell into it, yet there are hot springs right beside it.' I pointed to a couple of people standing on the riverbed in bathing suits.

As we started walking up the valley I noticed the man Tim had pointed out watching me, but he looked away every time I glanced at him and made no attempt to talk to me. He looked vaguely familiar, yet I was sure I didn't know him.

The glacier gave me the usual hit of well being and I stood for a moment enjoying the cold air swirling around my face. White ice flowed down between dark rock walls to pile up on the riverbed in a mass of twisted pinnacles and crevasses. It was a great body of frozen water and light, suspended above the river yet moving all the time.

No one spoke as we approached the glacier. People were usually awed by the sheer size of it. A pinnacle shattered and shards of ice bounced onto the rock, filling our vision with sparks of colour. People scrambled for their cameras. I cut steps in the ice, which was granular and easy to walk on. Sometimes it was like glass, and half an hour with the ice-axe made your wrists feel as if they would never stop vibrating. The tourist party followed and we threaded our way between pinnacles and across crevasses. I stopped so they could feel the frozen atmosphere and listen to the flow of water under the ice at our feet. They peered down sinkholes, past the crusty white rims to the deep blue ice below the surface. The glacier was the only thing that had made me feel better after my parents died. Crunching across the ice quietened my grief and drew away the pain. It was like a magic carpet: a place where sorrow did not belong.

The guy who had apparently wanted to talk to me pulled off his coat and tied it round his waist, gazing upwards towards the icefall. He seemed detached from everyone around him. Who the hell was he? While others took photographs he roamed across the ice, his body graceful and relaxed. Most people were a little uneasy on the glacier, but he looked as if he'd been here a hundred times before. I was puzzled because there was something familiar about him.

What had Tim been talking about? I felt cross. If this guy wanted to talk to me, what was stopping him?

He didn't come near me. I drove the tourists back to the village, collected their boots and snapped at Tim who, not surprisingly, looked rather hurt.

'Who was that guy?' he asked.

'I've no idea. He never spoke to me. Are you sure he asked about me?'

'Positive. He knew your name, knew you only worked part-time. What the hell's going on? Makes you wonder what he's after.'

I stared at Tim. He was right. It had not occurred to me that the guy might be sinister. He didn't look like some kind of stalker, but I still jumped as he approached my car a few minutes later

'Philippa. I'm Jack Browne.' He paused for a moment. 'I'm Kirsten's brother and I need to talk to you.'

Chapter 5

R wasn't looking for revenge.

That's the thing I find hardest to live with. If only I could say, 'R was mad. It was going to happen one day; I was just unlucky enough to be there.'

But that's not true.

I made R feel special. I took over an outrage that had nothing to do with me and helped transform it into an attitude that could kill.

R came to Lake Kaniere to heal, hopeful that solitude and a change of lifestyle would help. And it would have if I hadn't come along and suggested that there was another way.

No, I didn't suggest it. It's like what I said about a marriage going wrong: you don't see what you are doing at the time, and it is only when you look back that you may be able to see.

This is supposed to be a confession, but I'm finding it hard to say exactly what happened. It's been swirling round my head for so long it's become like an abstract painting. There's meaning there, but it's hard to see it. I've come to think that the only hope I have of understanding it is to trap it on paper.

It was madness, a folie a deux, which took months to explode into violence.

It happened long after the honeysuckle had gone, at a time when frost hung in the trees and the gravels on the lakeshore were locked in ice.

I can remember the blood melting the ice at the front door. But I can't remember the face of the person we killed.

...

'I wanted to talk to you on the glacier,' he said, 'but you looked too efficient and out of reach.'

I laughed. 'I wasn't feeling all that efficient. I spent most of the time wondering who you were. You look like her, you know.'

He looked sad. 'Everyone says that.'

I took him home. I didn't feel like hanging out in the village. Jack had been quite happy to come home with me and prowled round the living room looking at the mountain photographs on the wall while I searched the fridge for ideas for lunch.

'What an amazing place,' he said as I unearthed a tomato that looked as if had been through a nuclear disaster. 'It's more than just somewhere to live, isn't it?'

I was surprised at his perception. Our sprawling, impractical and interesting home was one of the things that had pulled me back from the edge when Susan and Liam had died. They'd put so much of themselves into it that it was as if some part of them was still here.

'I don't know what to say about Kirsten,' I said as I sliced cheese for sandwiches. 'Words are useless. She mattered to me, even if she was a lapsed friend.'

'Yeah. Kirsten wasn't easy to be around but she was straight.'

'Too much so at times. She knew where she was going when I flatted with her, and that was more than most of us did.'

'She thought she could change the world. But no one can.'

'They can clear up parts of it. Kirsten certainly did.'

'Yeah.' Jack smiled. 'Ironic that, when you think of our mother's attitude to Kirsten going into journalism.'

'What do you mean?'

'Justice Loraine Latimer wasn't keen on the idea of her daughter becoming part of the scum every court would be better off without. Not to mention taking what she saw as an observer's role in life. Rich coming from a judge, isn't it?'

'My ex-partner used to say that: always reporting, never doing. But the work Kirsten did was more than that. She exposed corruption and that's not just observing - it's action too.'

'Loraine didn't see it that way. She's a great director of other people's lives. Used to annoy the hell out of Kirsten.' Jack's tone was light yet I sensed something darker there too.

'Does your mother try and direct your life too?' I asked.

'Not my career – mainly because I've never had one. She was much tougher on Kirsten than she's ever been on me and it wasn't fair, really. Kirsten achieved while I let life happen.'

I laughed. 'I know the feeling.'

'But you've got a career.'

'A seasonal one. Yeah, I could guide full-time – if I ever decide I want to meet new people every day for the rest of my life.'

'What a prospect! So what else do you want to do?'

'That's the problem. I don't know. What about you, anyway?'

Jack grinned. 'Avoid ever doing the same thing twice. I get bored easily. I've worked in national parks – ski patrol, track clearing, rubbish collection, you name it. I just hope the casual jobs go on. I don't want a career. Getting locked into a system and dying of high blood pressure doesn't appeal.'

'You might look like Kirsten, but you don't sound like her.' I swallowed, remembering my driven friend. 'I'm not crazy about the average career track either. Now why did you want to see me?'

He'd been looking relaxed, but now his body stiffened.

'Ok,' Jack said after a brief silence. 'I wanted to talk to you about Kirsten's murder. I wondered if you saw anything, thought anything. I can't get a grip on why it happened and it's driving me mad.'

I felt dangerously close to tears. Ever since Susan and Liam were killed, my emotional threshold had been much too low.

'Philippa, I'm sorry.' Jack looked concerned. 'I should have rung you first, not just turned up on your doorstep. It's just that you saw Kirsten the day she died. I can't come to terms with it. I can't believe she's dead. I thought that you could tell me something, help me understand … oh, I don't really know what I thought.'

'It's fine – really, it is. I can't believe it either. I just wish I could tell you something that would help. But I can't. I only spoke to her for a moment.'

Jack paced round the room. 'You've heard the police line? That Kirsten was killed by some source, possibly an overseas media contact. That she was stirring up a story that was making things too hot for someone. So he or she killed her and tried to make it look as if she was the victim of a sex attack.'

'Yes.'

'It's a nice theory. The problem is, I don't believe it.'

'Why?'

'Lots of reasons. For one, Kirsten was strung up - she was bloody haunted by something, and that's not the way she usually reacted when she was chasing a story. You know the big one she'd just done on the paedophile ring? Well she was angry, focused and edgy when she was doing that, but she wasn't vulnerable. Do you know what I mean?'

'I do, actually. I wondered about that myself.' I described how Kirsten had been that morning at the lake and he listened without interrupting.

'I'm so angry with my mother.' Jack broke a silence that was just starting to feel uncomfortable. 'It's all there and she won't bloody see it. "Leave it to the police," is all she can say. A staunch believer in the system, is our Justice Latimer.'

'She's probably right. The police are the ones to solve Kirsten's murder, Jack. They've got science and technology on their side, not to mention professional investigating teams. I'm sure they won't just assume Kirsten was killed because of a story she was writing.'

'Yeah. If that were all, you'd be right. But there's something else - something I don't want to tell the police because it reflects on the person I loved more than anyone in the world.'

Jack sat down opposite me. He started to say something, then hesitated. He'd come all this way, but now he was here, he was no longer sure. I didn't blame him. And I certainly wasn't going to push him.

'Look,' I said, 'you're grieving and believe me, I know what that's like. Don't tell me any more. It's got nothing to do with me.'

'No, I do want to tell you. But it's hard.'

He did another restless circuit of the room, and sat down in the chair opposite me. 'I probably sound bitter about my mother. It's just, she knows what Kirsten found out about Dad, but she's not going to tell me. You can be too loyal. Or, in her case, too self-preservationist. I usually joke round with her and she likes having someone who shows her no respect - that's what I tell her, anyway.' Jack smiled without humour.

'If Kirsten had taken any notice of Loraine, she'd have made her life hell,' he said. 'She criticised her all the time, but she's been knocked sideways by her death. I was there when the police came. Thought it was to do with Loraine's work, yelled out to her "The police are here, Ma," or something equally stupid. She knew. As soon as she saw them she said, "Kirsten. What's happened to my daughter?" God knows how she knew. She might have been at the bench, sitting there listening to the facts. They talked about hammers and dental records, told her she would not be able to identify the body, that her daughter could've been raped, and she just sat there. Nothing seemed to upset her. Till they told her about the flowers. The killer scattered white daisies over her body, and that's the thing that made my mother fall apart.'

'There's something sick about that. That was possibly why. Or it could be they're the things that gave it reality. It's the little things that get you,' I said. 'When my parents were killed, I heard all the nasty stuff - about multiple fractures, ruptured organs, smashed-up bodies. I didn't cry until the police gave me two rock crystals they'd found in Susan's pocket. She'd promised to try and find them for Kate and me.'

Neither of us spoke for a few minutes. We had one huge thing in common: death.

'There's something more about the flowers, actually,' Jack said. 'We own a bach at Lake Kaniere - when the police went into it after

Kirsten was murdered they found a doll lying in the hallway with more of those flowers sprinkled all over it.'

I stared at him, shocked. 'That's obscene. Why?

Jack shrugged. 'It's one of many mysteries. But a pretty sick one.'

'Yes.' I couldn't think of anything more to say.

'Would you come over to Christchurch to meet my mother?' he asked. 'She seems tough, but she's devastated. It would help her to hear some of the things you knew about Kirsten.'

'I don't know. Would she want me to?' I asked doubtfully.

'It would help her a lot.'

I wasn't so sure.

'Kirsten found out something before she died. Something about our father. He's dead too and now I've got to live with the fear that some secret in his past caused Kirsten's murder. I need to know what it. It's buried there somewhere in the psychopathology of my family, and it's not something I want the police trampling all over.'

...

'What did she tell you?' I asked later. We were drinking red wine. Kate had come home from school, eaten dinner, sworn a lot and gone to bed. She had been very suspicious of Jack's sudden appearance and not at all friendly. I tried to ignore her and hoped Jack did not notice. We sat in the conservatory, watching the sky dull to steel as the light fell out of the day.

Jack sighed. 'You're lucky, you know that, Philippa? This place is a sanctuary. Home for me has always been a mansion without a soul.'

'Ah, but then you probably never had to light the fire every time you wanted hot water.'

'Do you?'

'Not now. But we did once. We were always running out of dry wood. What did Kirsten tell you?'

He sipped his wine and the relaxation went out of his face. 'Not much. And she wouldn't have told me anything if I hadn't seen her doing something strange one day. Kirsten trusted no one when she was onto a story, and she was no different with family secrets.'

'Why was she like that, do you think?'

'It was arrogance, in a way. Kirsten thought she could bear things better than other people.'

An unwelcome snapshot of my ex-lover Mark flashed into my mind. He'd told me the same thing soon after my parents were killed, when I'd said my brother Tom was better off overseas.

'What's wrong?' Jack asked.

'Oh. Nothing to do with Kirsten. Sorry, I didn't mean to interrupt.'

'Well, Kirsten wasn't exactly the sentimental type. Never kept letters or anything like that. Both our parents were hoarders and Kirsten was always on at them that the stuff in the attic was a fire risk. It's not as if she was interested in family history.' Jack smiled. 'I'm going around this the long way. I found Kirsten in the attic going through photographs and letters, sneezing like mad at all the dust she was raising.'

'And?' I asked after he'd stared into space for several minutes.

'She'd been strung out and upset for weeks. It started before our father died. He'd left years before that of course.'

'Left your mother?'

'Yeah. The deal was, no divorce and there won't be any haggling over money. Dad walked out and left Loraine with the house. It was more hers than his anyway. She didn't want a divorce; he promised to be discreet. It was all very amicable. They'd been on separate paths for years, then something changed and I don't know what it was. Something that made it impossible for them to live together any more. Dad probably had a lover. But anyway, Kirsten got upset a few weeks before he died, and I wanted to know why. No one should have been at home that day. Loraine was in court and I was meant to be away on a tramping trip. I gave Kirsten a hell of a fright when I appeared in the attic. I asked her what she was doing and she told me to leave her alone.

'Did she say any more?'

'Not much. I pushed her and the most I got out of her was that it was something to do with Dad. "I'll handle it," she said. "I could be wrong, and if I am you'll never have to know what I'm thinking now." Well, you can imagine how that made me feel. I nearly begged her to tell me, but that was a waste of time.'

...

We'd gone to bed about then. I was exhausted. I thought I'd pass out the minute my head hit the pillow but sleep wouldn't come. I thrashed from side to side, boring myself with my thoughts, but too tired to turn on the light and read.

Looking back on it now, I wonder how it would have been if I'd just gone to sleep that night, and if I hadn't seen what I did. Suspicion is a terrible thing. Once it's there it's hard to get rid of. You never really know someone else, and so you can never say 'That's wrong, they wouldn't do that.'

I wasn't worried when I heard the footsteps. After all the wine we'd drunk, it wasn't surprising Jack needed the toilet. My own bladder ached in sympathy, so much so that it took me a minute to realise he had gone in the other direction, towards the living room.

So he couldn't sleep either. It wasn't surprising. He was creeping, but that would only be so he wouldn't disturb Kate and me. If Jack was out there worrying about the thing he hadn't been able to tell me, perhaps I could persuade him after all. It was important, I was sure of that. I slipped out of bed, pulled on an oversized sweatshirt, and padded out to the living room.

Jack was there, but he wasn't staring into the darkness confronting his ghosts. He was wearing a head torch and in the light of the focused beam he seemed to be going through the contents of my desk.

I snapped the light on. 'What the hell are you doing?'

Jack whirled towards me, looking embarrassed. 'Philippa, this isn't as bad as it looks.'

'Yeah? You mean you're just looking, not stealing?' I was trying to sound tough but my voice was shaking.

'I'm not a thief. I didn't want to ask you, but there was something I needed to know.'

'What?'

'I would've asked you tomorrow. I couldn't sleep and - well, it's true that I wanted to come and talk to you about Kirsten. But I thought she could have told you more than you said.'

'She didn't have a chance. Look Jack, I want to know what you were doing snooping through my desk! I want to know exactly what you hoped to find.'

'Kirsten's notebook.' Jack looked as if he was willing me to believe him. 'She had it at the lake the day she was killed. The police told Loraine it was missing.'

'You thought I'd stolen it?'

'No! Not stolen. I thought Kirsten could have given it to you. I need to know what's in it, Philippa.'

'Why would I have the notebook? I'd have hardly told the police about it if I'd stolen it from Kirsten. Get out of my house, Jack. Get out right now!'

Chapter 6

We planned the whole thing and that makes it worse. If it had happened in anger, it would be easier to live with.

Of course fate played a part too. If we'd been left alone that winter it might never have happened but could have stayed where it belonged, a fantasy confined to our thoughts and never acted upon.

Guilt is terrible.

Why is it that people always need to talk about the things they should be silent about for ever? And why do they have to tell the wrong people? The people who are dangerous to them?

There was a right person to talk to in this instance. One who would have understood, absolved and carried the secret to the grave.

Another wrong choice. Just like me turning and talking to R that autumn day instead of running away.

It's frightening to think that something so monstrous can grow out of friendship. Something that takes on a life of its own and can't be stopped until it's too late for anyone. Just like we couldn't stop once I'd picked up the hammer that night.

It's hard to explain, but I don't remember much about the actual killing, though I'll never forget the mess we made.

'You've blocked it out,' R said to me next day, 'but I haven't. I can remember every little thing.'

'You'd do well to forget,' I said, 'otherwise the guilt will kill you.'

R laughed. 'Guilt's dangerous. And stupid. I'll never feel guilty. It was the right thing to do.'

I wish I were as sure.

R's view won't have changed. It's strange I can be so certain of it after all this time.

The eels could have eaten the body by now, but the hammer must still be down there somewhere. Under the black waters of the lake, wrapped in algae and wet darkness.

A reminder.

As if I need one.

...

I crawled back into bed, and the next thing I knew, it was morning and Kate was standing in the doorway. It took me a while to realise that my sister was checking up on me. Surely she didn't think that Jack and I were getting together? I'd wondered the day before if that was why she had been so unfriendly to him. She was wildly off target, but that wouldn't stop her.

'Where's he gone?' she asked me over breakfast.

'He had to leave,' I lied.

'What's he doing back here then?' she asked.

I spun towards the window to see Jack's car appearing in the driveway. 'Fuck," I said.

'What the hell do you want?' I asked as he appeared in the doorway.

'Philippa I can't just leave. I am really sorry about last night' Jack looked stressed but he stood his ground.

'What happened last night? Kate demanded.

I saw no reason to protect him. 'I caught him going through my desk,' I told her.

She stared at him looking as unfriendly as I felt. 'Why?'

Jack blushed. 'I thought Philippa had something belonging to my sister but I was wrong and I feel like a complete moron.'

'You are,' my sister told him.

'Yeah,' I said. 'So give us one good reason why we should ask you back into our house?'

Jack looked from one to the other of us. 'Look I am truly sorry – I was so wrong. But it doesn't alter the fact that I need your help. Even if you won't do it for my sake, will you do it for Kirsten?'

'She is past caring,' I said but I felt myself weakening.

Kate didn't relent, though. 'Philippa's boyfriend's coming here today,' she told Jack, giving him a cold stare.

I laughed. I couldn't help myself. Kate hadn't liked my journalist lover Mark at all while I was with him but now he was a preferred option to Jack. 'Mark is my ex-boyfriend, Kate,' I said. 'It's not a social visit: it's to do with his work.'

'He wants to get back with you.'

'Oh? And how would you know?'

'He wants to marry you.'

'Kate, would you give it a break?'

'Well I think you should get back together. You're both stupid.'

'Kate, go to school. And don't try to hand out advice on a thing you're far too young to understand.' There. I'd said the kind of patronising thing I'd vowed never to say.

'Bitch!' Kate stamped out of the room.

Jack had used the distraction to slide inside and sit down at the table. I glared at him.'

'So what does Mark do?' he asked.

I leaped to my feet, almost knocking my coffee mug to the floor. 'Jack that is absolutely none of your business!'

'Okay – sorry. Look it was a bad idea to come back but Philippa I need to ask you – will you still come over and see my mother?'

'You really want me to do that? I thought it was just a cover so you could go through my desk.'

'No! I am so sorry I did that. Please.'

I stared at him for a moment. 'Ok – but I'm doing it for Kirsten – not for you.'

'Philippa, I can't thank you enough. You don't know what it means to me. When do you think you'll be able to come over?'

'As soon as I sort out someone to look after Kate. Probably next week.'

'Thanks, Philippa.'

'It could be a waste of time. From what I know of your mother, she's hardly going to start confiding in me.'

'No. But there are other things. I want you to help me find out what this is all about. Kirsten said you were a pro at unearthing other people's feelings.'

'I wouldn't go quite that far. If you're serious about wanting someone to look into things you should hire a private investigator. Google someone. Or check out the Yellow Pages.'

He looked startled. 'I don't want to do that. I just wanted to talk to you really. And I know it'll help Loraine.

'Don't count on it.'

'You're a prophet of doom. Come on, I'm not that bad. Promise I'll never snoop through your desk again. Friends?'

I smiled reluctantly. 'Yeah. Now go. I've got a lot to sort out.'

Jack left and I felt confused. I liked him - even if I didn't trust him enough to tell him that Mark was coming to see me about Kirsten.

...

'Philippa, thanks for letting me come over.' Mark hesitated on the doorstep, obviously wondering if he should give me a hug for old times' sake. I stepped backwards onto Spree's paw. He yelped.

'Just come in.' I felt a surge of irritation.

'Where's Kate?' he asked.

'Out with Sally.'

Mark slipped his pack off his right shoulder, rubbing his wrist. 'Too much time at the keyboard. Don't laugh.'

'I wasn't going to. You should get out of the office and get a bit more exercise.'

Mark had aged and it shocked me. His face was thinner and there were dark smudges under his eyes. His hair was cut short in a trendy style unlike his former undisciplined dark mop, and there were lots of grey threads in it. He still wore jeans, but a pale blue shirt had replaced his customary T-shirt. The new woman, I thought, with a stab of jealousy, checking his hand for a wedding ring. There wasn't one. Those hands, those sensitive hands. I looked away, furious with myself.

Mark helped, by getting me angry before I'd even had the chance to offer him coffee.

'You're not going to turn into Nancy Drew over Kirsten's death, are you Philippa?'

'What do you mean?'

'Well, after last time ...'

'Last time one of my dearest friends had her life blown apart. What the hell would you know? You weren't here when it was all over, but I still haven't fully recovered from what happened. God, but you're a bastard, Mark.'

'Okay, I'm sorry. I mean it, Philippa. We always seem to get off on the wrong foot. I'm worried about you. And guilty. I should never have done what I did.'

'What?'

'You know. Abbie.'

'I never even knew her name.'

'No… well no reason why you should have.'

'Look, Mark, I hope you haven't come over here to fill me in on your love life. I don't want to know.'

'I don't have a love life, actually – it didn't last past a few weeks. I was so angry with you. I wanted to hurt you. But it was a bad mistake.'

'It's your life. You don't have to explain.'

'You're part of that life. Or at least I want you to be.'

'Funny, Mark. No one seems to be happy when they get what they want. I thought it was freedom I needed, but it's proving more complicated.'

'You're not free. Not as long as you've got Kate to look after.'

There was a time when I'd have been furious with Mark for making a comment like that, but I couldn't be bothered any more. He was right, after all.

'What have you been doing with your spare time?' I asked

'I haven't had much. I bought a house a few months ago, and it needs heaps of work, so I've been up to my eyes in sandpaper and paint.'

'And is it what you want?'

'What? The house? It's a good starting point. Affordable, 'cos it needs heaps done to it. It's an old bungalow, which needs megabucks to transform it into a character home. You'd like it.'

'Not all the work I wouldn't. I'll never forget the upheaval when my parents renovated our place.'

'You shouldn't let that put you off.'

I laughed. 'What's to like about house renovation? I couldn't be bothered.'

'You put a ton of energy into other things.'

I ground coffee beans. 'You always did want your own place, Mark, and I can understand that.'

'Yeah. Franz has always been that for you. I could never compete. It's the real love of your life.'

'You're out of date. Right now it feels more like a prison.'

He stared, which was hardly surprising. He'd had to put up with plenty of eulogies from me about the place I'd grown up in, my meaning of life.

'Because of Kate?'

'Yeah, partly. She's like I was years ago, so bonded to the place she thinks she'd die without it. She's lost her parents but she's still got her home and it's more than timber and corrugated iron. It's the whole environment, all the special places. It's how I felt myself, but now I'm not so sure. I feel trapped.'

'God, you're contrary, Philippa.'

'Thanks. True but not helpful.'

'You make it hard for yourself. You've got a problem with commitment.' Mark lifted a hand. 'I'm not trying to annoy you, it's just the way I see things.'

I swallowed anger, wondering if things could have been different between us if Mark hadn't been so brutally truthful all the time. He never retreated behind soft sentences, and given my own abilities in that area, it was ridiculous to be annoyed by him.

'I need to get away for a while,' I told him. 'Problem is, what am I going to do with Kate?'

'She could go to one of your aunts, surely?'

'No way.' As I spoke I remembered Jane Sherman, the woman who'd come to Franz for the lifestyle and was losing her sanity in a party house.

'What are you thinking?'

'Solutions.' I told Mark about Jane. 'The thing is, I don't like her.'

'Why? Because she's been force-fed to you, and you're going to show everyone they're wrong? Come on, Philippa. Don't let your stubbornness get in the way of a good idea.'

'Anyway, what are you doing here? You still haven't told me why you've come to see me.'

'You'd be good in the army, Philippa. You'd have the troops counter-attacking before anyone else knew there was a problem.'

I laughed. 'You go first. Then I'll tell you why I'm going away. The two issues just might be connected.'

'Yeah, I was afraid of that.'

I'd been controlling myself, though it probably didn't seem that way to Mark. I wasn't really interesting in revisiting our old differences. I wanted to know what Kirsten had told him.

'I saw Kirsten the week before she died' he said. 'She was back working in Christchurch. I hadn't seen her for a year or more, so I congratulated her on her paedophile investigation and - well you know how it is for journos: you don't spend much time thinking about a story once it's published, you're on to the next one. But that story was big. I was surprised at how she seemed to have moved right on from it.'

'So what did she tell you?'

'Not a lot. But I got the impression she was working on something even more painful than the paedophile story, and it's hard to think of much worse than that.'

'Could she have been personally involved this time?"

Mark stared at me. 'Possibly. I didn't think of that, but I did wonder why she was so uptight. She wanted something from me.'

'What?'

'Information. Kirsten was working as a freelance and she didn't have access to the kind of backup you have on newspapers - legal experts and that kind of thing. Though of course she had her mother. Justice Loraine Latimer.'

'Who she wouldn't have wanted to confide in.'

'Yeah. There's something odd about that family. Kirsten wanted some kind of specialist information, and she was up against pillars of the establishment. She told me she couldn't use her usual channels because her source would be in danger if anything leaked.'

'So she asked you?'

'Just if I'd do it. She didn't tell me what it was she needed to know. Told me she'd get back to me after she finished chasing Prince William around the country.'

'Why ask you?'

'And you tell me I'm tactless! You're right, though, I'm not a leading-edge journalist like Kirsten. Maybe that's why she asked me. She didn't want anyone with a high profile getting involved with what she was doing. She wanted a good footsoldier, I guess.'

'There'll be more to it than that. Think about it, Mark. What are you an expert in?'

'Nothing. I'm just a general reporter.'

'And where have you been working for the last ten years? Christchurch. That's what you've got expertise in. You know the people, know the way the system works. You don't have to be a media star to have a lot of useful inside information. You always undersell yourself. If Kirsten was about to hit on you for information, she was doing it for a damn good reason.'

'The problem is, I've no idea what.'

'Have you told the police?'

'Yeah. They weren't all that interested. It's pretty nebulous after all.'

'So why come and tell me? I thought you disapproved of me playing Nancy Drew.'

'Sorry. I shouldn't have said that. I guess I wanted you to know because you were a friend of Kirsten's. Also… '

'Also you thought I'd be well on my way to some left-of-field solution by now. And you thought you'd "one-up" me by telling me the police are right: that Kirsten was killed because of a story she was investigating.'

'Philippa, that's not true! I can't really explain - I guess I'm upset about what's happened and I wanted to talk to you about it. And I meant what I said on the phone. I do want to talk about us.'

'There's not a lot to say. We both messed things up. Do we have to keep on analysing it?'

'I want to give it another chance. We're good together, Philippa.'

'We're not. You want marriage and children. All the conventional things. I don't know what I want, but never that.'

'I'm not sure about what I want any more. I pushed you too hard last time. I just want to be with you - sometimes, if that's the way you want it. No big life changes. No pressures.'

'Mark, if you accept that, you'll be making all the sacrifices. And why should you? You haven't changed. The same problems will come back again.'

'You've met someone else, haven't you?'

'No. I'm not bloody interested in anybody else. Relationships are way too much trouble.'

'I see. Well, I can't blame you. Not after what I did.'

'For God's sake, Mark, it's got nothing to do with you. It's me. The choices I've made.'

'So what is wrong? I can tell something is?'

I sighed. 'Just life. Tell me more about Kirsten.'

'She was extreme - well you know that. She'd go to the end of the line and back for a story. She put herself in danger sometimes, but no one could warn her off.'

'Why did she go freelance?'

'More freedom. She scared off a few editors in her time. They couldn't control her and she never trusted them, so it was a bad combination. She refused to discuss work in progress, and her loyalty was always to her sources, never her boss. She went to prison rather than identify a source once.'

'Really? I never heard about that.'

'She wasn't in for long. The guy in question came forward in the end. It was a fraud case, I think. So now it's your turn, Philippa. What are you planning?'

'I've just met Kirsten's brother Jack. He thinks she found out something terrible about their father and he's scared it's connected to her murder. He came over here to talk to me'

'So what does he expect you to do about it?'

'Nothing really. But he does want me to go and meet his mother.'

'I hope you're joking. You don't know what the hell you're getting involved in. There's something wrong with that family, Philippa.'

'That's Jack's point.'

'Kirsten knew more about it than you can ever hope to - and that didn't stop her being killed. If that's the reason – but it's far more likely to be to do with her work and that's obviously what the police think. Leave it to them.'

'I can't. Kirsten was my friend .'

Philippa – stay out of it – there is something really wrong here,' Mark said.

Chapter 7

I knew as soon as I saw R that day that something had changed.

I'd been expecting it, in a way. We'd talked about everything, we were as close as it was possible for two people to be, yet we came from different worlds and I always knew it could fall apart one day.

The person who had ruined R's life was here. Drinking tea. Talking about the lake. An ordinary person who didn't really look like a monster. But I knew all about acting.

'Why come here?' I'd asked when R and I were alone.

'To try and get rid of the guilt. It makes me laugh.'

'Isn't that what you wanted?' I was puzzled. At the time, repentance could have made the difference.

'I'm not the one being apologised to. I'm just the confidante,' R's tone was hard.

'What else is there to be guilty about?'

R took a long time to tell me. By the evening we were in a new and frightening phase of our friendship. Before it had been fantasy. Now it was real.

We knew we could do it, that we should do it. We'd just been given a perfect justification. If we didn't stop this person, the hurt would go on, spreading like ripples on the lake, reaching out for other lives to maim.

R was the victim I cared about, but there were others.

Looking back on it I can't believe our arrogance, our belief that it was our

duty to take another human life. That's something that should be left to God.

'Let's do it tonight,' R said.

...

Mark was being ridiculous. He knew less about Kirsten's family than I did, and that wasn't a lot.

So why was I worried? Because I'd believed him? I was glad I hadn't told Mark about Jack's secrecy, not to mention his midnight search of my desk.

The party house was quiet today. I'd rung the hotel where Jane Sherman worked and found out that she had the day off. Obviously none of her teenage housemates were in residence as the stereo was off. I waited for someone to answer my knock, looking in through the open sliding door at synthetic orange carpet, a Formica table, a collection of beer cans in the window alcove, and several cracked and shapeless black vinyl chairs. It was the kind of cheap furniture that no one would choose to live with, and it was depressing. There was a radio playing somewhere in the background. I could hear the well-modulated tones of a male newsreader.

I was about to walk away when Jane appeared, dressed in track pants and a sage green sweatshirt, her hair wrapped in a towel.

'Have you been waiting long? I was in the shower.' Jane looked surprised to see me, and given that I'd been less than friendly last time I'd seen her, I could hardly blame her.

It had been nagging at the back of my mind for weeks, the feeling that Jane had seen something important the night before Kirsten was killed, yet I'd been reluctant to talk to her. Now I had to. And it wasn't the only difficult thing I had to ask her.

Jane made coffee, then took the towel from her hair and rubbed it dry. She gave me a wary look, and I suppressed a pang of irritation as I balanced my coffee mug on a stack of newspapers by my chair. What the hell was wrong with me? She was sitting on the other side of the room, yet it felt like she was invading my personal space. Considering that I was in her house, uninvited, that was rich but I couldn't shake the feeling. Stop being so stroppy, I told myself. There is nothing wrong with this woman. You're the one with the problem.

'You must wonder why I'm here,' I said.

'Is it to do with Kirsten Browne?'

'Well, yes, partly. Look, I was rude to you on the glacier that day and I've got no excuse for it. I'm sorry.'

Jane shrugged. 'It doesn't matter. I wasn't trying to be inquisitive, it was just...'

'You noticed something, didn't you? Well you started to tell me about Kirsten having a heavy discussion with someone.'

Jane looked at me for a moment, her face serious and her shoulders slumped. She looked as if she was well used to receiving bad news. 'I saw her, yes. I'd gone up to Lake Kaniere to get away from Franz for a few days. This household gets to me at times. I've got a tent and I often go off camping on my own. I was looking for solitude – I had no idea Prince William was going to be there.'

'You must have got soaked camping in that weather.'

'Yes, I did. It was fine the evening before though, and after I'd set up my tent I went for a walk round the lake. That's when I saw Kirsten. It was late evening and there was no one else around. I was about to go down to the jetty when I heard voices - and the sound of a man crying.'

'Who was it?'

'I couldn't see his face. He was wearing a dark coat with the hood up and he was sitting at the end of the jetty facing out into the lake. But I saw Kirsten. She looked towards the road but she didn't seem to notice me. Then she put her hand on his arm and started talking to him.'

'What did she say?'

'I couldn't hear her words but it seemed quite intense. It wasn't... well it didn't seem like she was soothing him as much as explaining something. He stopped crying but he didn't say anything. I didn't hang around. I didn't want them to see me. But I was puzzled.'

'No wonder you were curious about her when you saw her next day. That reminds me. I saw a person in a raincoat turning away and walking off up the road. I couldn't see if it was a man or woman, but Kirsten was angry - said she wished people would stay out of things they didn't understand.'

'It was a man,' Jane said. 'I don't know who it was, but I saw him as he turned away. He was wearing a coat with one of those hoods you draw right round your face so I couldn't see his hair. The only reason I know it was a man is because his chin was covered in stubble, like he hadn't had a shave for a few days.'

So presumably it was the same man?'

'It has to be, doesn't it?'

I sighed. 'This gets stranger by the day. Kirsten lied to me, or at least implied she'd arrived that morning on the media bus. But she was there the night before, and was secretive about it, so it looks like the person she came here to see wasn't one of the paparazzi hanging around Prince William. And for some reason she needed to hide the fact, even from a lapsed friend like me. Why?'

'I don't know. I should tell the police what I saw. But there's something else you want to say to me, isn't there?'

I was startled and all my old unease about Jane came flooding back. 'How do you know?'

'I don't. Sorry, I don't mean to come on too strong, but you seem tense, like there's something on your mind.'

There was, of course. And I'd never been good at hiding my feelings. Why was I so jumpy around this woman? There was no need to be. No one in the village spoke badly of her, and if there had been something wrong, local intelligence agents Jem and Angie would have been onto it before now.

'I'm sorry,' I said, 'but I'm not used to people reading my feelings. There is something actually. Nothing to do with Kirsten.' I had not considered whether to tell Jane about Jack, but my subconscious had made the decision for me.

'Then what is it?' Jane looked puzzled.

'I have to go away from time to time and I need someone to look after my sister. I'd heard you weren't all that happy living here and wondered if you'd be interested in living with us. Rent-free in exchange for looking after Kate while I'm away. Our house is huge and you'd have plenty of space.'

Jane's face lightened as if a huge anxiety had been lifted, and I'm not sure how she did it because she didn't smile. 'That would be wonderful.'

'You haven't met Kate yet. You'd better come for dinner first and see what you think. She isn't easy.'

'We'll get on fine. I know we will.'

I wasn't so sure.

But she was right.

...

For a year I'd been needed and felt trapped. Now I wasn't and it made me resentful. There's no pleasing some people.

Even Spree seemed to like Jane better than me. As for Kate, she'd defected the night Jane came to dinner and followed her round like a puppy the day she moved in.

'Leave Jane to get settled,' I'd snapped. 'She doesn't need you hanging around all the time.'

'She doesn't mind. She likes me and I like her. So there, Philippa.'

Jane was a great cook. She dug out and cleaned baking tins which had grown cobwebs after years in the cupboards. She had a bread-maker, and the yeasty fragrance of baking loaves filled the house each day, a welcome change from the bread on offer at the local store. Jane told ghost stories, completing her conquest of Kate. She was careful around me, perceptive and always ready to give me the space I needed.

It would have been easy to give in, to enjoy Jane's friendship and trust her. So why didn't I? I'd been bloody-minded all my life, but I was pushing the limits further than usual this time. Mostly I thought it was I who had the problem, but occasionally I felt sure I was right to doubt Jane. She never gave me the slightest reason for it, but the feeling was there all the same.

'When are you going away, Philippa?' Kate's voice was incurious.

'Tomorrow,' I said, making up my mind. 'If Tim doesn't need me, that is.'

Jack had rung a few days before and I'd been vague about when I would go over to Christchurch. 'You're welcome to stay with us,' he'd said.

I'd quickly refused. Part of the attraction of the break was the prospect of a few days on my own. Staying with Loraine Latimer was not the kind of relaxation I had in mind. I planned to check into a motel and do my own thing.

I rang Tim that night. He sounded relaxed about my increasingly frequent breaks from work.

'Now would be a good time, actually, Philippa,' he said. 'There's no one much around this week, but we've got a few big tours booked for the week after.'

'I'll be well back by then,' I promised.

Kate was at school and Jane at work when I loaded up the car. Spree, who usually gazed at me as if I'd stolen his best bone when I got in the car without him, was calm today. He was spread out in a patch of sun, and did little more than wag his tail at me. It was getting bad when I was upset because a dog wasn't emotionally blackmailing me. Get a grip, Philippa, I told myself.

It was a while since I'd been to Christchurch and it felt good to be on the road with no fixed plans and no real commitments. I let my mind drift as I listened to U2's powerful song of death and friendship, written for their New Zealand-born roadie killed far from home. One Tree Hill was a long way from here, but the music prickled the nerves on the back of my neck. I thought of my dead parents, of the Auden poem made famous again by 'Four Weddings and a Funeral' – and of Kirsten.

I turned inland from the ragged breakers of the Tasman Sea, and drove through the rainforest towards the mountains. Fallen trees hung like straws from the slip faces and mist rose from the deep pools of water down in the Otira Valley. Rocks the size of cars could crash out of the hillside without warning here. In the past, storms had done massive damage to this fragile road, but today it was hard to imagine, with a clear blue sky and sun reflecting light off the snow on the scarred mountaintops.

I wasn't especially looking forward to meeting Loraine. Jack had persuaded me against my better judgement. I hardly needed Mark to remind me that this was a family with secrets. Why should Loraine Latimer welcome me?

A breeze stirred the tussocks on the pass. It had been breathless in the valley but now the cool mountain air washed through the open windows onto my face.

I drove fast through the high country, passing erosion-scoured hills, steel coloured lakes and rock outcrops, before descending onto the Canterbury plains. On my side of the mountains most of the land was wilderness, but here few acres escaped cultivation. Civilisation reached out and before I knew it I was surrounded by the city - leafy trees and grand houses - or overbridges, industrial sites and railway yards. It was all in the way you approached it. Today I was chasing culture so I took the left turn.

I hoped Jack would be alone. I wanted time to familiarise myself before confronting Loraine. Their street wasn't hard to find, and the house was set well back behind a high wrought-iron fence and an avenue of oak trees. It was built of cream stucco with a burnt-orange tiled roof and black window frames with diamond-shaped leadlight windows. My clapped-out Toyota seemed out of place on the smooth oval parking area outside the front door. Jack appeared from the garden.

'You look hot,' he said as he led me into the house, across thick crimson and blue Persian carpets in the wood-panelled entranceway, to a large kitchen. An espresso machine and other state-of-the-art appliances contrasted with the antique oak dresser in the corner but the effect wasn't discordant. I perched on a high kitchen stool and watched Jack pouring orange juice into frosted glasses. He seemed uneasy.

'Look,' I said, 'if you think this is a bad idea, just say and I'll go. I've been thinking about it on the way over. I don't see why your mother would really want to meet me.'

'She does, though – she's looking forward to it. I have been too. Don't go, Philippa, I haven't changed my mind for a minute.'

'What's wrong then?' I thought but didn't say.

He reached into a high cupboard for biscuits and his T-shirt came adrift from his shorts revealing a tanned back. He was hot – in more ways than one. I cursed myself, trying to delete the thought from my mind.

'Are the police making any progress?' I asked.

'No. Or if they are they aren't saying a lot. Someone comes and talks to us most days but it's bloody frustrating – they can't tell us much. They talked to the overseas journalists but they didn't seem to get anything useful from them - and of course they're long gone. Now the police seem to be concentrating on Kirsten's other work. They came here looking for her computer flash drives but that was a waste of time. She never kept anything important here.'

'How's your mother standing up to it?'

'You'd never know with Loraine. She's not showing much emotion and she's back at work as though nothing ever happened.'

I shivered. 'Don't be too hard on her. I did that too when my parents died. Working helped. Anything rather than being alone with my thoughts.'

'Yeah, I guess you're right.' Jack didn't sound convinced.

'When will she be home?'

'Soon, probably. Let's go outside.'

I followed him through a maze of polished wood, antique furniture and formal living rooms to a leafy conservatory. It was a relief to get outside. It was a beautiful house, but not the kind of place you could relax and live in. I kept expecting someone to appear and tell me to get back behind the ropes.

There was something wrong with Jack. As I turned back from the garden I surprised a grim look on his face, and although he erased it with a smile it was obvious his mind was not really on me. It was the cat who confirmed it, appearing out of nowhere and rustling the bushes behind Jack's head. The colour drained from his face and he sprang round, laughing with embarrassment when he realised what it was.

'Jack, what's going on?'

'Well, this probably sounds like advanced paranoia but I'm almost sure someone's following me. I was out late the other night visiting friends on the other side of the city. Someone followed me home - I tested them out by doing some pretty weird detours.'

'Was there anything else?'

'Yeah. Little things. Someone shone a torch on my bedroom window a few nights ago. And the phone calls. Always at times when I'm here on my own, like there's someone watching the bloody place. I've looked and haven't seen anyone around, but they wouldn't be by then, would they?'

'What does the caller say?'

'Nothing the first couple of times. Then this mad laughter. Today they talked for the first time - "Don't even try to work this out, Jack - you can't change history." Weird.'

'Male or female?'

'Hard to tell. Same with the laughter. It was androgynous. I think that's the thing that freaked me out most.'

'Something else happened just before I came, didn't it?'

'How can you tell?'

'Body language, I guess.'

'Well yeah, there is something else. Could have been done any time in the last couple of days but I've only just found it. Someone's taken an axe to my antique sailing boat. It's only a kid's toy, but it's a family heirloom. Loraine gave it to me years ago.'

'Why didn't you tell me?' I hadn't heard Loraine approaching and neither had Jack, judging by the startled look on his face.

She stood in the doorway, tall in a charcoal grey suit. Silver-rimmed glasses shaped like bird's eggs hung from a chain around her neck and her fingers, ears and wrists were weighted down with silver jewellery. As she moved the reflections from her disc shaped earrings made shapes like bruises on her neck.

'You know me, Ma. I hate to worry you.' Jack's tone was light but I doubted that Justice Latimer was fooled. Her face was oval and looked young and unlined in the leafy light of the conservatory. Her dark hair was sculpted around her face, the kind of cut which would need weekly attention to keep looking right. She seemed angry but as Jack lifted a hand and grinned, her face relaxed into a smile. She was a beautiful woman, with a face and body as perfect as a stone sculpture and probably not much more yielding.

'You're ridiculous. You must tell me these things. I do tend to find out, you know.' She glanced at me and I felt as if I was a piece of conservatory furniture that wasn't right for the setting.

'This is Philippa Barnes,' Jack said. 'Kirsten's friend. The one who...'Loraine held out her hand and I shook it, surprised at the strength of her grip. 'Thanks for coming. I'm sorry not to greet you in a friendlier manner. But Jonathan's words shocked me.'

'Me too,' I said.

'Sit down, Ma, and I'll get you a drink. Usual?'

'Yes, thank you. What about you, Philippa?'

'We've got the lot - beer, red wine, sav, spirits, you name it. What'll you have?' Jack asked me.

'A sav, thanks.'

Jack left and Loraine and I sat in silence. I didn't know what to say. Loraine took the initiative and I was grateful.

'So what do you do, Philippa?'

'I'm a glacier guide. At Franz Josef.'

Her right eyebrow lifted slightly and I imagined her sitting at the bench listening to an unlikely piece of evidence with just this kind of expression on her face.

'An interesting part of the world,' she said after a brief pause.

'It is rather special. Have you been there.'

'Years ago. I don't get out of the city much these days. Unfortunately. I used to enjoy the outdoors, but there's never enough time now. You have an unusual job. Do you like it?'

'Most of the time. It can get a bit stressful.'

'In what way?'

'The access to the glacier has been a bit dangerous lately. And you have to deal with people from all cultures and all types of fitness. It's not easy.'

'No. I can imagine. You knew my daughter?'

'She and I flatted together years ago.'

Loraine didn't respond and it was a relief when Jack reappeared with our drinks. Whisky on the rocks for Loraine and a bottle of sauvignon blanc for him and me. I sipped appreciatively. There was a lot to be said for quality, but my enjoyment of the wine was tempered by Loraine's scrutiny.

'I feel terrible that I didn't go into the bush that morning and look for her,' I said. 'I knew she hadn't come out of the track but I didn't do anything.'

Loraine sighed. 'It's not your fault. You'd have probably been killed as well. Whoever did this was deranged. Tell me: what did she want to talk to you about?'

'I don't know. She was asking me about how I was coping with my sister – our parents were killed in a climbing accident; Kate's only eleven. Then Kirsten said – as if the two things were related – that she wanted to talk to me. But I can't figure out what the connection was.'

Loraine sipped her whisky and looked at me for a moment. 'Did she seem upset?'

'Not about that – I had the feeling she was happy about whatever it was she wanted to talk to me about. Yet at the same time she was jumpy and stressed.'

'And you have no idea why?' Loraine's tone was soft.

'No.'

'This notebook you saw. What exactly did she say about that?'

I was starting to feel as if I was in the witness box. 'Something about it being a record of a journey to hell.'

'And no, Ma,' Jack said as Loraine opened her mouth to ask more. 'Philippa doesn't know what she meant. I've told you all this.'

'I needed to hear it myself.'

I hesitated, then said: 'I'm really really sorry. Kirsten was special.'

Loraine's lips quivered, but her eyes were steady. 'Thank you. I didn't realise quite how special my daughter was. Suddenly she's gone and I'll never really know her.'

'You and she were alike in a lot of ways, Ma.'

Loraine sighed. 'You're wrong. We weren't alike at all.'

Jack looked as if he was about to argue, then shrugged. 'Whatever. Tell me, Philippa, do you think it's strange we didn't have a public funeral?'

'I hadn't really thought about it,' I said.

'We were selfish.' Loraine's glass rattled as she set it down sharply on the patio table. 'I couldn't face it, but I realise now that it was unfair. Kirsten's friends had the right to grieve as well. I'm going to organise a memorial service for her. When I can get my head together.'

'Don't do it unless you want to,' I said.

Those two coffins sinking into the wet West Coast soil.

Kate's white face.

Red flowers.

All those eyes looking.

All those people talking.

Judging.

I shivered. Loraine was staring at me.

'I'm sorry. It just reminds me …'

'You poor child. Jonathan told me about your parents. I don't know how you stayed sane. Your sister is a very lucky girl.'

'I don't think so,' I said. 'We're keeping afloat, but only just.'

Jack put his hand on my arm.

We all sat in silence for a few minutes. Then Loraine stood up.

'The boat. Is it badly damaged?' she asked. The softness had gone.

'Not irreparable. But it'll need a lot of work.'

'And how did this intruder gain access to the house? I take it the boat was inside.'

'I keep forgetting to lock the conservatory door when I go out. I'll be more careful now, Ma, don't worry.'

'Honestly, Jonathan. And the telephone calls? How many have you had?'

'Five or six.'

'Probably just a crank.'

'If so, it's a crank who knows me. He - or she - knows my name. The laughing was the worst thing. It sounded way out of control.'

'We could get a trace put on the phone,' Loraine said, 'but chances are the caller's using a throwaway cellphone, so that would probably be a waste of time.'

'Have you told the police?' I asked.

'No. What's to tell? It's all pretty vague.'

'You've got someone stalking you. Someone who's prepared to smash up an antique to make a point. Get real Jack: you've got to do something,' I said.

'It'll be a crank,' Loraine's tone was dismissive. 'I've had some experience of them in the past. Once they've played out their pathetic dramas they move on to other things. None of this sounds seriously threatening. It's just a nuisance.'

But she was wrong. The 'nuisance' was going to get a lot worse if only we had known it.

...

I lay in a claw-footed bath, a glass of red wine at my side, and counted the blue and white tiles on the wall. The scent of flowers and lawn clippings drifted in the open leadlight window.

They had asked me to stay and I'd said yes.

I didn't want to analyse why.

Kirsten could have lived here yet she'd chosen to slum it on the wrong side of town in a flat that should have been condemned. I could see why. There was nothing spontaneous about the well-oiled luxury of this mansion. Everything was too perfect. It wasn't a home. There was nothing left to achieve here.

It was different being a visitor, to have escaped from work and feeding the chooks, fights with Kate and all the other trivia that made up a normal day. And there was Jack. I stretched and turned on the hot tap with my big toe, wondering what he was doing.

What was I doing?

Jack interested me. He was the free spirit I'd always wanted to be.

Yes, and there was more.

He was so bloody attractive. I'd been cynical and off men for months. I'd felt sorry for my friends when they got involved with someone, knowing they'd pay for their highs: that ultimately relationships could be an emotionally crippling waste of energy.

And here was Jack short-circuiting my common sense.

Lust. It was down there with maternal urges. Biological traps, both of them. Traps I was far too sensible to fall into.

Yeah, right.

I dragged my reluctant mind onto other things.

I'd been wrong. Loraine Latimer had loved her daughter. Her quiet understated grief was sadder than hysterical emotion would have been. I remembered Kirsten's bitter words about her family and shivered. No more chances.

And there was Jack. He was being stalked, but I was puzzled rather than worried. With hindsight, I can hardly believe that I felt so casual about it. I guess I was too convinced that Jack was ignorant of whatever it was that had caused Kirsten's death to believe he also was under threat.

The room was almost dark when I dragged myself from the tub, wrapped myself in a thick white towel, and leaned out the window. The garden below was in deep shadow and the only sound was the rustle of leaves in the oak trees. It was hard to believe this place was in the middle of a city.

I dressed and padded along the hallway to my bedroom, settling into the queen-sized guest bed with a book. I had no idea where Loraine or Jack were sleeping, and was starting to think I had the upper floor to myself, it was so quiet. I jumped when someone knocked on my door. Jack slipped into the room, dressed in shorts and T-shirt, his wet hair plastered against his head.

'Settled? You look it,' he grinned. 'I've been out running.'

'Weren't you worried about your stalker?'

He laughed. 'I was, yes, but I told myself not to be stupid. Ma wasn't worried, and she's usually over-protective.'

Her attitude had puzzled me but I didn't feel like going into it with Jack. 'You didn't see anything while you were out?'

'Nah, nothing. God, I'm unfit. Took me forever to get round the park. I'll go and have a shower then I'll bring you a nightcap. That's if you don't mind company for a while?'

'No' I said. I didn't mind it at all actually. In fact … I went back to my book but my mind wasn't really on it. Jack eventually reappeared in jeans and a clean shirt, carrying a glass of red wine for me and a can of beer for himself.

'I could get used to this kind of luxury,' I said.

'My mother has a good cellar. So we might as well make the most of it. Philippa, thanks for coming. I do appreciate it, you know.' Jack settled himself beside me, stuffing a pillow into the small of his back and leaning back against the headboard.

'I don't know if it helped, really.'

'It did, believe me. I couldn't believe how much she opened up to you. And when she started talking about memorial services and friends' rights to grieve I almost fell off my chair. '

'Actually, I liked your mother.'

He laughed. 'You sound surprised .'

'Yes well...' I was embarrassed and Jack noticed and laughed all the more.

'She liked you too.'

'We've got something in common. Death.' I felt drained all of a sudden. I wanted him to get out of the room, to leave me to sleep. But at the same time I wanted… something else.

I'd been uptight, prickly and alone for months. Suddenly I wanted someone close to me.

Jack was looking at me.

I shivered as he touched me.

'You needn't worry about Loraine; she's at the other end of the house.' His reassurance was unnecessary. He slipped his hands under my night shirt as we kissed, and after that I don't think we'd have heard a burglary going on in the next room.

Unfortunately the outside world came even closer. We were naked and tangled in the blue linen sheets when the door swung open and Loraine stood in front of us.

'Jonathan, there's someone outside!' she said.

...

We crept downstairs, Loraine leading the way, straight backed in a burgundy dressing gown. No one said a word. Jack glanced at me, his expression amused, but he was the only one of us smiling.

I wasn't scared. The prowler outside didn't seem anywhere near as real as my embarrassment. This was the kind of thing that happened when you were a teenager, not when you were in your twenties. Actually it had never happened when I was a teenager.

We stopped beside a window in the downstairs hallway, and Loraine leaned her face against the glass. There was no sound outside and just as I was wondering if Loraine had invented the prowler to check up on her son, Jack stiffened beside me.

'There's someone out by the pool,' he said. 'Either that or the shadows are moving.'

'Should we ring the police?' I said.

'Not yet.' Loraine's tone would have frozen a bank robber. Her shoulders were taut as she sheltered against the window frame, staring out onto the darkened lawn.

'Shit!' Jack said. 'They'll get out the gate. I'll run out onto the street and see ...'

'No! Stay here, Jonathan.' Loraine reached out with her left hand and flicked a switch. The lawn was flooded with light. 'These should have come on automatically. Did you turn them off before you went to bed?'

'No. Why should I?'

'Did you leave the door unlocked when you went out running?' Loraine opened it as she spoke. 'You did, of course. Well, someone was watching you again. I ...' Her sentence was choked by a stifled scream.

Jack's car was silver under the floodlights. The headlights were smeared bright red with blood.

Chapter 8

I watched them talking and was jealous, despite everything I knew. R played a good part that night. Sad, hurt, but still loving. Ready to forgive.

Yes. Jealousy was part of it. I wonder why it has taken me so long to admit that. I've always know that jealousy is a sick emotion, and I can usually control it, but that night I could feel it radiating from my body like heat.

R recognised it and smiled.

Our victim recognised it and thought I was mad, that R needed protection from me.

What a joke.

This story is like one of those magic wooden boxes where you press a button and it opens to reveal a smaller box. There are so many layers to our crime. So many people affected. None of whom are innocent except those who were born later, and even they...

It's a help to write it all down. I don't know what I'll do with this record when I'm finished. I hope then I'll be brave enough to die, but I won't take this confession with me. I'm writing it for those who need to know. But I'm digressing.

R was enjoying the act that night, and we'd all had too much to drink. I don't know when I felt our plan slipping away, but I knew that unless we did it then, we never would.

R smiled as I picked up the hammer, reached out a hand as if to stop me then shrugged and withdrew. I struck the first blow, but R helped. God, but it was hard. A healthy human being does not die easily.

I'm shaking. Decades too late. I have to put down the pen and wait for my hands to be still. Because I'm back there as I write, watching the light flare and die in the Tilley lamp, smelling the metallic scent of kerosene, watching our victim die. A scene I've played so many times, but one which never loses its impact.

The worst thing of all was the expression on our victim's face as I lifted the hammer. There must have been fear, but that's not what I remember.

That look of revulsion. Towards me. Not R. Me.

...

'I don't know what this is all about,' Loraine said, 'but I think it would be best if w all forget what we've seen tonight.'

'Get real, Ma.' Jack looked annoyed. 'We should call the police.'

'And play into the hands of whoever did this? They're getting desperate. Pushing harder for a reaction. I won't give them the satisfaction.'

Jack opened his mouth to object, but something in Loraine's expression stopped him.

'This kind of thing has happened to me before,' she said. 'You know that, Jonathan. It goes with my career. I was harassed years ago and went to the police. All it did was increase the problem. It was never solved.'

'It's not you being threatened this time, Ma.'

'Of course it is. You're my son.'

'It might surprise you to know I have my own existence too, Loraine. You're assuming too much.'

'You have someone with a grudge, then? Is that what you're saying? Who, then?'

'Obviously it has something to do with Kirsten's murder.'

'Don't be ridiculous, Jonathan.' But by the look in Loraine's eyes I could tell she had already thought of this.

'Loraine, someone's blood is smeared all over my headlights and you don't seem to think it matters. Well I'm sorry, but I don't agree with you,' Jack snapped.

'Of course it matters. The point is not to let it matter too much. I don't intend to be driven crazy by some sick person. And it won't be human blood. This is a tacky little drama and I refuse to get involved in it. But I'll get the blood tested, if it makes you feel any happier.'

'It's the least we should do. We're going to look really good if it is human and we haven't bothered to report it.'

'I'll take that risk. Now go back to bed.' Loraine glanced at me for the first time and, oddly, she looked amused.

I didn't feel all that amused as I crawled back into bed, but I was past thinking about Jack's body. Loraine's reactions were all wrong. I knew all about detached parents, but if something like that had happened to Kate, Tom or me, mine would have been horrified. Okay, so Loraine made tough decisions in her job, and she could have made plenty of enemies, but it didn't seem normal to shrug off bloodstained headlights as a prank.

She had been shocked when she first saw them, but her recovery was quick, and she was quick to deny Jack's suggestion that it could be connected to Kirsten's murder. Why?

I gasped as something moved in the darkness and Jack slipped into bed beside me.

'Now,' he said, 'where were we?'

...

In trouble was the obvious answer. It was nine o'clock. The window was wide open, and sun poured onto the end of my bed. Jack had been gone for ages. I'd mumbled something about being up soon three hours ago, and then fallen back into a sound sleep.

I was surprised to hear voices as I approached the kitchen. Loraine should have been gone by now. Jack was leaning across the table talking to a blonde woman. I hesitated. Their voices were low and intense. I was about to turn away when Jack glanced up and noticed me. He grinned. His visitor turned towards me, revealing a heart-shaped face with laugh lines around the eyes. She had looked young from behind, but I realised she was probably Loraine's age. Her skin was weathered, as if she had made no attempt to protect it when she was young. There was character in her face and her eyes were intelligent.

'This is Philippa,' Jack said. 'My godmother, Helen.'

We shook hands. Who was she? I'd seen her face before, but I could not place it. She noticed and looked amused rather than puzzled.

'I've just been telling Helen about what happened last night. And about my mother's total indifference.'

'And I've been telling him he's too hard on his mother.'

'I'm too hard? Come on, Helen. That word takes on a whole new meaning anywhere near Loraine.'

'Have you ever wondered why that is? People are made, you know, Jack. We very rarely just are.'

'You know what your trouble is? You're too kind.'

Helen didn't smile. 'I'm not, actually. Your mother stands her ground, Jack, and sometimes she can seem harsh. But she is loyal beyond question to those she cares about. She has been a good friend to me down the years.'

'I just can't make her out sometimes.'

She shrugged. 'Loraine's had some hard things to live with.'

'It's always the excuse, isn't it? I don't notice empathy having much effect on her when she's sentencing.'

Helen looked at me and her expression was troubled. 'Forgive this, Philippa. Jack and I have always sparred, but now isn't the time. Are you here on a holiday?'

Our talk became general, and I had the feeling she was not just asking questions for the sake of it. She seemed really interested, especially when I explained my home situation.

'Your sister sounds bright. You're lucky. I wanted a sister so badly when I was a child.'

Jack drifted off somewhere. Two hours and several cups of coffee later I'd told her just about all there was to tell about my troubled relationship with my sister, and felt as if an infection had been drawn from my heart. But Helen evaded any discussion about herself. I was glad to have her there, as I felt awkward with Jack after what had happened between us last night.

'Who is she?' I asked when she had gone. 'I've seen her before but I can't place her.'

'You really don't know?' Jack was amused.

I shook my head.

'Helen Grenville.'

'Helen... Not the Helen Grenville?'

Helen Grenville had stood for parliament in the last election, winning a landslide victory for Labour in a seat that had always been held by National. Her election promises were simple and unusually sincere. 'Children are disenfranchised at a time when they are most vulnerable. I speak for them,' she had said in her election-night speech. I was no admirer of politicians but I believed her. She had since disappeared from the podium. She was too busy out there working with disadvantaged children and community groups to have any time for grandstanding.

'She's had a sad life,' Jack said. 'She wanted children but she could never have them.'

'She sounds close to your mother.'

'Yeah. They've known each other for years. Though you'd have to wonder why. They've got zero in common.'

We looked at each other. Suddenly there was a chasm between us and I didn't know what to say to him. He grinned at me and reached across the table to touch my arm. 'About last night…'

I could feel my face going red but he pretended not to notice. 'I wasn't planning that, you know, Philippa. But I am glad it happened.'

I looked at him for a moment then smiled. 'Me too. But I don't want you to think …'

'Hey I don't think anything bad. I know you had a tough relationship break a while back but I have the sense you're over it. I haven't been with anyone for a couple of years now and I liked you the moment I saw you. I was telling myself to do nothing about it but I guess I couldn't help myself.

Well when he put it that way there seemed no good reason not to do it all again.

'Jack, do you really have no idea who Kirsten's boyfriend was?' I asked some time later.

He yawned and sat up in bed. 'I'd have said there wasn't one. It was one of the first things the police asked and everyone said the same. My sister seemed to have given up on men.'

'But?'

'But there was one after all. Had to have been. She was two months pregnant.'

'Really? I don't believe it! Is that what she wanted to talk to me about? She wanted to talk to me about something personal, not about her investigation. After all what would I know about the criminal underworld? I'm a glacier guide buried in South Westland'

'Since when have you been an expert on pregnancy?' Jack looked surprised. 'You haven't got a baby hidden away have you?'

'God forbid. But I am learning fast what it means to be tied down. In my case it's an eleven-year-old sister. Kirsten met Kate at the lake that day, made one of her tactful remarks about what a tie it must be, and immediately said she wanted to talk to me about something.'

I thought for a minute, and then said: 'We were talking about relationships - general stuff, you know. Well, you know what Kirsten was like: useless when it came to men.'

'You can say that again.'

'But she told me that day she'd finally got that part of her life sorted out, even though it had thrown up a whole new lot of problems. Maybe she meant she'd met the perfect man, but was pregnant as a result.'

'If he was so perfect why hasn't he come forward? And why was it such a big secret?'

I shrugged. 'He could have been married.'

'Yeah, well that's what Loraine thinks.'

After that we had got up and gone out for coffee. We talked about ourselves as you do when you've just fallen into bed with someone and I was feeling good about it all. Jack looked puzzled as we approached the house.

'Ma's home,' he said. 'Strange. She should still be at work.'

Her car was outside but Loraine was nowhere to be seen. The doors were wide open but there was no sign of her in the living rooms or kitchen.

'I'm going to have a shower. Grab a drink if you want one,' Jack said.

I wandered round the house trying to make up my mind what to do. I felt lethargic and suddenly depressed. I wandered into the formal dining room, running my hand along the length of the gleaming rimu table, and paused beside a bookshelf. Most of the classics were there, bound in navy leather. Jane Austen, George Eliot, the Brontes and a full set of Dickens. The book on West Coast mountaineering looked out of place. I picked it off the shelf and thumbed through it. As I did so, something fell out. I stared down at the pressed flower lying on the floor. It was small, white, with a yellow tinge around the edges. An everlasting daisy, just like the ones that had been found on Kirsten's body. But this flower was very old.

I picked up the flower, staring at the tiny white petals as I remembered what Jack had told me. About the flowers on Kirsten's body. About a doll on the floor of the bach, similarly decorated. And here in this house was a flower of the same kind. One that had been saved years before. It had been significant to someone. But who?

Loraine had reacted to the flowers on her daughter's body. I thought it was just because it was sick, but what if they had been placed there as some kind of signal to her? Jack could be right. Kirsten's murder could be linked to something that had happened in her family.

But was I letting myself be influenced by his complicated view of things? After all, what he'd told me about Kirsten's secret lover suggested another possible motive for murder: her pregnancy.

Kirsten's lover probably knew about the story she was researching. So had he followed her to Lake Kaniere and killed her? I laughed at myself. I'd been reading too much crime fiction. But if he was innocent why hadn't he come forward? The police would be following up this angle, surely?

I'd tell Jack what I thought and go home. Before I got in any deeper. I'd found nothing to suggest his theory about his sister's murder might be true. Nothing except one faded flower.

And bloodstained headlights. Not to mention the rest of the harassment Jack had experienced. I was not convinced at all by the way Loraine had downplayed the whole thing.

I jumped as I heard footsteps on the stairs. They went past the open doorway and paused in the hallway. Loraine. I remained standing still. It did not occur to me that Loraine had no idea I was here. Not until I heard her pick up the phone. I leaned against the wall, my senses prickling. There was something furtive in her movements, something that alerted me. I don't know what it was.

'Helen?' I heard her say. 'Where have you been? I've been trying to ring you all day.'

There was a long pause. 'Don't I know it.' She sounded angry. 'No, I can't do that. Helen, I'm not going to the police. They know I can't. But I know what they did.'

There was another long pause, then Loraine sighed. 'Oh, Helen. They'd better not try me any further. I don't know how much more I can take. The thing is, there's no way out of this one. Not unless ... Helen, there's someone here.'

I froze, but she was not talking about me. I heard a door bang, then the sound of footsteps in the hallway. 'You there, Ma?'

'It's Jack,' Loraine told Helen, 'I'd better go.'

'Don't hurry.' Jack appeared at the doorway and then he saw me hiding behind the wall.

It still makes me feel cold thinking about that moment.

The expression on his face was not surprise, or even anger. He looked as if he hated me.

...

'What the hell were you doing, Philippa?' he asked a couple of minutes later. He'd retrieved the situation well, walking through the dining room to the outside door, beckoning me to follow him. The look of hatred was gone almost as soon as had come, making me wonder if I had really seen it. I followed him outside, shaken. The only good thing about the situation was that Loraine could have had no idea I had been there.

'What's your problem, Jack?' Suddenly I was furious. I was tired of all the crosscurrents, angry with myself for getting sexually involved with Jack, angry with him for making it happen.

He looked embarrassed. 'I'm sorry. But when I saw you there, eavesdropping on Loraine, I was angry.'

'Why? You want to know why Kirsten was murdered. You think some family secret is the key. You've involved me in this. You can't blame me for listening if I hear something interesting.

'Philippa.' Jack put an arm round my shoulders, but I shrugged away from him. 'Sorry,' he said. It's just, Loraine doesn't know what this is about either.'

'How do you know that? If it isn't about her, then it could involve your father. That's what Kirsten told you. If anyone's likely to know about his past it's your mother.'

'Yeah. But even if she does, she wouldn't talk about it on the phone. She could have walked in there and caught you.'

'You're right, that was careless.' I made a huge effort, forced my mind of the look he had given me and changed the subject. 'That book on mountaineering in there. Whose is it?'

'What? Oh... Dad's, I guess. It wouldn't be Loraine's. He must have left it behind when he moved out.'

'He did a bit of climbing on the West Coast, didn't he?'

'Every spare weekend when he was young. That's why we have the bach at Lake Kaniere. We never go there now. The place has been closed up for years. Dad used to take Kirsten and me there when we were kids.'

'What about your mother?'

'Can you imagine Loraine slumming it in the bush? Not exactly her scene.'

'I wonder if Kirsten stayed there the night before she died.'

'No. The police checked that. Said it looked as if no one had been near the place in years. I think she was staying with someone who has the key to this whole damned mystery. That's why ...'

'Why what?'

'Nothing.'

'Jack, I'm sure your mother knows something. Her reaction to those bloodstained headlights proves it. I think she knows who is doing this.' I wasn't going to tell him what I'd heard her telling Helen, but that conversation had intrigued me. So much for not getting involved. 'I wouldn't mind having a look at your bach at the lake.'

Jack shrugged. 'You won't find anything there.'

'Maybe not. But I could spend some time there, talk to the locals and that kind of thing. There could be someone there who knows what's going on.'

'Philippa, I'm sorry.' He reached forward and kissed me, and I managed to stay frozen for all of half a minute. I looked at his face and saw the sadness in his eyes.

'What is it?'

'Nothing. Honestly.'

I didn't believe him. There was something he wasn't going to tell me. But why? He was the one who had got me involved, after all. In more ways than one. He could be right. His father could have been involved in a crime that had led to Kirsten's murder. If it came out, Loraine's reputation would be seriously damaged. So it was fair enough for him to be protective of her, fair enough for him to be angry with me for spying on her. But to look at me as if he hated me? The man who had been acting as if he was in love with me the night before? It didn't make sense. I hadn't imagined his look. And I could think of no reason for him to be so upset with me.

'I think I'll go home today,' I said. I'll stop at your bach for a night on the way through if that's okay?'

'If you like. But it'll be pretty musty. And there's no power.'

'I'm a glacier guide, remember. It won't be worse than the average mountain hut.'

'You're angry with me, aren't you?'

'Yes. And with myself.'

'Philippa. Don't be.' He laced his fingers in mine and bent towards me.

'Getting together with you has complicated things.' Despite myself, the knot in my throat started to dissolve. I didn't know what was worse, lust or weakness, but if I spent another day with Jack my personality would be in shreds. Everything was warning me not to trust him, yet I'd have gone back to bed with him just like that.

'Stay. One more night.'

'No. I can't. There's Kate, don't forget. I haven't got unlimited time.'

'No. Of course you haven't. Let's have today, though. And dinner tonight. My treat.'

'Okay.'

The cafe was expensive and despite all my injunctions to myself, I started to relax, but was glad to recognise a few survival skills struggling back into view. I heeded them. Even when my car wouldn't start.

We stood in the darkness. 'Take my car,' Jack said. 'That's if you really insist on going tonight. I'll bring yours over when it's fixed and we'll swap.'

A few minutes later I was driving out of Loraine Latimer's gate, and was too busy concentrating on the unfamiliar car to take any notice of the headlights behind me. I was in a city, after all. I turned west, looking forward to the long drive through the mountains. I needed space more than anything right now.

Loraine definitely knew something. What had she said to Helen? That she knew what someone had done, but there was no way out of the situation. So did that mean she'd do anything to protect her reputation, even if it meant her daughter's murderer going unpunished?

I flicked up the rear-vision mirror to cut back on the glare from the headlights behind me and slowed to allow the car to pass me. Instead it slowed and fell behind me. I began the drive up onto Porters Pass, climbing steeply into the night-blackened mountains. Tussocks glowed silver in the headlights and a strong wind tugged at the car. There was no one on the road except me and the car behind. At this time of night it would be no fun to break down, and it was reassuring to know that help was only a hundred metres or so behind me. The driver was keeping well back, obviously happy to follow at my speed.

So what had I found out? Kirsten's family had a bach at the lake, yet Jack was sure she hadn't stayed there the night before her murder. She must have known someone else there. I thought of Simon and Ali, and the obvious stress they'd been under. Were they involved in some way? They lived there after all. Could Simon be the father of Kirsten's baby? I'd already wondered if they'd been lovers. He could have killed Kirsten to stop Ali finding out, just as she could have seized the chance of coming to the lake to tell him about her pregnancy. Jane had seen her with a distressed man the night before she died. It was possible.

The car following me had drawn closer, the driver not bothering to dip the headlights. Feeling uneasy I pulled over again to let it pass, but instead it fell back.

Or had Ali killed her? How would she have responded to the news her husband had fathered Kirsten's child? Especially if Kirsten was determined to bring the relationship out in the open. Ali didn't seem especially happy with Simon, but that didn't mean she'd stand by and let him leave her. But if she had done it surely she wouldn't have gone and "found" the body next day.

Limestone outcrops like castle turrets stood out in the moonlight and I slowed down, tempted to stop for a walk. Then I remembered the car following me and changed my mind. The car was quite a way behind me, but only sporadically out of sight.

No. I didn't believe Ali or Simon had killed Kirsten to prevent anyone finding out about her baby. There were too many other things involved. Like the daisies and the link to Kirsten's family. But most of the connections were at Lake Kaniere, a place Loraine Latimer never visited. So what was the truth of these hints of something wrong in Kirsten's family? Not to mention that she had apparently uncovered it while researching some major public scandal. Something as bad as a paedophile ring. Something that haunted her in a way no other story had done. And something that forced her to seek help from my ex-lover Mark, because there were powerful people involved and she couldn't use her usual channels of information.

Ali was an alternative lifestyle artist and her husband seemed like a retired nobody. They'd been living at Lake Kaniere for years. It seemed unlikely they could have had the kind of influence Kirsten had talked about.

Then there was the woman in the canoe. Sam Acheson. I'd only seen her for a minute but there had been something in Ali's manner that made me curious about her. What was it I'd thought that day? That there was something about Sam that Ali didn't want me to know. Had Kirsten come to the lake to see Sam? If so, why? And what did Ali have to do with it? Was Sam the killer and Ali her concerned friend? I had too many questions and some of these ideas were starting to seem left of field. But if the lake was the place to begin my search for answers so too were the lives of its people.

I drove through the sleeping village of Arthur's Pass, wondering what it would be like to live in a cleft between the mountains, down in a valley where you never saw a decent expanse of sky. People raved about this place but it always made me feel claustrophobic.

As I reached the top of the pass, I was startled to notice the car that had been following suddenly close in on me. I put the car down a gear to slow down as I negotiated a steep slope, trying not to think of the how little stood between the road and the rocky riverbed far below. The car behind me closed in, nudged my bumper, then accelerated, and I felt myself being pushed towards the edge. I wrenched my wheel round and slid back onto the road, accelerating and racing downward as the car came after me.

I felt another sharp bump and screamed as I wrenched the wheel away from the edge. I glanced in the mirror and was was momentarily blinded by the dazzle of silver light.

My heart hammered as I slid on downwards. I knew the road well, but that gave me little advantage.

Again I felt a sickening crunch as my pursuer rammed the car. Again I wrenched the wheel away from the edge. Terrified, I glanced in the mirror and saw something strange. The lights of my pursuer had turned away from me and were lighting the road edge instead. The car must have spun at the same time as I did but it had gone further and was not moving. Stuck?

I wasn't going to hang around to find out.

I raced onto the viaduct, too busy looking at the road to spare a glance for my pursuer.

Skidding off the viaduct, I tore down the last pitch of the pass and raced out of the valley at a speed I'd never travelled at before. There were no lights behind me any more.

I was safe. My body sagged against my seatbelt and I began to shake all over.

Maybe I'd found out too much after all. Or maybe my pursuer thought he was following Jack. If so, it was time Loraine Latimer started worrying about her son.

Chapter 9

We wrapped the body in an old tarpaulin, tied it up with ropes and weights, and carried it down to the boat.

It had been blowing an easterly for days and the lake had been like a sea, but it calmed that night, and the only sign of the storm was the wrack of leaves and twigs plastered along the shoreline.

I rowed until I noticed R was shivering, handed over the oars and shivered myself. We said little as we rowed through the oily black water, the cold air stinging our eyes as we watched the mountains gleam white in the moonlight. We had a long way to go. To a place where the lake was deepest.

Lake Kaniere fills a trough carved by a glacier during the last ice age, 14,000 years ago. It's so deep it's undiveable, or it was then. Maybe someone will be able to get down there one day and find the body.

It was a beautiful night, cold and clear, the only sound the creak of the oars and splash of water against the sides of the boat.

After a while I took over the oars again and R leaned back in the other seat, trailing a hand through the water. 'It feels as thick as blood. But it's the wrong colour, and cold.'

I shivered.

We reached the place. Where the mountains were overlaid by the crowns of the rimu trees. An illusion, of course. The mountains were much higher.

I could go to the exact spot again now. I can remember every line, etched sharp in the winter moonlight.

If you tried to dump a body out of the light aluminium boats of today everyone would end up in the water. But our old wooden boat was so steady, so safe. We watched the bubbles swirling as the water closed round the body.

R laughed. 'Ashes to ashes. Mud to mud.'

I shivered again, looking down into opacity, wondering how long it would take the body to reach the bottom.

People say the lake's bottomless. But that's ridiculous. No glacier carves its way into infinity. There has to be an end to all that water somewhere.

'Amazing Grace'. I can't listen to that song now, but there was a time when I loved it.

R sang it as we rowed home. It seemed right then. Now it seems evil

...

I'd lost my pursuer in an old car that shook if you drove at over one hundred kilometres an hour. I tried to laugh but didn't fool myself. I was scared. Okay, so my attacker also drove a slow car. It hadn't stopped him killing Kirsten. And it could be he was only trying to scare me. Successfully too.

He? Stop being sexist, Philippa. It could easily have been a woman.

Jack must have been the intended victim. It was dark. I was in his car. He'd already been targeted by some maniac.

The big question was, why?

Kirsten had known she was in danger and she'd known the reason for it. Jack, unless he was a great actor, had no idea.

I was at home in my own bed but I still felt cold. A late night visit to a decrepit bach at Lake Kaniere had not been tempting after my drama on Arthur's Pass. I crept into a sleeping house, smelling the aroma of freshly baked bread in the kitchen. Spree had scrambled out of his beanbag to greet me, but Kate and Jane slept on. I'd crawled into bed, but was too strung out to sleep. My thoughts were taking me anywhere. I remembered Loraine's promise to get the blood on Jack's headlights tested. Had she? My mind charged on from one useless speculation to another, and it was a relief when

Kate appeared in my room a few hours later. After what I'd been through, her style of cross-examination was easy to take.

'Are you screwing him?' she asked.

'Why would I be?'

'That's where you were, isn't it? With him?'

'Yes, but not for the reason you think. I went to see Kirsten's mother – she wanted to meet me.'

'Oh yeah? What about Mark? Sally says you'll have to have sex with someone before you can forgive him.'

Sally was eleven. At her age I'd known vaguely what sex was, but had no idea how useful it could be for emotional game-playing.

'Who says I've got anything to forgive with Mark? We both decided to split.'

'He was sleeping with someone else, though. I heard him tell you.'

'And you told Sally. Thanks a lot, Kate.'

'Well, how else are we going to learn things?'

'You could try Sally's brothers. Their love lives would leave mine for dead.' I yawned.

'They never yell them out for the whole world to hear like you do.'

It sounded hostile, but it wasn't really. My sister was looking positively benign compared with how she'd been lately. And she hadn't sworn once.

'How are you getting on with Jane?'

'She's really nice. I hope she stays with us forever.'

It was a depressing prospect.

'She bakes great cakes. And bread. Every day. And she tidies things no one else has looked at in years.'

'Like what?' I was instantly suspicious and Kate noticed and backed off. I didn't push her, but the thought of Jane investigating every corner of our lives, duster in hand, didn't appeal to me at all. I didn't know what she was after, but there had to be a reason why she'd been so keen to move in.

I was being paranoid. Jane needed somewhere quiet to live. She was efficient and liked a tidy house. That was all.

Kate sat on the end of my bed and wrapped her arms round her knees. 'Mark rang,' she said, 'and I gave him your phone number. Did he get you?'

'No. What did you tell him?'

'Nothing.'

I'd only been in Christchurch for a couple of days but it felt like I'd been gone for weeks. My mind and emotions had been through the wringer, and Mark's critical but honest attitude might have helped me. The thought surprised me.

'It's funny he didn't text you. He sounded worried,' Kate said.

What if he had? What if Jack had checked my phone and deleted the message? If I went on this way, I'd start thinking the pigeons perched on the telephone lines were there to spy on me.

'Mark's busy,' I said, not convincing Kate or myself.

'I like him,' she said.

'You didn't when I was going out with him.'

'He's better than that Jack. He's weird. Jane thinks so too.'

'And what the hell does she know about him?'

'Just what I told her. She said you're at risk at the moment because you're vul- something.'

'Vulnerable. Thanks for the psychoanalysis, Kate, but I don't want you talking about me to Jane or anyone else. Her opinion isn't worth having. She doesn't know me.'

'She might know you better than you think,' my sister said.

It was a worrying thought.

...

'Kate's a great child. I've really enjoyed being with her.' Jane sliced into a new loaf. My stomach rumbled.

I'd returned from my run to find Kate had left for school. The kitchen was clean and the smell of freshly ground coffee filled the room. I was feeling better and determined to stop being paranoid about everyone around me. My resolve had faltered when I found Jane at home on a day off, but her bread helped.

'She seems happy. She's stopped swearing,' I said, wishing I didn't feel so grudging.

Jane smiled. 'Not entirely, I'm sorry to say. We had a visit from some Jehovah's Witnesses a few days ago. I'm sure they left convinced there was no hope of salvation at this place.'

I laughed, despite myself.

'She's protective of you,' Jane said.

'Kate? She's just stroppy.'

'Anyway, I thought I'd go off for a walk. You'd probably like a bit of space today.'

'Thanks.' I was surprised by Jane's sensitivity. 'Actually I have to go away again soon. Probably tomorrow. I've got a bit of time off work. Is that okay with you?'

'Of course. Kate and I are doing fine. I don't work at night, so she's only alone for an hour or so after school. And Sally's been here most days.' Jane's voice changed slightly, and I looked up, interested. She hesitated for a moment. 'I probably shouldn't say this, but I don't find Sally all that easy to have around.'

'No. She can be pretty blunt - and wildly imaginative. Hasn't always done Kate a lot of good. But she's a personality. You can't help liking her.'

'Yes.' Jane's voice was full of doubt but she said no more. After she'd gone I tidied away my breakfast things, and retreated to the conservatory with another mug of coffee.

Should I go to the police and tell them I'd been rammed on Arthur's Pass? Probably, but if I did it would open a whole can of worms with Jack and Loraine and I didn't feel up to it. There was one thing I should do. End my liaison with Jack. It was complicating things and clouding my judgement. I didn't need Kate to tell me I was on a road to nowhere. It was interesting that she thought he was a creep while I though him the most attractive man I'd ever met. One of us had to be wrong. I remembered that look he had given me when he found me listening to Loraine's phone call and wondered again what it meant. I was certain I hadn't imagined it. No. There was no future in a relationship with Jack. A lot of it was about plain lust. It's an occupational hazard when you're celibate for too long.

It is ridiculous how sure of yourself you can be at times. I really thought I'd done it that day - got Jack out of my system and moved on.

Spree came flying into the room, tracking soil across the floor, and leapt up for a pat. I caught his mood and chased him outside, tearing round the lawn a few times until we both collapsed in a heap.

I had to do something. I was here on the West Coast with time on my hands. If I could figure out what had happened maybe I could figure out Jack as well. Was he on the level? Was it worth trying to find out?

Assuming it was, the first thing to do was find the person Kirsten had come to the lake to see. It could have been a convenient meeting place with someone who didn't actually live there, but it seemed unlikely. Her family had a long-disused bach there, and if some secret in their past was at the heart of Kirsten's murder, Lake Kaniere had to be more than a casual meeting place.

Ali had lived there for a few years. She must know most of the locals by now. I would talk to her again, but the person I really wanted to see was the woman in the canoe, Sam Acheson. It had been there on the edge of my mind every time I thought of her. Some connection that seemed important. I sighed with frustration. The more you tried the less you remembered.

The year I'd flatted with Kirsten had been one of my photography years. It's something I used to do in stages. Accumulate packets of indifferent photos then give up on it for a few years before I got the bug again. They never made it to albums but ended up scattered through my various boxes of papers. It was worth a search, I thought without enthusiasm. I spent the next two hours sitting on the floor exhuming my past. It was depressing to say the least. I flicked through photos, letters and various other detritus, and was so busy reflecting on the trivia of my life that I didn't miss the thing that should have been there.

There were no photos of Kirsten apart from one of us all sitting round the kitchen table drinking wine. I pushed the last box back under my bed and escaped into the fresh air, vaguely trying to recall what was missing.

Yes. I'd been through six boxes of junk which hadn't been opened for years and hadn't sneezed once. That was what was missing. Dust.

Someone had been through my boxes recently. And I was willing to bet it wasn't Kate or Spree.

...

'Did I give you a fright?' Sally Stuart looked pleased. She enjoyed having an impact. I sat up yawning. My night slithering down Arthur's Pass had caught up with me and I'd gone to sleep in the sun.

Sally sat down beside me. She looked deceptively ordinary, a solidly built girl with a freckled face and a shaggy mop of brown hair. She was dressed in a faded blue T-shirt and jeans ripped at both knees, and looked the tomboy she was. The thing that didn't show was her imagination. Or her willingness to try anything. Security had been tightened at the airport a few months ago after one of the pilots caught her trying to get into a helicopter. She wanted to see what it was like but she didn't plan 'flying it or anything,' she had told him.

Soon after that she'd gone religious, but her interpretations of theology would have curdled the blood of the most rampant born-again Christian. It had taken me a while to get over some of the images she'd thrown up to Kate of souls trapped in the rotting bodies of unbelievers. Our parents' deaths had been hard enough to cope without this kind of nightmare fodder.

But Sally wasn't as out of touch with reality as she seemed, and occasionally scored a direct hit on some aspect of human behaviour you'd think was well beyond a girl of her age. Like my sex life, for example.

'I was hoping to catch you on your own,' she said. 'I'm worried about Kate.'

That was rich, coming from the source of ninety per cent of my sister's fears, but I said nothing.

She glanced at me, making sure she had my complete attention, and must have been satisfied because she looked pleased. 'It's that Jane. She's after something.'

'Why do you say that?'

'You don't like her, do you?'

God! Was the child a mind reader too?

'I… well, I hardly know her. But she seems okay. Kate likes her.'

'Yeah, you got that right. Waste of time talking to her. I tried.'

'What makes you think there's something wrong with Jane?'

'I've never liked her. People in this village are fools.' Sally sighed as if the stupidity of the world was too much to bear. 'No one's as good as everyone thinks she is. I was onto her long before she came to live with you. She prays a lot.'

'Prays?'

'In church when she thinks no one's around. Comes out crying sometimes. I've never been able to get close enough to hear what she says, but it must be bad, don't you reckon?'

'It doesn't sound the best. I didn't know she was religious.'

'You got that right. She's not. If she was she'd go to church when there were other people there, not just sneak in on her own.'

'Different strokes, Sally. People have different ways of expressing things.'

'Nah. I reckon she's done something real bad and she's praying for forgiveness.'

And I was leaving this woman alone with my sister! My stomach churned. You're listening to Sally Stuart, I reminded myself. If half of Sally's theories had proved right over the last couple of years there wouldn't be many local people not in prison by now. All the same …

'She's good with Kate. She's not her target.' Sally looked reassuring, and I was annoyed she'd noticed how much she had got to me. 'I think she likes Kate actually. But she's using her so she can get close to you.'

'Why would she want to do that?' I asked, thinking of my dust-free boxes.

'I don't know. But she's always looking through your things. Kate's so dumb sometimes, she just doesn't see it.'

'What things?'

'Your desk. One day when Kate wasn't here. I watched through the window. Jane went through the lot: every drawer and every pigeonhole. I watched her for ages.'

...

I had to laugh. Two people had now searched my shambles of a desk. I hoped they'd had fun among the MasterCard receipts, household bills and other bits of paper too boring to think about. The main items of interest were Kate's school reports and my bank statements. All they proved was that my sister had ability but wouldn't use it, while I had no money but spent it anyway. Well worth snooping to find.

If only my life was as interesting as everyone seemed to think.

I drove into Hokitika, enjoying the blast of sea air outside the supermarket before fighting my way through a crowded checkout. A few minutes later I was driving towards the mountains, winding up my window as the bush enclosed me. I'd left Hokitika in sunshine, but as I got closer to the hills the day got greyer and I wondered if it was going to rain.

What did I hope to find here in the place that Kirsten had died? There was a mysterious woman in a canoe who might have known Kirsten, a couple with marriage problems who could be hiding something about her murder, and an old family bach. Tenuous? Very.

But I was stubbornly sure this mountain lake was integral to the crime, not a randomly selected murder site.

I drove slowly beside the lake, looking for the bach. I had expected a ruin, so was pleasantly surprised at what I saw. The dilapidated weatherboards were virtually stripped of paint and the bush had grown close to the windows, but there were no gaping holes in the walls or flapping sheets of corrugated iron on the roof. The driveway was almost too narrow for the car, but I was pleased to notice the bach had an internal garage.

As I opened the front door the old metal hinges seemed to gasp. I jumped. The hallway was dark, and the boxy ground-floor rooms weren't much better. I stood still listening to the branches scratching the windows. The place was dry and still. It seemed as if it was holding its breath, waiting for something. Get real, Philippa, I told myself, forcing my feet onwards.

There was dust everywhere, except for a small patch of floor at the foot of the stairs which looked as if it had been brushed recently. I squatted by it, puzzled. There was nothing there, and no apparent reason to sweep such a small part of the hallway.

There was less dust upstairs and I chose a room where the air seemed fresher and spread out my sleeping bag on the bunk. There was more light coming in the window than in the rooms downstairs, but the dark matchlined walls canceled it out.

I clattered downstairs to a kitchen that looked retro enough to be a museum exhibit. The black-and-white lino was scruffy and full of holes, dust was thick on the wooden table, but the cast iron stove looked magnificent - big enough to live in, though obviously not functioning. I set up my tramping Primus on the wooden bench and hummed to myself as I heated water for coffee, trying to break through the sense of sad expectancy the bach seemed to exude. The view didn't help. The kitchen window looked over a wilderness of rank grass flanked by a ragged semi circle of olive-green rimu trees. I opened a cupboard and jumped backwards at the small white shape I found there. It was a naked porcelain doll. The same doll that someone had left on the floor for Kirsten's family to find?

And then I heard someone at the door.

…

Ali was holding her jade pendant in both hands. It reminded me of the day I'd met her on the Kahikatea Walk just after Kirsten's murder. She looked relieved when she saw that it was only me.

'Philippa! I was just trying to decide if I was game enough to come in and investigate or whether I should wimp off home and get Simon. No one's been in this place for years.'

'I'm staying here for a few days.' I'd thought about what I was going to say to Ali and anyone else I needed to talk to about Kirsten's murder. That Jack and I were friends, and he'd offered me the use of his family bach. It wasn't that I distrusted Ali, but I thought I'd find out more if I seemed only casually connected to Kirsten. I had no official authority to run around asking questions, after all.

'Kirsten's brother.' Ali sounded thoughtful. 'He must be going through hell. Were they close?'

'Not especially. But he's worried her death is connected to something in their family's past.'

'That's ridiculous. Kirsten was surely killed over a story she was writing. She struck me as a young woman firmly rooted in the present day.'

'I didn't realise you'd met her.'

Ali shrugged. 'I hadn't. But I have been keeping up with the news about her since. The media have had a field day. Not often they turn up a real live whodunit with one of their own.'

'No. Would you like coffee?' I asked her.

'Surely you haven't coaxed the black stove to life?'

I laughed. 'No. I've got a Primus.'

'Okay, thanks.' She seemed reluctant as she followed me through to the kitchen and I wondered why. She ran her fingers through the dust on the table and peered out the window. 'God, what a miserable place this is. No wonder no one uses it. Is Jack meeting you here?'

'I hope so. Depends if he can get away.' What a good liar I was turning into. 'There was something I wondered about, Ali. That woman in the canoe. Sam. Do you know much about her?'

'Why? What do you want to know?'

'It's just … I've seen her before somewhere. It's been puzzling me.'

'She's a sad woman.' Ali sounded relieved at my explanation and I wondered why my question seemed to have worried her.

'Sad?'

'She was quite famous once. One of the country's leading naturalists. Now she's an alcoholic on a make-work project with no future.'

'Has she any family?'

'None that mean anything to her. She told me they'd cast her off, but I think it was the other way round.'

'What does she actually do here?'

'She's doing bird studies for the conservation department. A bit of a come-down for a woman with a doctorate in zoology. She could have had a top job in any university or chosen any field study she wanted, but instead she threw away her career and took jobs anywhere she didn't have to meet people. She worked as a firewatcher in a tower in the middle of a forest before she came here.'

'Did she know Kirsten?'

'Why should she have?'

'Jack thinks his sister came to Lake Kaniere to meet someone.'

'Why should it be her?' Ali's voice was sharp. 'It can't have been, anyway. Sam was away when Prince William came to the lake. I gave her a ride to town to catch the bus a week or so before. She didn't come back till the day after the murder.'

'I wasn't suggesting that she killed Kirsten.'

'No? What were you suggesting?' Ali noticed my surprise and looked embarrassed. 'Sorry, Philippa, sorry, I'm hyped up. The truth is, Sam's a wonderful person and I don't want to see her hurt by life any more than she already is.'

'Kirsten stayed with someone the night before she died. Jack wants to know who.'

'Well it wouldn't have been Sam even if she had been here. She's camping in a possumer's hut up the side of the lake. It's a two-hour walk from here. There's no road access.'

What is it you don't want me to know about Sam, Ali? I said to myself as she walked down the driveway. What are you hiding?

...

I turned onto my side and unzipped my sleeping bag. The room was hot and airless, but I didn't dare open the window because of mosquitoes. It was midnight and I was still wide awake. I was nervous.

There was some link between Sam and Kirsten. Ali's evasion made me even more determined to find out what. The thing was, it was something I already knew. But my mind would not cooperate.

I slept and dreamed I was swimming out into the black water of the lake as the moon lit the mountains and sky. It was warm. Unreal. There was a fire on the lakeshore. I swam towards it, watching golden tongues of flame grabbing black branches and smothering them, and listened to the crackle of the fire as it moved eerily over the lake towards me. There was a loud cracking noise.

I sat up in bed. The noise was real. I jumped out of bed. My room was on the same side of the house as the kitchen and I peered out of the window onto a moonlit patch of lawn. Someone was standing on the edge of it and as I looked stepped back onto something that cracked underfoot. A person in a hooded raincoat was staring at the bach. I could see the pale blur of a face and shrunk back behind the window frame.

I was terrified. It was two o'clock in the morning and some maniac was out there staring at the bach I was alone in.

I scrambled into my clothes, pulled on my running shoes and crept down the stairs to the kitchen door. I was relieved to see that it was locked. When I peered out the window again the person was gone.

He wasn't after me, I told myself. My car was invisible in the garage, I'd been in bed asleep. There was nothing to suggest there was anyone in the bach. For some reason this person – Kirsten's killer? – was hanging round her family bach in the middle of the night.

But why?

Chapter 10

The Cousteau team went to Lake Kaniere a few years ago. They landed their floatplane at the south end of the lake and did a dive.

I was living in another part of the country then, and I walked into a dairy to confront a headline: 'Gruesome find in Lake Kaniere'.

I felt sick.

...

There was one thing I could do. Eliminate a few potential prowlers.

I had lain in bed after the prowler had gone, wide awake and uncomfortable in the musty air. After an hour of sleeplessness I got out of bed and switched on my phone. There was no signal. I swore, scrabbled in my wallet and found a handful of loose change. I had only a few dollars, but wouldn't need much. I dressed quickly and let myself out of the bach, glancing uneasily up and down the road. There was no one around and I relaxed, savouring the fresh night air. A full moon lit the road and the sky glowed. The phone wasn't in a proper box, but inside a cupboard mounted on a pole and it was an old-fashioned coin model. I picked up the clunky bakelite receiver and held it to my ear, relieved to hear the dial tone.

I glanced over my shoulder as I dialled the first number, uneasy, though I'd heard no sound. Anyone would be able to see me in the moonlight. But it was a risk I had to take. The phone rang unanswered as I counted the seconds it would take to get from Jane's bed to the phone in the hallway. Sally's tales of Jane's tear-soaked guilt no longer sounded crazy. I had to know that she wasn't extending her guilt trips further to firelighting rituals at Lake Kaniere.

Where was she? As the phone kept ringing, I imagined Jane fled, Kate dead, Spree strung up by his paws out in the shed. Stupid, I know, but it was the early hours of the morning and I'd had a strange night.

'Hello?'

I jumped as Jane answered the phone, then waited until she spoke again. I put down the phone and my heart was thumping. Not her. Thank God.

Was the prowler the killer? It was certainly possible. And if so, it couldn't be Jane. I imagined her standing puzzled and perhaps scared in the hallway, imagined Kate awake and curious.

I picked up the receiver and dialled again.

'Loraine Latimer. Who is it?' She sounded annoyed, as well she might, at being awakened at two o'clock in the morning. I replaced the receiver.

So neither Jane nor Loraine had been at the prowling near the scene of the crime. But I had no way of knowing about Jack. There was no point ringing his cellphone – that wouldn't tell me where he was.

Jack didn't kill his sister, I told myself, shutting the phone box and walking back to the bach. But I couldn't still the doubts. I recalled his look of hatred when he found me eavesdropping on Loraine. I shivered.

I didn't understand him and it worried me.

...

Sometime before dawn I awoke again to the sound of mosquitoes and it came back to me. The link between Kirsten and Sam. It was so ordinary. Kirsten had written a magazine feature on Sam's work with endangered species. I'd read it on the plane as I flew up to Auckland a year or so ago.

I didn't want to ask Ali how to find her, given her defensive answers to my questions about Sam. I'd just have to try and meet her by chance, a slightly difficult task given that she travelled by canoe. She lived out in the bush somewhere round here. She could have been the prowler. Though I couldn't imagine why.

Kirsten had come here to see someone. It could have been her. Why not? At least they knew each other. It might mean something.

A truck with a Department of Conservation logo on its door pulled up beside me, and a guy about my age climbed out. He dragged a lawnmower off the back. His long brown hair was tied into a ponytail with a leather bootlace, and he wore baggy khaki overalls which flapped against his skinny frame.

'Hi,' I said.

He nodded.

'You might be able to help me,' I said. 'I'm looking for someone. Sam Acheson.'

'Yeah.' He bent to his mower, unscrewing the petrol cap, and looked round vaguely for his can of petrol. I passed it to him.

'Sam.' His voice was bland. 'Yeah, I know her. Doesn't like people much. You want to see her?'

'If I can find her.'

'Could be out on the lake. Or at her hut.'

'Where is it?'

'What?'

'Her hut.' I tried to keep the impatience out of my voice.

'Oh. Yeah. Up the far end of the lake track. Take you a couple of hours to walk to it.' He sounded dubious. 'Likely she won't be there.'

'Well, thanks. It's worth a try.'

He turned away from me, and started the mower.

I went back to the bach and packed myself some lunch. It would not be a waste of time even if I didn't find Sam. I needed some exercise. I strode through the bush, pausing to look at lake views when the track passed close to the water. I'd had a headache and my senses felt dull, but after an hour in the bush I felt fresh again. I stopped for a while, perching on a rock, and gazing across the lake onto purple hillsides, and lifted my face to the breeze. Small waves splashed at my feet, and I heard the high clear note of a bellbird.

After a while I scrambled to my feet and headed back into the bush. I arrived at the hut before I expected to, and paused for a moment, suddenly frightened at what I was doing. No one knew I was here except a guy who would have forgotten me the moment he turned to start his lawnmower.

There were plenty of spectacular lakeside building sites available, but the hut was jammed in the middle of a dense stand of second-growth bush. It was built of corrugated iron and was small, dark and mean, its tiny window jammed open with a stick and mosquito netting nailed across the window frame. An open padlock hung from a metal loop on the door.

I knocked. There was no answer.

I waited a moment, then forced my way through black supplejack vine, stumbling out onto the lakeshore and blinking in the sudden dazzle of light. This was better. I sat on the shore, wrapped my arms round my knees, and looked around me. A large hook was nailed into an overhanging tree and a coil of yellow nylon rope hung in one of its branches. There was no sign of Sam's canoe.

I ate my lunch, feeling jumpy. It was amazing how much noise you noticed in the bush when you were feeling edgy. I wasn't in any mood to enjoy the sun, and the constant sandfly bites added nothing in the way of relaxation. I scrabbled in my pack and hauled out my map. This beach was called Lawyer's Delight. Though what there was to be delighted about I couldn't imagine. Even though I couldn't see the hut from the beach its spirit seemed to radiate, depressing the whole area.

Sally Stuart would be proud of you, I told myself. It's sunny and the views are great. What's your problem?

Sam Acheson had been brilliant and she'd ended up living here. Brains guaranteed you nothing. The more you had, the greater was the scope for grief.

I killed my millionth sandfly and scrambled back through the supplejack to the hut. I put my hand on the door and hesitated, tempted to go in, to escape the sandflies if nothing else, but if Sam returned and caught me there it wouldn't get things off to a great start. I contented myself with a look in the window, and saw a bunk with a dark brown sleeping bag spread out on it, an unpainted wooden table, an ash-filled grate and a rough shelf crammed full of books. Tins of food were stacked on the bench, heavy raincoats and bush shirts hung from nails on the wall, and a half-empty whisky bottle sat on a stool by the bunk.

A twig snapped behind me and I whirled round, heart thudding.

'Hello?' I called.

There was no reply.

I went back to the lakeshore, feeling spooked and depressed, covered as much of myself as I could to escape the sandflies, and tried to read my book. I'd chosen badly. Patricia Cornwell's graphic tale of young lovers being murdered in remote woodland settings didn't make me feel good about being in the bush on my own.

It was getting late. If Sam didn't arrive soon I would have to leave. The thought of a torchlight retreat back to civilisation wasn't appealing. I stretched out on the shore, shielding my eyes with my arm, and tried to enjoy the sun. It didn't hang around for long. Clouds rolled in and Lawyers Delight Beach grew cold.

I heard her before I saw her. A paddle slapped the water and I turned towards the sound and watched the canoe slide out of the dusk. I wasn't trying to hide, but was out of Sam's line of vision, and she didn't notice me. She jumped out and bent to pull her canoe onto the shore. I called out to her and she jumped. She was small and slim, her body lost in black track pants and a blue-and-black checked bush shirt which enveloped her to the knees. Her hair was long and grey, and swung in heavy plaits, framing her face.

'Who are you?'

'I'm sorry.' I moved towards her, then hesitated. 'I'm Philippa Barnes. I didn't mean to startle you.'

'Just like the other girl.' Sam clutched the yellow rope so tightly her knuckles gleamed white. 'Are you a tramper?'

'Not exactly. I'm staying at a bach at the other end of the lake.'

As I spoke, I noticed the sky had become black and some heavy drops began to fall.

'How do you think you're going to get back there in this?' Sam's voice was unfriendly and she turned towards her hut, gesturing with her arm that I should follow her. As we stepped inside the rain poured down, the noise on the corrugated iron was deafening. 'You can't go back tonight.' Sam looked less than pleased. It'll be dark soon too.'

'I've got a torch,' I said. 'I'll be fine.'

'It wouldn't be safe. I suppose you'll have to stay here.'

I'd had more tempting offers, but the though of battling my way through a storm wasn't appealing either. How could I have been so stupid? The weather had been deteriorating and it should have been obvious what was going to happen. Admittedly this was extreme. There was a sudden flash of light then such a crack of thunder that I expected the rocks to come tumbling off the mountains. Sam seemed impervious to the noise. She lit the fire and turned on her small gas cooker.

I'd come here to see the woman but now I wanted to run. It was illogical. Sam was obviously not pleased to find herself lumbered with a guest, but this was hardly surprising and it didn't make her an axe murderer.

'You haven't a lot of room,' I said.

'Oh, I've enough. There's an old sleeping bag.'

She said nothing more and her refusal to let me help with dinner made me uncomfortable. I perched on a stool as she threw things into a pot, feeling like the worst kind of optional extra. The tiny hut didn't offer any scope for getting out of the way. I was surprised at how good the stew smelled, a combination of tomato and basil reminding me of some of my favourite Italian dishes. I was starving, and enjoyed every mouthful of the brimming tin plate of food Sam served me. She tended the fire and made me coffee but it was obvious she didn't want to talk. It would have been difficult anyway given the storm outside. An especially loud crack of thunder made me jump but Sam showed no reaction at all.

She cleared away the plates, again refusing my offer of help, then looked at me without saying anything for a few minutes. I felt uncomfortable, and was angry that I'd let the situation slip so totally out of my control. What could I possibly say to this woman?

'Even though I'm a scientist, I find myself believing things that are irrational.' Sam reached forward and threw another branch onto the fire, then turned to look at me. 'That girl – I thought you were her.'

'What girl?' I asked, though I knew.

Sam's hands were trembling. 'The one who was killed. Kirsten. She was there waiting for me just as you were. For a moment I thought she'd come back.'

'When did she come and see you?'

Sam turned away and poured whisky, handing me a glass. I sipped and coughed, while she knocked back a swallow big enough to stun a horse. 'A month before she was killed. More, maybe. It's hard to remember.'

'You weren't at the lake when she was killed?'

'No.'

'Why did she come and see you?'

'Why do you want to know?'

'Kirsten was my friend.' I took another cautious sip and gazed into the fire. 'Her brother thinks she found out something terrible before she died. Something about her father.'

I turned and met Sam's eyes. Her face was frozen.

'You talked to her before she died. I don't want to push you, but it would help her family. They need to know what she found.'

'I have nothing to tell them.' Sam's voice was hard.

'Did you know Kirsten's father? Alex Browne?'

She looked away from me and rummaged in a pack, pulling out an old sleeping bag. 'I've got a foam pad you can lie on,' she said, 'and if you sleep near the fire you'll be warm. I'll be gone when you wake. Go back to where you came from and tell no one where you've been.'

'Why?'

'I can't tell you. I spoke to Kirsten. It did her no good.'

'Why was she killed?'

'I have no idea.' Sam's face was like stone.

'Do you know who killed her then?'

'No. No. I wasn't here. All I did was fill her last weeks with pain. That's a worse crime. The other would have been quick.'

'You think she died because of something you told her?'

'I tell you, I don't know!' Sam touched my shoulder and gazed at me, as if willing me to believe her, then relaxed and turned away from me and slipped out into the night. She returned minutes later, climbed into her bunk, and turned her face to the wall. The smell of alcohol permeated the night air.

Sam was either crazy or an integral part of the crime. It was too hard to imagine anything else in between.

I watched her leave next morning, while pretending to sleep. She hadn't told me the night before when her mind was relaxed with whisky. She would not do so now.

As light crept in through the small window, I scrambled out of my sleeping bag. My body and head ached. I felt as if I'd had a night on the town, and struggled to remember the disturbing serial dream I'd had during the night.

I looked over my shoulder and hesitated. I was about to do something terrible. Sam had taken me in and fed me, but she had refused to part with her secrets. So I was going to search her hut.

It didn't take long and I found nothing. Her books were mainly natural history texts, stained with water and soil from time in the outdoors. There was no laptop, only her handwritten log of bird species, which was meticulous. I found no other writings. No letters linking her with Kirsten. No photographs.

The only thing of interest in the hut had been clearly visible all the time I had been there. It was a hooded Gore-Tex raincoat, hanging from a nail on the wall. It looked similar in design to the one worn by the prowler I'd seen at Jack's bach, but coats of this kind were as common as pairs of jeans on the West Coast.

I made myself a mug of coffee, ate a slice of Sam's camp-oven bread, and stepped out into a cool morning. There was no trace of last night's storm. I wandered along so lost in thought that I hardly noticed the scenery. Had Sam canoed down the lake to prowl around Kirsten's family bach, and if so why? It had been a moonlight night. I imagined her slipping away, out onto the silver water, and paddling back up the lake to this hut. It was possible. She'd been at the lake. She was strung up and guilty about what she had told Kirsten. But I did not think she had killed her. And I didn't think she really knew why Kirsten had died, though she possibly thought her knowledge had triggered the murder.

Sam was frightened. Had someone warned her off? And if so, what about? I came out onto a rocky headland, and blinked in the sudden dazzle of light on the lake. I sat on a rock and gazed across the water to the purple hills on the far shore.

There might be someone else at the lake who knew. I remembered the crying man. Then my mind spun in a new direction. The only person who had witnessed that encounter was Jane. She could have been lying. What if it was Jane who Kirsten had come to the lake to see? Jane had seen me talking to Kirsten, and had since become involved in my life. No. She had tried to become involved long before Kirsten had actually died. She'd been looking for a quiet house to live in for ages before this event. There was no way she could have known that Kirsten and I would meet and talk that day, and if we had not done so there was absolutely nothing to link Kirsten with me. So where did that leave me? I didn't know.

Jane had searched my house, even though there was nothing for her to find there. And she was at the lake when Kirsten was murdered. I remembered something else. Jane had claimed she hadn't known Prince William was coming to the lake, but the woman was a news freak. She bought all the papers. I noticed this without registering its importance. So she must have known about the prince's visit to Lake Kaniere. The newspapers had been full of it.

And this woman was at home with my sister!

I was surprised when I reached the end of the track. It had seemed to take forever to reach Sam's hut, but I'd been so locked in doom and gloom mode that I'd not noticed the kilometres slipping by.

Jack's bach was like a luxury motel compared to Sam's hut. I wandered round the damp rooms, collecting the possessions I'd strewn around, boiled water for coffee, and sponged myself clean-ish at the sink, hoping no visitors would come along.

I felt more and more keen to be gone. I needed to get home and find out if my sister was all right. And find out what Jane was after. She was connected in some way. How could I have failed to notice her lie about the royal visit?

I had to get home. Now.

Chapter 11

Eels. That's all it was.

They had found massive eels living in the dark waters of the lake.

'If people knew what was in that lake they'd never swim in it,' one of the divers said.

Eels wouldn't have eaten it though. They can't easily tear bits off fresh human bodies and they don't like rotten meat. I knew at the time that we couldn't rely on them to get rid of the evidence. We wrapped and weighted the body well, but material and ropes can rot. You can never be sure with water.

We weren't worried about it at the time. There was too much to do. The blood-stained hammer was easy. We'd thrown it into the lake.

But the living room. We'd turned it into an abattoir.

And the car. We had to make sure it was found far away from Lake Kaniere.

'I'll take it to Christchurch and abandon it. Then I'll come back,' R said.

I was frightened. R was going and would be lost to me forever. It had all been for nothing.

It must have shown in my face.

'I won't leave you,' R said.

I took it to mean never.

...

How could I have left Kate alone with Jane? Okay, she was bloody-minded and often treated me as if I was the worst thing that had ever happened to her. She was happy with Jane. But I'd known Jane was searching my house, and I'd gone off and left my vulnerable young sister alone with her.

Come on, I thought, as the car jerked its way up to 80 kilometres an hour. I planted my foot on the accelerator, but it made no difference. There was no hurry, anyway. Kate would still be at school. Hopefully Jane would be at work. If she was I was going to do some snooping of my own.

I was sure now that Kirsten had been using Prince William's visit to the lake as a cover for some kind of personal investigation. She'd gone there before, to visit Sam Acheson. And had found out something, which was more than I had done. But Sam hadn't been there when Kirsten was killed. Jane had been. She'd seen me having an intense discussion with Kirsten that morning. And she had needed to find out why. Then I'd played into her hands by asking her to move in with Kate and me. She'd fed me a few hints about Kirsten, knowing I'd want to learn more. I'd taken the bait and she'd given me the story she'd prepared for me. About a man crying on the jetty. It was very neat. I'd already met a man from the lake whose life seemed to be falling apart. Somehow Jane knew about him and had set him up as a decoy.

I didn't know why, but it was making sense so far. Jane had killed Kirsten for reasons unknown, and she had a conscience. Sally Stuart had seen it in action.

Jane knew I was involved with Kirsten's brother. She would think that any contact was dangerous. She wasn't without aces though: she had my sister's confidence. Kate made me vulnerable. If I ordered Jane to leave, Kate would oppose me every step of the way. Jane could use Kate to force me to back off. It would be easy.

My imagination was so active by the time I got home that my head was humming with tension. It was a relief to find nothing wrong apart from three uprooted azalea bushes lying on the front doorstep. Spree had been gardening again. He met me with enthusiasm, shedding crumbs of soil, his eyes sparkling.

'You're terrible,' I told him.

His eyes sparkled as he jumped all around me.

Jane wasn't at home.

I hesitated outside her bedroom door. I could ring her workplace on some pretext and make sure she was there. But if Jane was as devious as I thought, this would alert her at once. Her bedroom was at the far end of the house. So I'd have time to get out if I heard her coming. I wasn't happy with my security arrangements but they were the best I could come up with.

My obsession with Kirsten's murder was turning me into a suspicious cow with a nasty habit of snooping. I should ask Tim for a permanent job on the glacier. At least that would keep me busy.

Jane had the room that had once been occupied by my brother Tom. She'd cleared away his junk, but her own possessions didn't occupy much space. Two work uniforms hung in her wardrobe, along with a black dress, a charcoal suit and a pale blue dressing gown. Her drawers were only half full, and each contained an open cake of soap to keep the clothing smelling fresh. Jane mostly wore jeans or track pants and sweatshirts, and these were neatly folded and ironed. There were no personal letters in her desk, just a stack of bank statements and miscellaneous bills.

She had a small collection of books, propped on top of her chest of drawers between brass bookends. Most of them were hardback editions of early New Zealand fiction. I picked up Sylvia Ashton-Warner's Spinster, the story of an inspirational teacher working in the backblocks. There was an inscription on the flyleaf. It was in pencil, and I had to strain my eyes to read it: 'Jane, you have the imagination and the will. Let your mind soar. It's the path to freedom. Love, Margie.'

Jane had been a teacher – an inspired one, from what I had heard. Why had she turned her back on it? Who was Margie? Someone who'd been close to Jane. But no longer. There was no one special in Jane's life. 'I'm alone,' she'd told me around the time she moved in. 'Everyone important in my life has gone away or died.' There'd been no self-pity in her words. They were a flat statement of fact.

I was so lost in my thoughts that I didn't realise Jane was back until she stepped into her room. Her desk was still open; her book was in my hand.

It was lucky I had a career as a glacier guide. Because I wasn't doing well as an amateur private detective.

...

'What are you looking for?' Jane didn't sound angry. But she was watchful.

I looked at her for a moment. 'I'm not sure. But there has to be something, doesn't there?'

Her eyes flicked away from me, and she sat on the side of her bed, smoothing an already immaculate cover as she did so. 'Why do you say that?'

'Because I don't like being used. I've been stupid enough to let you make the most of my weaknesses. But don't think I'll take it if you hurt my sister. Leave her out of whatever you're doing, Jane.'

'Kate has nothing to do with anything. I promise.' She looked upset.

'She'd be a useful tool to use against me. But I'll fight you. And I'll win.' I hoped I sounded more confident than I felt.

'I'd never do that. What do you know, Philippa?'

'Enough to be damn sure I shouldn't have left you alone with Kate. You've lied to me, Jane. While I – fool that I am – didn't trust you, but put it down to my own nasty nature. You went to Lake Kaniere to meet Kirsten. You knew her, and you knew she was going to be there as a journo that day.'

Jane laced her fingers and clenched them, then looked me in the eye and nodded. 'I did lie to you. I'm sorry. At the time it seemed ... necessary. But I didn't kill her. You have to believe that.'

'Why? I have to hand it to you, Jane, you are some strategist. Tell me something. Why did you want to move in here? You were sowing the seeds round the village weeks before Kirsten died. Before you even realised I knew her. Or do you know something I don't?'

Jane sighed. 'Moving in here had nothing to do with Kirsten. That came later. I had no motive for coming to live with you and Kate other than the need to get out of that awful staff accommodation. You've got to believe me, Philippa. It's the truth.'

I stared at her. 'So when you found out I knew Kirsten …?'

Jane sat down on the edge of her bed and wrapped her hands round her knees. 'I can't deny that it added to my incentive to move in. I thought you knew what Kirsten was doing. I wanted you to trust me. Because I need to know …'

'You expect me to trust you?' I paced across to the window, and spun round to glare at Jane. 'You've been through all my things looking for something. You've done all you can to alienate me from my sister …'

'I haven't. I haven't. A relationship with a sister is special. I've done wrong, Philippa, but I haven't done that. I've tried to help you with Kate. I've talked to her about how much you've done for her. Sometimes we'll only listen to outsiders. I think Kate's listened to me. That's been my payback to you. I've been deceiving you, but I've done all I can to make things better between you and Kate.'

'So is it me who's driving you to cry in church? I can't believe I'm etched that deeply on your conscience.'

'Oh.' Jane looked shocked. 'How do you know that?'

'Someone saw you.'

'Yes. I should have realized. Small towns. It's so easy to be seen when you think you're alone.'

'So?'

She sighed, got up from her bed, and shut her desk. When she turned, her shoulders were slumped and her face sad. I felt like a bully but wasn't going to give up now.

'I'll make coffee,' I said, 'and then we are going to have a talk. We must.'

'Yes. You're right.'

Jane said nothing as I made the coffee, and her face was like a mask. You're giving her plenty of time to prepare another lie, I told myself crossly. We moved out into the conservatory, sipping our coffee in silence for a minute. I glanced at the mountains. Some days they made life seem impossible. Beautiful, yet so high. A great barrier locking me into a life I loved – yet one I could never escape from. I felt a twinge of empathy for Jane, and it was strange, because she still hadn't told me anything.

When she started talking her voice was low. I had to strain to hear it.

'Kirsten came to me. A year ago, maybe more. I hope this doesn't make you angry, Philippa, but I've seen you doing just what I did. You've blocked the pain your parents' death has caused you. But one day you're going to have to deal with it. It won't go away.'

My eyes filled with tears, and I scrubbed them away with my fists. I said nothing.

'At least you know what happened.' Jane leaned forward in her chair and looked at me. 'So you have closure. I don't.'

'What do you mean?'

'I lost someone once, and I've never found out what happened to her. Margaret.'

'The inscription in your book?'

'Yes. Margie gave it to me not long before she disappeared.'

'Who was she?'

'My sister. That's what I meant when I talked about you and Kate. Sisters. The relationship is precious, no matter how volatile it may be. And it's irreplaceable.'

I put down my coffee mug. 'What happened?'

'Margie was fifteen years old. I was two years younger, her confidante. But she didn't tell me enough. She walked out of the house one day and never came back. She'd told her parents she was going away with a girlfriend. But she was meeting her lover.'

'You knew that?'

'Yes. But I didn't know who he was. Just that he was a lot older than she was. And that she was sleeping with him, even though she was underaged.'

'She told you that?'

'Yes,' Jane slipped out of her chair and started pacing, picking dead leaves off one of the plants. 'There were times when it frightened her - times when she needed to talk. No one would have believed it, but under her confidence – no, that's too mild a word – her radiance, she was vulnerable.'

Jane smiled, but her eyes were bleak. 'I was frightened for her, but she laughed at my warnings. Then something changed. She was worried, scared. And she wouldn't tell me why, though she'd told me everything before. I came home one day and she was on her own. She was playing Verdi's Requiem. And she was radiant again. The old Margaret. She told me she'd sorted out her problem. That she was happy. And that she was going away with him for the weekend.'

'Did she tell you where she was going?' I stripped a leaf to the spine, watching her face.

Jane shrugged. 'To a West Coast lake. He knew someone with a bach there. Or perhaps he owned it. I never found out. Margie was a city girl, and she wasn't excited about his choice of location for their weekend. "Think of me hidden in the bush and pity me," she said. "He needs to go there, and I find I can't deny him. Not after what's happened." She wouldn't tell me any more. I decided he must have been the one with the problem she'd been so worried about. Not her.'

'So she went, and never came back.'

'The police did everything they could.' Jane perched on the edge of her chair. Her voice was flat. 'But there were no leads. I'd never seen the man, and I didn't know his name. As for the bach – well, it could have been anywhere. I'm sure now that it was Lake Kaniere. The police searched a lot of places. And found nothing. But they weren't convinced she'd even gone to the West Coast. They thought he could have lied to her, taken her somewhere else and killed her there.'

'But why?'

'All kinds of reasons. He was having sex with an underage girl. He could have been married. She could have been pregnant. And Margie wouldn't have gone away quietly if he found her a nuisance.'

'How did you stand it?'

'I just had to. There was a massive search. Murder wasn't common in those days. There were sightings all over the country, but they were more a reflection of public interest than anything important. She just vanished. Well, that's not true.' Jane gave a harsh laugh. 'She was so alive, she left a residue of herself in every corner of our lives. It was impossible to believe she was dead. But she must have been. Because she was happy with her family. She had an adoring younger sister, indulgent parents. No. If she was alive, she'd have told us. I'm as sure of that as I am of anything.'

A high and excited bark echoed across the paddock, and Spree tore past on a mission I didn't like to speculate on. I walked to the glass doors and peered out. He had vanished.

'Where does Kirsten come into this?' I thought of her long-disused bach at a West Coast lake, of a possible scandal involving her father.

'As a reporter.' Jane's voice was hard. 'She found the newspaper reports on Margie's disappearance and came to interview me. She was researching a big story and thought my sister's disappearance was connected to it.'

'What kind of story?'

Now Jane was breaking a spray of leaves from the wisteria and shredding them one by one. 'I don't know.'

I didn't believe her.

'I asked, of course. But Kirsten told me it was part of a far-reaching scandal, affecting people in powerful positions. She said – how did she put it? – that Margaret's was one of the worst stories, but there were other tragedies. That the knowledge was dangerous, and she wasn't ready to tell anyone.'

'Didn't you push her?'

'You knew Kirsten. Did you ever get anywhere pushing her to do something she didn't want to do.'

'But Margaret was your sister. You had the right to know.'

'Kirsten saw that. She told me she needed to think, and arranged to meet me a few days later. She was sympathetic, but very much in reporter mode – detached but determined. But something changed in those few days. Kirsten always dressed well. She wore designer jeans and jackets, things that looked casual, but also elegant. But she met me in town in an outfit she could have painted the house in. Dirty old jeans, a sweatshirt torn at one elbow, and she had dragged her hair back into a tight ponytail. Her eyes – you know how expressive they were.'

I nodded. Kirsten had once told me what a handicap it was. 'You can control your tongue, but not your eyes,' she'd said.

'Her eyes told more than her clothes. She was in pain. And she was dirty. She smelled of sweat. That wasn't like Kirsten.'

'And?' I said after a long silence.

'And, nothing. She didn't tell me much, just that things were worse than she'd thought. "There's more pain in here than I've seen before, and some of it's mine," she told me. She said she was putting the whole story on tape, as she didn't want to endanger anyone else by telling it to them. She said she knew a place where the tapes would be safe. I really pushed her, but she would only say that she could do nothing until after she had covered the royal visit. "Guess where Prince William is going?" she said. "To a scenic little place called Lake Kaniere. A place that is my idea of hell."'

'You must have been living in Franz by then?'

'Yes. I'd organised time off work to go to Christchurch and see Kirsten. I was angry when she refused to talk, but nothing I said made any difference.'

'I wonder if she did record it all on tape.'

'Yes. I'm sure she did.'

'Well, the police obviously haven't found it.'

'They probably don't know where to look.'

'And you do?' I must have sounded disbelieving.

Jane looked tense. 'I do, actually. It's only a vague idea, but it's something. She told me she had a friend who lived on the Otago Peninsula, that she was going down there before she came to the lake. She told me she was leaving the tape with someone she trusted, someone none of her friends or family knew.'

I rubbed my hands across my face and sighed. 'She knew all there was to know about keeping her sources secret. Otago. That's a long way from Christchurch. I wonder ...'

'What?'

'She had a lover no one seems to know anything about. I wonder if the tapes are with him.'

Jane stared at me. 'It's possible. She was so careful. She didn't even tell me whether the friend was male or female.'

'So,' I dragged my thoughts back to Jane, 'you went to the lake to try and make her talk.'

'Yes. But it was no use. I didn't know she was going to be there the night before the royal visit, so it seemed like a stroke of luck when I saw her on the jetty. I waited until the man left, but I had to keep well back, so I didn't see who he was. Then I followed her.'

'Where to?'

'I wish I'd been more subtle. If I'd found out where she was staying, I might know more than I do. She saw me. And she went off her head at me. Told me to leave her alone, that she had enough to cope with without having to nursemaid me through my pain. I left her. There was no point pushing it. I went back to my tent and lay awake all night wanting to die.'

Spree reappeared. He was soaking wet and looked at peace with the world as he came marching through the open conservatory door and flung himself down on the floor at my feet. I gave him an absent minded pat.

'I wonder if she was staying with Ali McKee,' I said.

'Ali? Oh, the artist. I don't know. Why should she?'

'Ali lives there. Not a lot of people do. But she says she never met her, and I've no reason to think she was lying. I can't see her as a key person in a web of scandal, that's for sure. She's not a person in a position of power. And neither is her husband. You're sure you don't have any idea what the scandal was, Jane?'

She hesitated. 'No.'

Again I sensed she was holding out on me, but there wasn't much I could do, apart from sitting in silence for a moment, hoping she'd crack. She didn't.

Instead there was a crash of steel as Kate arrived and threw her bike to the ground. She rushed into the conservatory, doing a little dance to avoid a re-activated Spree.

'Philippa, you're back. I've got heaps to tell you. Guess what Sally's brother's done ...'

We were back in the familiar world of village gossip. But something was different. Kate was pleased to see me.

...

The goodwill lasted for one hour and fourteen minutes. I was just getting used to it when it fell apart.

Kate and I were replanting Spree's uprooted azaleas when we heard the car. We'd been having a great old yarn about nothing much, and Kate seemed happy. Her expression changed as she recognised my car and its driver.

'What's that bastard doing here?' she asked.

I felt angry too. Jack had just wrecked a rapport I hadn't enjoyed with my sister in months. He hadn't bothered to ring, he'd just turned up. I watched him climb out of the car, feeling about as welcoming as Kate looked. But I couldn't sustain my anger. I'd told myself it was over: that lust-driven relationships ended in disaster every time, that I needed to distance myself from Jack to be objective about what had happened to Kirsten. It took just one look at the guy to sabotage all that. Really admirable.

'Hi, Philippa, Kate,' he said, presenting me with a bottle of wine and Kate with a Toblerone chocolate bar. 'Look, I'm sorry about turning up unannounced, but I just decided to come straight away when the garage rang up to say your car was fixed.'

Kate wasn't bought. She handed the chocolate to me and disappeared inside.

Jack's smile faded. 'Philippa? What's wrong?'

'I … Nothing.'

'There is something. What?' He tried to put an arm round me, but I shrugged away, and bent to shovel soil onto the last azalea.

'Someone tried to run me off the road on Arthur's Pass.' I looked at him and swallowed, wondering what was happening to my mind. I hadn't planned to say that. It just came out of nowhere.

'What?'

'They followed me from your place. The night I left.'

'Why didn't you tell me?' He was close again. I felt his breath on my arm.

'I haven't told anyone. I was terrified. Out of control. The only way to deal with it was to forget it.'

'Oh, Philippa. You're unhelpable, do you know that?' There was laughter in his voice, but concern too. Not guilt. I was sure then that it couldn't have been him, and wondered how I'd ever suspected him. I told him the whole story, struggling to keep my voice calm. Silver light, a narrow road plunging into rocky infinity. I'd have nightmares about it until I died.

Jack looked dubious. 'Are you sure it wasn't just some mad bastard trying to overtake you?'

Suddenly I was furious. 'Of course I am sure! You think I wouldn't know the difference? This freak rammed me about four times!'

'Okay – sorry, Philippa. It just seems so mad. But it's obvious when I think of it. It was supposed to be me, he said. 'You were in my car, only days after some lunatic smeared its headlights in cow's blood. Yeah,' he smiled at my expression of surprise, 'that's all it was. Loraine was right. Take one kilogram of prime steak, and you've got a tremendous horror tool.'

'Oh. Well, good.' I wiped the shovel on the grass, then leaned on it and stared at him. 'I guess I didn't really think it was human. But it was still sick.'

'Yeah. Look, Philippa, nothing's happened since. Bizarre, isn't it? It all happened over the space of about ten days, and now it's completely stopped. I thought it had ended with the smashed boat, but now you tell me what's happened to you … well it must be connected, don't you think?"

I stared at him. It was strange that the harassment had lasted for such a short time.

'Look, what have I done to upset your sister?' Jack changed the subject. 'She looked at me as if I was the worst thing she'd ever seen.'

'She's taken it upon herself to be keeper of my morals. She only likes my boyfriends when they're history. They're never any good at the time.'

'So – we're not history?' He smiled. 'I thought it was all over when you ran out on me like that.'

'It was. Is. You're ruining my objectivity.'

'I don't think so. You're stronger than that.'

I opened my mouth to argue, but Kate's arrival forestalled me. 'When's dinner?' she asked.

'Now, if you like.'

'What are we having?'

'Stir fry? Something easy.'

'Yuck.'

'I've got a better idea.' Jack grinned at Kate and she glared at him. 'Why don't I shout you both a meal? Out somewhere.'

Kate gave a grudging smile. 'Cool.'

'What about Jane?'

'She's not home yet. We can leave her a note.'

'Well, okay. It sounds tempting, I must admit. You can have first shower if you like, Kate. I'll phone and book a table.'

An hour later Kate was enjoying steak and chips while Jack and I tucked into carbonara washed down with red wine. Tables were jammed close together in the cafe, and its French windows were thrown open onto the street. There were a lot of people in the restaurant, but Italian music drowned their voices. Jack glanced around and smiled at me.

'What?'

'It just seems incongruous. Italian music at Franz Josef Glacier. It doesn't quite fit.'

'No.' I laughed. I sipped my wine, and ate garlic bread, feeling relaxed. That didn't last long.

'How did you feel when your sister was killed?' Kate was staring at Jack.

'Kate, for God's sake ...'

Jack lifted a hand to interrupt me. 'I don't mind talking about it. I felt awful. I still do. It's not something you get over in five minutes.'

She looked thoughtful. 'No. But some days are okay. Some days I don't think about my parents at all.'

'I haven't got that far yet.'

'But your sister was murdered. That's worse than just dying.'

'Yeah. You know there's someone out there who's responsible. But it doesn't change things, really.' Jack pushed his plate to one side. 'The loss is the same. Whether its murder or an accident, you'll never see that person again; you'll never have that last conversation. That's what is hard to live with.'

Kate put her elbows on the table and cupped her chin in her hands. 'Did you love Kirsten?'

He hesitated. 'I don't know. We weren't close. Sometimes I didn't like her much.'

'I loved my Dad. I didn't love my mother as much. A lot of the time I didn't even like her.'

I stared at Kate, my wine forgotten. She'd never told me, and I'd never guessed. But I should have. Susan had been as remote as the glacier breeze, while Liam was an in-your-face enthusiast, dragging you into impractical dreams you didn't want to be part of. He wanted you to be there. I'd never known what Susan wanted.

'Philippa's been better to me than Mum.' It's lucky Kate wasn't looking at me. I'm sure my face would have reflected my disbelief. 'But one day she'll get married and she won't want me any more. Nor will he.'

'That's not true,' Jack said, as I opened my mouth and shut it again. 'You have to trust the people you care about. Philippa's not the sort to turn her back on her mates.'

'And I'm not getting married,' I said. 'Not now. Not ever.'

Jack lifted his wine to his lips and grinned at me. 'Yeah. I think I've got that one.'

'You're okay after all,' Kate threw Jack an embarrassed look. I told Sally you were a creep. I'll have to text her when we get home and tell her you're not.'

'I'm sure the good news can wait till tomorrow,' I said.

'Hey, it's okay for you. My character's the one facing ruin, not yours.' Jack said with a laugh.

We drove home in silence. There were no lights on and I wondered what had happened to Jane. Spree's welcome was muted, and Kate looked exhausted. They disappeared into her room, and I stood in the dark hallway thinking. About what I shouldn't do.

I'd been attracted to Jack, and mostly it had been about lust. But that had changed. Now there was more. He looked at you as if he hated you, I reminded myself. You did not imagine that. It happened. And you still don't know why. He's hiding things from you. There are things going on that you don't understand. Stay away from him

I thought of Mark, recalling the strange blend of friendship, sparring and physical attraction that had bound our relationship together for years. We'd been comfortable. There was nothing comfortable about my feelings for Jack.

'Philippa?' He was beside me in the dark. 'Any chance of a bed?'

'Yeah. I'll show you the spare room.'

'I'd rather see yours.'

'Shhh. You'll wake Jane.'

'Here, isn't it?' He opened my bedroom door and I followed him inside.

'No,' I whispered. 'We can't. We've got to stop this, Jack.'

'Why?'

'Because ...' My heart rate had sped up, and I reached up and put my arms round his neck. It wasn't a conscious decision. It just happened. His body quivered against mine, and we stood there in silence for a minute, maybe more.

'We shouldn't do this.' I pulled away from him and turned on the light.

His hair was rumpled, and his face was serious. 'Jesus, Philippa. What do I have to say to convince you that I'm crazy about you?'

'Just be honest with me.'

He winced. 'I am. Just give me time. There are dark places in me that I don't understand. I can't explain them. I don't know what they are.'

'You were great with Kate.'

'She's good value. I like her.'

'She believes in good guys and bad guys. You've changed categories. Now all you need is Sally Stuart's approval.'

'It's yours I want. Come here, Philippa.'

I smiled at him, as I reached up to touch his face, running my fingers over his eyebrows, then down to his lips. He put his arms round me. We looked at each other and I flinched at the sorrow in his face. I was well qualified to recognise it. It had hung around me like a river mist since my parents' death, blowing away for a while, then stealing back just when I was starting to hope I was getting over it.

We undressed and I turned out the light. Jack followed me across the room, and touched my shoulders, turning me to face him, as he bent to kiss me. We stood for a long time in the warm darkness, exploring without any need for words. After a while we moved to my bed and made love slowly, stretching out every sensation.

As day spread its first light into the room, Jack raised himself on one elbow and looked at me.

'Help me, Philippa. Will you?' His expression was sad. I'd never seen anyone look so alone.

Chapter 12

It wasn't sexual. That's what I thought at the time. But it could have been. Perhaps if R and I had made love, I'd have been able to move on. Instead of being caught for decades in the aftermath of an emotion I'd never fully understood.

'Sleep with me,' R said that night, when we returned frozen and exhausted from our journey on the lake.

We huddled together to get warm.

R slept. I didn't.

R dealt in emotion. I understand that now. Few people can shape others to their will the way R did. Even now I admire that. It awes me.

I was scared of emotion. I knew its power and turned away from it. R was wiser, recognising that emotion, used properly, could create rather than destroy.

Emotion was power.

But not for me.

...

'Help? How?'

Jack climbed out of bed, and pulled on a pair of shorts. He did not look at me, and when he spoke his tone was light. 'Oh, you know. Who wouldn't need help with a family like mine? I was rambling last night, Philippa. Ignore me.'

I waited but he said no more.

I dressed feeling grumpy. Even the aroma of Jane's bread didn't help.

'That smells divine,' Jack said, as I rummaged in the fridge for yoghurt.

'Yeah. All down to our resident superwoman.'

'Don't you like her?'

'Let's go for a walk.'

'What? How about some breakfast first?'

'Humour me!' I snapped.

Jack lifted an eyebrow, then shrugged, following me outside without any further complaint. We wandered along the road for a few minutes in silence. I watched the mist shimmering on the paddocks, thinking. I had to tell him about Jane's link with Kirsten.

His face tightened as I spoke, but he said nothing until I'd finished.

'So we're back to some public scandal. Something that involves my family. But what is it? What the hell is it?'

'Well, perhaps your father was Margaret's lover. But I don't know' I hesitated, 'I'm not really convinced of that. Look, Jack.' I stopped and turned to look at him. 'You're not going to like this, but your father has nothing to lose if it's true. He's dead. But your mother? What'll it do to her?'

'What are you saying?'

'I'm wondering if we've been looking at this the wrong way round. If the secret involved Loraine instead of your father.'

Jack's eyes froze. 'Are you suggesting that Loraine killed Jane's sister? That's ridiculous.'

'Don't tell me not to be ridiculous. You want me to help you find your family secret, but only if you can handle what it is. Get real.'

'Yeah. I'm sorry, Philippa.' He tried to put a hand on my shoulder, but I spun away from him and started walking back towards home.

'You're right,' he said after a few minutes of silence. 'Loraine is involved. In the fallout, whatever it is. But there's no question it was about Dad. Kirsten told me it involved him. She never even mentioned Loraine.'

'Did she ever mention Jane?'

'Who? Kirsten? No. Not to me. She hasn't always lived here in Franz Josef has she?'

'No.' I picked up the paper at the gate, and glanced at the headlines, wondering why I didn't cancel my subscription. Jane devoured it, but I only skimmed it. It was part of my morning habit, even if it wasn't quite up there with the first coffee fix of the day. 'Jane's a special-needs teacher, and a gifted one judging by the way she's turned Kate round. Jack, what's wrong with you? You looked sad beyond anything before.'

'There's nothing.' He looked uncomfortable. 'It's just – there's been a bit too much death in my family lately.'

That was true, but I knew he wasn't being straight with me.

'I wonder who Kirsten left the tape with,' he said after another uncomfortable silence.

'Her lover, maybe.'

'We don't know his name. We don't know what he does. We don't know who he is. We'll never find the guy.'

'Maybe not. Jack, one other thing. Why do you think whoever was harassing you has stopped?'

'I don't know. There's been nothing since – well, since what happened to you on the pass. Philippa, I've been thinking about that. It was the worst thing by far and it was intended for me. Whoever it was wanted to kill me. And they got you by mistake. I feel terrible about it.'

'It wasn't your fault. What have you done to make someone want to kill you?'

Jack rubbed his face with his hand. 'I don't know. They must have thought I'm involved in whatever my sister was doing. As if.'

'And now they don't think that?'

'Well, it's stopped, hasn't it? I'm bloody angry with Kirsten, if you want the truth. She was too arrogant to let anyone in on what she was doing, but you and I have both been harassed because of what she found out. You could have been killed. God, Philippa, if that had happened ...'

'It didn't. But I agree with you. Kirsten's left us with a load of trouble. I wish we could find out who her lover was. I'll bet you anything he's the one with the tape.'

'If Dad killed Margaret, it'll be all there,' Jack said. 'Kirsten spared no one. Not ever.'

...

Kate had beaten me to the crust and looked pleased about it. She waved it at me as I walked into the kitchen, then howled with indignation as Spree took it from her hand.

'Serves you right for gloating.'

'It was my turn to have it.'

'Tell that to Spree. He's not the most fair-minded of animals.' I laughed.

'Why are you in a bad mood?'

I sighed as I poured cereal into my plate. 'No reason.'

'Last night was fun.'

'Yeah.' It was an effort to remember the evening. A lot had happened since, and not much of it was good. 'You liked Jack, didn't you?'

Kate frowned. 'He's okay.'

I was perversely pleased I wasn't the only one whose goodwill seemed to have evaporated.

'Where is he?' she asked.

'In the shower.'

'Do you like him?'

'Yes. Unfortunately.'

'Why unfortunately?'

'Because that's the sure route to disaster. It was last time, anyway.'

'With Mark you mean?'

'I guess.'

'When you wouldn't marry Mark, was that because of me?' My sister was buttering her toast and she didn't look at me.

'No. Kate, you must never think that. Never. I meant what I said last night. I don't want to marry anyone. I've seen what it does to people.'

'What?'

'Oh ... You compromise and compromise. Till it kills your soul.'

'What?'

'Put it this way, Kate I haven't seen many good role models for marriage. Besides, I'm happy with my life the way it is. Mostly.'

Kate put her elbows on the table and stared at me. 'I thought life was s'posed to be fun when you grew up.'

'So did I. And it is, so long as you keep your feelings under control. Which is what I intend to do. Have you seen Jane?'

'No. She must've gone for a walk. She's got the day off.' Kate glanced towards the door as Jack appeared, his hair tousled and wet from the shower. She looked him up and down and he smiled at her.

'Talked to that friend of yours yet?' he asked.

'Sally? No. I'll see her at school.'

'You still going to tell her I'm okay?'

'Mightn't have time to talk about you at all.' Kate got up from the table and dumped her plate and glass in the sink.

'You'd better get moving, Kate. You'll be late for school,' I said.

'You can talk. You're the one who slept in.' Kate peered into the cupboards and emerged with an armload of cake tins. It was yet another reason for having Jane in our lives. I no longer needed to feel guilty about Kate's lunch. She was the envy of the school these days.

I sat back and concentrated on my coffee, while Jack and Kate talked a lot of nonsense. After a while my ill humour cracked and I started to smile.

Then I saw Jane.

She stood in the doorway, staring at Jack. I saw the shock in her face. Then she turned and ran to her bedroom.

...

'Jane? Can I come in?'

She opened her door. She was pale, and her eyes slid past me, peering down the hallway. 'Where is he?'

'He's taken Kate to school. She was too late to ride her bike. Jane, what's wrong?'

'It's him,' she whispered.

'What?'

'He's the guy who was at the lake that day. The one Kirsten was talking to.'

'On the jetty?' I stared at Jane. 'But you told me you didn't see his face.'

'I didn't. Not then. But I saw him the next day. So did you.'

I remembered Kirsten's angry face as she watched a raincoat-clad figure turn and walk away from her. 'You told me you hardly saw him. How can you be sure?'

'I just am.'

I thought of something. Jane had been out the night before. She hadn't talked to Kate or me. 'You don't know who he is, do you?'

She shook her head.

'He's Jack Browne. Kirsten's brother.'

She looked amazed. And I was sure it wasn't an act. But right now Jane's honesty wasn't the first thing on my mind.

I was sleeping with Kirsten's brother. I was in love with him. But he'd been lying to me ever since we met. He did know something. And he'd been at Lake Kaniere the day his sister was killed.

...

'Why didn't you tell me?'

Jack looked hassled as he climbed out of the car. 'I don't know. I lied to the police about where I was. So I thought it was best to keep to the same story with everyone. After all, I didn't find out a damned thing by going there.'

'So what were you doing?'

He sat on the car bonnet and looked at me. 'I knew Kirsten had some other reason for going to Lake Kaniere. I knew it involved

Dad. She wouldn't tell me. I just decided I'd had enough. I went there to make her tell me.'

'Why would she tell you then when she hadn't before?'

'I don't know. I was desperate. Can't you understand that? I guess I thought I could surprise her. Follow her and find out who she was meeting.'

'But you didn't.'

Jack sighed. 'Like I said, it was a total waste of time. I was going to talk to her that morning, but there were people everywhere, and she gave me a welcome which would've made a born-again Christian throw away his Bible.'

'So what did you do?'

'Went home. I was furious with her. I just walked away. While Kirsten was being murdered, I was driving back to Christchurch, hating her.'

'You've got an explanation for everything,' I said, 'but each time you hold back a bit of the truth.'

'What do you mean?'

'Oh, stop playing games! Kirsten told you something. That's why you look so sad – so bloody haunted – when you think no one's watching. Well I've had it, Jack. You can forget our relationship, and I'm going to forget trying to help you. I can't find the truth if you keep lying to me.'

'Lying? How?'

'Oh, for God's sake! She told you something that upset you badly that night at the lake. And if you won't tell me what it was I'm not going to waste my time trying to find out from other people.'

'You're talking in riddles.' He looked puzzled as he clambered off the car bonnet and walked towards me.

I folded my arms and glared at him. 'Kirsten told you something the night before she was killed. I don't believe you've forgotten it.'

'Philippa, I wasn't there. I drove to the lake the morning she was killed. The night before I was at home. Watching television with Loraine.'

'You were seen at the lake.'

'I wasn't there.'

'Yes you were. Crying on the jetty.'

He looked at me as if was mad. 'Who told you that?'

'Jane.'

'She thinks she saw me? Crying?' He shook his head.

'Kirsten was telling you something you didn't much like, apparently.'

'That woman must be crazy. I wasn't there. How many times do I have to tell you?' His eyes caught mine.

I didn't believe a word Jack told me. So why did I believe this? Jane hadn't seen the face of the crying man but she'd assumed it was the same person who had angered Kirsten the next day. And so had I. But suddenly I knew we were wrong.

In the house the phone started ringing.

...

'Philippa? It's Loraine Latimer. Is my son with you? I can't reach him on his cellphone.' She sounded hassled.

'I'll get him,' I said.

Jack gave me a haunted look.

'It's your mother,' I told him.

He looked irritated as he took the phone from my hand. 'Loraine? What's wrong?'

He didn't speak much after that, and when he did his voice was soothing. 'Come on, you're over-reacting ... Well, not till tomorrow ... Okay, okay, I'll come today.' He glanced over his shoulder and caught me staring, then turned away. 'Listen, Loraine, chill out, you're doing yourself no good. Pour yourself a whisky, d'you hear me? Okay, see you later.'

'What was that about?' I asked when he returned to the kitchen. There was no point pretending I hadn't been listening.

'I'm not sure.' Jack sat down at the table. 'Loraine's almost hysterical. Over a bloody break-in.'

'At your house?'

'No. At Kirsten's flat.'

'What was stolen?'

'Loraine didn't seem to know. But for some reason it's upset the hell out of her.'

'Is that why she wants you to go home?'

'Yeah.' He got up and paced round the kitchen, then sat down again, rubbing his face in his hands. After a minute he looked at me and shook his head. 'Kirsten's murdered and Loraine takes it on the chin. I'm hassled by some lunatic who gets off on smashing antiques and splashing blood on cars, and Loraine acts like she's been taken to a bad movie. Then Kirsten's flat is trashed and she falls apart. I don't understand her, and I don't think I ever will.'

I stared at him. 'Perhaps there's something else. Something she doesn't want to discuss on the phone.'

'Like what?'

'God knows. You'd better get home and find out.

'That's the other thing. She wants you to come with me, Philippa.'

Chapter 13

'I despise guilt,' R said. 'It's hypocritical, revolting and useless.'

'That doesn't stop it being real.'

'Why? Why do you feel guilty?'

I was silent. I couldn't explain that the thing eating me had nothing to do with the cold way we'd planned the murder. I didn't feel guilty about that.

It was my loss of control. And I don't know if I felt guilt. Or if it was just a sick knowledge that there was something wrong with me.

When I'd picked up the hammer I hadn't been thinking of the way in which R was betrayed. Nor had I thought of the others whose lives had been ruined.

I'd struck those blows for myself. To stop the person I loved slipping away from me.

But I didn't own R.

Murder was never going to change that.

...

'Why does she want to see me?'

'She didn't say. But she said it was important.'

I spooned coffee into the filter machine. 'And you didn't think to ask why?''I didn't have the chance to ask her. She was doing all the talking.' Jack came and stood beside me, touching my shoulder so I was forced to turn and look at him. 'You're mad with me and I don't blame you. I should have told you I was at the lake. But I wasn't thinking straight. And I wasn't planning on falling for you.

It's complicated things. There's nothing else I'm holding out on. I have no idea who killed Kirsten. Will you still help me?'

I sighed and pulled away from him. 'Yeah. We should never have slept together.'

'Don't reduce it to that, Philippa. What we have is important.'

'It'd want to be. Because it's causing one hell of a lot of trouble.'

He laughed. After a minute I managed a grudging chuckle.

'There's another small problem,' I said. 'I don't know if I should leave Kate alone with Jane again.'

'Bring her with us.'

'Your mother would be thrilled with that.'

'Well, to hell with her. She's the one who's asking favours.'

'I can't, anyway.' I handed Jack a mug of coffee. 'Kate's at school. I can't haul her out of the classroom unless I make up some story and ask her to go along with it. And I won't do that.'

'Okay. But surely she'd be safe here. You don't really think Jane killed Kirsten?'

'Not really. Even if she thinks your father killed her sister, I can't believe she'd have killed Kirsten. Not unless she's crazy. And there's no way she was prowling round your house smearing blood on your headlights. She was at home with Kate. No, I think Jane's a victim. Not a killer.'

'So what's the problem?'

I put down my coffee mug and stared at Jack. 'The problem is that I'm surrounded by people who haven't been straight with me. You. Jane. It's made me a bit suspicious.'

'Yeah. I'm sorry. But I've told you everything I know. And Jane – well, I don't think you can blame her for not telling you about her sister straight up. Would you tell her your secrets?'

'No. But I wouldn't have talked my way into her house and searched through her things either.'

'Not even if you were sure she knew something vitally important to you?'

'Okay, okay. But there wasn't anything to find. As you should know. You were the first one to search my desk.'

Jack looked embarrassed. 'I'd forgotten that.'

'I hadn't.'

'Philippa.' He reached across the table for my hand. 'I didn't know you then and I really did think you might have Kirsten's notebook. Things have changed now – I think I'm falling in love with you.'

I snatched my hand back. 'I wish you wouldn't use that word. It's meaningless.'

He raised his eyebrows, but said nothing.

'I wonder what your mother knows about Kirsten's death,' I said by way of changing the subject.

Jack's face closed. 'Nothing.'

I stared at him.

He was the one who broke eye contact.

That didn't make me any happier.

...

Tim was talking to me on the phone. He was sounding irritated and I could hardly blame him.

'From next week I'll be here, I promise,' I told him.

'Okay. I know we're not busy at the moment, but there have been a couple of days when I could have used your help,' he said after an uncomfortable pause.

'I'll stay now if you need me,' I'd said. In some ways it would have been a relief to tell Jack where to get off, and to resume my normal life.

'No – you're okay,' Tim said. 'There's nothing big coming up in the next week or so that I know of.'

Jack and I drove to Christchurch in convoy. I'd been glad to travel separately, but as I began the steep drive up the gorge onto Arthur's Pass my fingers tightened on the wheel and my heart rate sped up. I kept looking for a car to appear out of nowhere and try to push me over the edge. Ridiculous. But fear usually is.

I drove through the mountains, blotting out thought with music, descending slowly onto the Canterbury Plains. Jack soon disappeared in front of me. I took my time. I wasn't in any hurry to see Loraine Latimer.

I arrived before she did. Jack was pacing round the house, flinging open windows even though it wasn't all that hot. I opened my mouth to comment, then shut it again. I didn't know what he was thinking, but it was obvious it wasn't pleasant.

There was a crunch of gravel outside, and seconds later Loraine appeared in the hallway. She was immaculate in a charcoal suit, and her hair looked as if it had just been styled. She didn't look like the stressed-out wreck I'd been expecting. She smiled.

'Philippa. Thanks for coming. I ...'

'Why didn't you tell me my father was a killer?' Jack's voice was quiet, yet it chilled the room.

'Hello to you too, Jonathan. What are you talking about?' Loraine dumped her briefcase onto the floor, and turned towards the light. I'd been wrong. The strain was there after all. Power dressing couldn't hide everything. She'd applied her mascara carelessly, and spilled droplets highlighted the crows' feet under her eyes.

'You know.' Jack's tone remained frozen. 'You know all about what happened to Margaret Sherman. Don't you?'

Loraine gazed at him for a moment, then shrugged and turned towards the kitchen. 'I think we could all use a drink. Philippa, I appreciate your coming. There are a few things I'd like to talk to you about.'

Loraine poured whisky for herself, then opened a bottle of cabernet sauvignon and handed it to Jack. He turned his back on her and spent longer than necessary looking in the cupboard for wineglasses.

'Cheers.' Loraine lifted her glass to her lips. 'You must be wondering what this is about. I believe the police will solve my daughter's murder. I have to believe that. But things are more complicated than I realised.'

I glanced around the kitchen. It was in a mess. The floor was unswept, and the benches littered with dirty dishes. An open cereal packet, a loaf of bread and a carton of milk sat on the kitchen table.

Loraine noticed me looking. 'Forgive the mess. I've been busy. And the cleaner is sick. Come through to the lounge and I'll tell you what's happened.'

'Yeah, Ma. And not before time. Because I've had all the secrecy I can take. It's caused a hell of a lot of grief.'

'It's not as simple as that.' Loraine's voice was sharp.

We followed her into the lounge in silence. There was more evidence of disarray. Papers were piled on the desk, the heavy green curtains were not pulled back properly, and a basket of washing lay in the middle of the floor. I perched on the edge of an armchair, hoping I wouldn't spill my wine on the rich cream upholstery. I glanced at an oil painting of a night sky that hung over the fireplace. It was abstract and looked careless. Thick black brush strokes were cut with silver lines. It added to the impression of restrained gloom. I thought of Ali's painting of the glacier. She had taken similar materials and conjured up ice and rain-washed bush. Much more to my taste.

I felt myself smile. Loraine gave me a quizzical look. I could see why. There hadn't been a lot to laugh about so far.

'I want to know about Margaret Sherman, Ma.' Jack had not sat down.

'I don't know who you are talking about.'

'Come on. You know what Dad did.'

'Do I?'

'He killed her, didn't he?' Jack set his glass on the windowsill and locked eyes with his mother. She didn't flinch.

'Philippa's talked to Margaret's sister. Margaret vanished thirty years ago. After a secret meeting with her lover. At his bach at Lake Kaniere.'

I opened my mouth to object. Jack was pushing the truth a bit here. He glared at me.

'I ...' Loraine pushed her fingers hard against her cheeks. She bent her head so I could not see her expression, but she couldn't hide the way her body shook. 'Jonathan, that is the most ridiculous thing I ever heard. And I've heard some great stories in my time. Your poor father. He was no saint, but ... oh, this is too much.' She looked up and I was shocked by the expression on her face. She was laughing.

Jack didn't falter. He waited until his mother was silent. 'It's time you accepted reality, Loraine. Kirsten had found out what Dad did. And that's why she died.'

'Yes?' Loraine turned the word into a weapon.

'She had found out something terrible about Dad. I think this is what it was. That he killed Margaret.'

'Then you think wrongly. I knew your father. We had no secrets, not in the end.'

'You can't be sure of that, Ma.'

'Oh yes I can. And don't ever doubt me.'

'So why did you drag us over here?'

Loraine drained her glass. 'I'm trying to tell you. But you're being somewhat aggressive, my dear son, and you are distracting me.'

'Well, the floor's yours.'

Loraine smiled at him. 'Actually, I want Philippa's help.'

'Why?' I asked.

She stood up and walked over to her desk, scrabbled through a handful of papers, and extracted one and handed it to me. 'I found this in the wreckage at Kirsten's flat. I don't know what it means. But it worried me.'

The note was typed on an ordinary sheet of computer paper. 'Your daughter is dead, but her secrets are alive. I know where the tape is, and when the time is right, I'll bring it out and take your world apart. Stone by stone. Catch me if you can, Judge Latimer.'

Jack leaned over my shoulder and read the note. 'Why threaten you?' he asked.

'Why do you think? A family scandal won't help my career. Your father and I never divorced. Any mud thrown at him is bound to catch me too.'

'So now you're saying he did do something.'

'Of course he did. But he didn't murder his lover, I can tell you that.'

'What did he do?'

'I don't know.' Loraine crossed her legs and leaned back in her chair. She looked exhausted.

'Come on, Ma, don't take me for a fool. You and he went along separate tracks for years, but you stayed together. Then something changed. Something made it impossible for you to live together.'

She laughed, but there was no humour in it. 'Yes, and can't you guess what that was?'

'He had a lover?'

'Why him? It could have been me.'

Jack stared at her. 'Yeah. So was it you?'

She shrugged. 'It hardly matters now. One of us forgot the rules. That's all you need to know. It's irrelevant, anyway.'

'Kirsten didn't think so.'

'Then she thought wrongly.'

'What do you expect Philippa to do?' Jack asked.

She looked at him for a moment, and then turned to me. 'I want to find this tape before the police do. I do not intend to spend the rest of my life being blackmailed. But I can't look for it myself. Not if I want this to stay a secret. Philippa, Jonathan told me you have a friend who's a journalist? Someone Kirsten talked to before she died? I'd like you to try and find the tape for me. With your friend's help you may be able to do it.'

'I've got no idea where it is.'

Loraine leaned forward, and her eyebrows seemed to arch higher. 'No? Then why are you hesitating?'

I felt as if I was being drawn into her mind. 'It's just ... Well, Jane Sherman – Margaret's sister – thinks it could be with someone who lives on the Otago Peninsula.'

'But you don't know who that is?' Loraine reached for her glass, frowning when she noticed it was empty, and glancing at Jack. He ignored her unspoken hint.

'It's possible they're with her lover,' I said.

'And we don't know who he is.'

'No.'

'Margaret Sherman. Who is she?'

'Give it a break, Ma. As if you don't know.' Jack paced across the room, and looked out of the window for a moment, before turning to glare at his mother.

'I don't know,' she said. 'Philippa?'

I told her Jane's story. Loraine's expression changed as I spoke. From distaste to recognition.

'Oh yes – it was in the 1970s. I do remember. The papers were full of it. They never linked her disappearance to Lake Kaniere. No ... But they did link it to the West Coast.'

'How can you be so sure Lake Kaniere was never mentioned?' Jack asked.

'Because of your father, of course. I knew he had a bach there.'

'You weren't married then.'

'No. But we did know one another.'

Jack poured me more wine, then picked up his mother's glass and retreated to the kitchen for the whisky bottle. Loraine didn't seem to notice. She sat still, one arm trailing along the back of her chair. Her eyes were wide and her face was tense. It was as if she was watching a picture unfold. I wished I could see it too.

'What are you thinking?' Jack reappeared with a hefty glass of whisky.

She took it as she returned from wherever her thoughts had taken her. 'Nothing.'

I did not believe her. She had realised something. Something important. But she wasn't going to tell us what it was.

'Where's Dad in all this?' Jack asked.

'I don't know.' Her voice was low. 'He had a lot of friends. Any one of them could have used that ghastly bach for an assignation. I hated the place. So gloomy, surrounded by all that bush. Alex took me there once, soon after we married. I've never been back. Why haven't we sold it? We never use it.'

'Ma.' Jack looked at his mother and I was surprised to notice his anger had gone. 'You're going to have to face it. Kirsten wasn't in ruins over one of Dad's old mates. It was him. She told me it was.'

'She was wrong.' Loraine lifted a hand to stop him interrupting. 'Someone made her believe it was Alex, and the story must have been good. Kirsten was no fool. Yet someone convinced her that her father murdered that girl.'

'Who?'

'I don't know. But believe this, Jonathan: Your father was a good man. He didn't kill anyone.'

...

'Do you believe her?'

We were in the corner of a dimly lit wine bar. The tension in my head was dissolving under the influence of background music and anonymity. Jack looked exhausted. His anger had gone, but not the uncertainty. Or the fear.

'I did, actually,' I said. 'She sounded sincere. But you've got to remember she became a judge by being a good lawyer. An advocate. In this case for her husband.'

Jack laughed without humour. 'Yeah, she'd have stunned Dad with that performance. Made it sound as if her marriage had a heart and soul after all. Problem is, if Dad was such a good man why did she throw him out?'

I hesitated. 'Something connected in her mind when I told her about Margaret.'

'What gives you that idea?'

'The look on her face. Of recognition.'

'Recognition of what?'

I sipped my wine. 'I don't know. But I have the feeling it could explain a lot.''Well, if she doesn't want to tell us she never will.

Philippa, while you were in the shower she told me she's organising the memorial service for Kirsten. Can you stay?'

'When is it?'

'On Friday.'

'Three days. I don't know, Jack. I shouldn't be so long away from Kate. And there's my work …'

'It's a chance to say goodbye to Kirsten.'

'Yeah.'

Behind us a group of people burst out laughing. I envied them. It would be good to be having fun somewhere. I smiled to myself.

'What?' Jack asked.

'I'm descending into self-pity mode. Nothing a good night's sleep won't fix. It's good of your mother to organise this. It won't be easy for her.'

'No. All in the interests of closure. Unusually considerate of her.' Jack's voice was hard.

'She's right, though. The people close to Kirsten do need that.'

'Jack traced a pattern on the table with his finger. 'Who were they, though, Philippa? Kirsten was respected and well known. But not loved.'

'There was one person ...'

'Who hasn't come near us. Who Kirsten guarded like a state secret. It's not my idea of love.'

'Listen Jack.' I leaned towards him. 'Don't take this the wrong way, but when I knew Kirsten she never talked much about her family. Perhaps she said nothing to him either. You can't measure his feelings for her by the fact he's never made himself known to you. What was there for him to gain if he did? Kirsten was dead. All he'd have done would be to step right into the firing line.'

'Yeah. Wonder if he listened to the tape? It makes me bloody angry to think some stranger knows exactly what my father did, when I don't.'

'Don't think about it. If you do, it'll drive you crazy.' I reached across the table for his hand. I saw his vulnerability and it frightened me. It loosened a wave of emotion inside me, and that frightened me even more. I didn't understand what I was involved in, yet my feelings for Jack were spiralling out of control. It served me right for being so cynical. Until I met Jack, I'd thought myself capable of dealing with emotion. Free falls weren't part of the deal.

'What are you thinking?' He stroked my wrist.

'Nothing very sensible.' I yawned. 'Let's go home. I need to sleep. My brain's getting looser by the second.'

'I doubt that. And I can think of something more healing than sleep.'

'So long as we're not interrupted by prowlers again. I feel like a precocious high-school girl, sleeping with you in your mother's house.'

We crept into the house and crawled into bed. I relaxed against Jack enjoying the feel of the familiar angles of his body, but our lovemaking was unsatisfactory. His touch was intimate, yet I sensed that he wasn't really there.

'What's wrong?' I whispered.

'Nothing. It's you. You're tense.'

I pulled away from him.

'Philippa? I'm sorry. It is me. Not you. And I don't know what's wrong.' His body trembled against mine. 'Don't leave me. I need you.'

We slept, but I had a lot of bad dreams.

...

Over the next few days we talked but resolved nothing. You don't when you're holding out on one another. If it hadn't been for Kirsten's memorial service I'd have left. And I would, just as soon as it was over, I told myself as I sat in a pew in the middle of the church.

'How's it going with Jack?'

I jumped as Mark sat down beside me.

'What do you mean?' I greeted him.

'You and Jack. There's something going on between you, isn't there? You look terrible, Philippa.'

'I'm upset about Kirsten,' I snapped.

I'd insisted on sitting apart from Jack. I wasn't family, and there was no way I wanted to be conspicuous in the front row.

I turned away from Mark and glanced around the crowded church. Two tweed-suited women shared a pew with a youth trapped in skin-tight black leather. A goth in purple and black held a baby to her breast. There were more conservative-looking people up the front, probably Loraine's friends. A man with neat wings of white hair, parted exactly in the middle, fiddled with an earphone. Judging by the rapt look on his face it was for a radio, not a hearing aid. There was nothing going on in the church to encourage that kind of attention. Mournful music was skirling out from somewhere in uneven blasts, while a robed figure at the altar did something to the candles. I noticed a large group of people about Kirsten's age sitting across the aisle from me, probably her journo friends. I knew none of them.

I glanced towards the watery light filtering through the stained-glass windows. It did not warm the church. I shivered and Mark moved closer. I edged away and got a grim look from the pearl-wrapped woman on my other side.

Jack and Loraine sat alone in the front pew. I could just see the backs of their heads. They didn't move at all.

After a wait that seemed to last for ever, the minister appeared, clad in a flowing white robe, his face raised. He had visited Loraine the day before. Jack was not invited to participate in their discussion about Kirsten, so we'd gone for a walk and returned to find them still talking, their voices low and intense.

'A lovely man,' Loraine had said when he'd gone. 'He cares. You can tell by his eyes.'

It had not been my impression. He struck me as cold and knowing, and my unease returned as I watched him standing amid the trappings of Anglican worship, yet somehow apart from it.

'The Reverend Roxborough. Interesting,' Mark said.

'What do you mean?'

'Kirsten was an atheist. He wants to be a bishop. I don't quite see the connection.'

The pearl-wrapped woman glared at him.

'Friends,' Reverend Roxborough established control with that one word. 'We come together today to remember Kirsten Latimer Browne. A special young woman. A person whose integrity shone. A seeker of truth. She never claimed a belief in God. Yet she lived by His most sacred principles. She tried to make the world better. Her path was not through traditional religious worship. We must all find our own way. Kirsten's example was one any person would be proud to follow. I want everyone gathered here to take time now to remember Kirsten. Silently and in your own way.'

The words were great. So why couldn't I like the man? I watched as he stepped down from the altar to stand in the aisle beside Loraine and Jack, his head bowed as if in prayer.

I thought of Kirsten. Remembered the way she'd been the morning she was killed. White-faced and haunted. She would have hated being praised like this. She'd never sought personal recognition. But she didn't exist any more, so people could do as they chose with her memory. In some ways this carefully choreographed memorial service was the final indignity. An arrogant attempt to erase the hurt and cruelty. Kirsten had died in torment. She would not have chosen a service like this. She would have asked for the truth. And somehow I was going to find it for her.

She was gone forever. I bent my head as tears carved warm tracks down my cheeks. It had been a mistake to come to this service. I felt as if I was colluding with those who sought to turn her into a sanitised example to us all. It was as if she'd slipped further away than ever.

The words kept on flowing, and none of them touched the Kirsten I had known. None of them gave her life. We sang hymns and bowed our heads in prayer, but for me at least, there was no sense of healing.

Jack looked haggard as he walked out of the church. He turned to speak to a woman. It was Helen Grenville, his godmother. The woman I'd last seen sitting in Loraine's kitchen, her blonde hair loose and sparkling, her face full of life. Today her expression was blank, as if she had gained no comfort from the well-oiled memorial service. She wore a severely cut blue suit and no jewellery apart from a single strand of pearls. As she clenched her hands together in front of her stomach I noticed her papery-looking skin and ringless fingers. She was looking at Jack and didn't notice me, but I recalled the way she'd drawn me out about Kate and a slight warmth crept into my chilled feelings.

Mark followed me outside and showed no sign of leaving. I kept away from Jack. I did not want to have to introduce them. I was angry with myself. There was no reason why I should feel guilty, but I did. Mark said nothing and that made me even angrier.

'Are you coming to the wake?' I asked him.

'Yeah. Philippa, there's someone I want you to meet.'

'Who?'

'Jan Barker. One of my workmates. She knew Kirsten. That's her over there, getting into the green Skoda.'

'Would she know anything about Kirsten's lover?'

Mark shrugged. 'Maybe. She was closer to Kirsten than anyone else in the office. God, that service was false. Kirsten would have hated it. Cover up the foibles of the family with hymns and prayer, and everyone's happy.'

'They're not the worst family in the world,' I said, 'but I agree with you about the service. Kirsten would have been furious to see us sitting there with prayer books. Talk about missing the point.'

'If you don't mind me saying so, so are you, Philippa.'

A breeze stirred the trees in the churchyard and the oak leaves clashed softly over our heads. I glared at Mark. 'What do you mean?'

He lifted a hand. 'Just that Jack Browne has taken over your life. And it's not making you happy.'

'You're wrong.'

'You look terrible, Philippa. Do you want to talk about it?'

'No, I bloody well don't.'

Mark looked ready to argue, but after glancing at me he changed his mind, following me to my car in silence, and climbing, uninvited, into the passenger seat.

'So you want a ride too?' I said.

'If you're offering. Doesn't matter, though.'

'Are you trying to be annoying?' I crunched the gears of my long-suffering car.

'No. I'm depressed about you.'

'Well don't be. I'm fine.'

'If you're in love, I hope never to catch the disease, Philippa. It looks painful.'

'I'm not in love.' I ran an orange light and felt childishly pleased as Mark clutched his seatbelt. 'But I'm not as in control of things as I like to be and it's making me stroppy. So keep your six dollars' worth of advice for the Salvation Army. And leave me alone.'

'Okay.' He hesitated. 'But he'll hurt you.'

I glared.

Mark whistled as I turned into Loraine's tree-lined driveway and pulled up beside a BMW.

It was a relief to get inside and blend into the crowd of people, especially after I managed to lose Mark. I looked around for Kirsten's journalist friend, Jan Barker, but could not see her. Jack wasn't in evidence and neither was Loraine, but the party was going on well without them. I sipped a glass of red wine and tried to listen to the talk. None of it seemed important. There were no insights into Kirsten's inner life to be had from this gathering. A group of people standing near to me were talking loudly about someone's marriage problems.

I hovered on the edges of lots of pointless conversations. Real private investigators always learned something useful at parties. But all I was getting was a headache.

The real drama was happening in the kitchen, but I never thought of looking there. I stumbled on the end of it when I went out in search of a glass of water.

Loraine, Helen Grenville and Reverend Roxborough were sitting at the table, their heads bent together and their voices low. They jumped when I walked in, like children caught in the matron's torchlight during an illegal midnight feast. Loraine was glittering, defiant. Helen had been crying. And the minister looked as if he'd run out of prayers. His face was hard.

Someone moved behind me. Jack stared past me, to the three people seated around the table. His face was white and his eyes were as cold as the stones under the glacier.

...

'What was that about?' I didn't look at Jack, but lifted my face to the grey evening sky, smelling leaf mould and listening to the sound of the branches shifting in the breeze. We'd escaped from Kirsten's funeral party and walked to the park without talking much.

'I don't know,' he answered after a long silence. 'Loraine was angry. And that bastard who thinks God is his personal ticket into the best houses in town – he's not fit to breathe the same air as Helen.'

'I wonder why she was crying.'

'I have no idea, but I don't believe she's involved in whatever led to Kirsten's murder.'

I scuffed through a drift of russet leaves. 'She must know something, though.'

'Yeah. I think she and Dad were lovers. I think that's why Loraine kicked him out. And it looks to me as if Loraine might have been taking a great deal of pleasure in telling Helen about Dad's sordid past.'

'But why tell her now? It wasn't the most suitable time. Your house was full of people ...'

'Because my mother is running scared, that's why,' Jack interrupted. 'Maybe she thinks Helen knows something about what Dad did. If so, she'd be none too gentle in her enquiries. But there's one thing I don't understand: our man of prayer. Where does he come into it?'

I shook my head. 'Jack, there's something else that doesn't fit. Something I've been meaning to ask you. Do you know Sam Acheson?'

'No. Who's he?'

'She. I met her at the lake. She's a scientist. Lives in a hut in the middle of nowhere. Kirsten went to see her a few weeks before she was murdered. Sam told her something, but when I went to see her she wouldn't tell me a thing. Sam was as nervy as hell. Told me to go away and tell no one I'd talked to her. She scared me a bit too.'

'Sam Acheson.' Jack looked thoughtful. 'The name does sound vaguely familiar, actually.'

'It did to me too.' I stopped under an oak tree and ran my fingers over the rough bark. 'It took me ages to make the connection. Kirsten had done a magazine feature on her work. I read it a year or so ago. But there's obviously more to their relationship than that. Sam was terrified about something.'

'Do you reckon she saw Dad kill Margaret Sherman?'

'She wouldn't have been living at the lake then. She was a woman with a bright future once. Now she's an alcoholic and she's scared of ghosts.'

'Sounds more like she's scared of someone who's still alive,' Jack said.

We walked in silence for a few minutes. Sunset reds seeped through the cloud and the leaves glowed with gold.

'Kirsten never told me.' Jack thrust his hands into his pockets and frowned. 'I must have seen the article. That's the only reason I'd remember Sam's name. I'm positive Kirsten never suggested any link with Dad. I'd have remembered that. All the same ...'

'Yes?'

'There was something. Kirsten ... Yeah, I remember. She had to go and live in the bush for a week with some nature-loving type when she was writing a story. They were somewhere near your place, actually. Doing kiwi surveys. Kirsten did tell me about Sam, said she'd insisted that Kirsten should experience life in the bush to get the right feel for her story. It wasn't my sister's scene, but she went along with it. She only told me because she wanted to borrow a sleeping bag.'

'And?'

'Kirsten brought it back to me. I was living at home. Between jobs.' Jack didn't say anything for a while, then turned and smiled at me. 'You've got to remember, Kirsten and Loraine fought a lot. So what happened probably had nothing to do with Sam Acheson. I certainly didn't think so at the time.'

'What did happen.'

'Loraine and Kirsten had a fight. I came home and they were screaming at one another. It was awesome. But they wouldn't tell me a thing.'

Chapter 14

We'd worked together and achieved our goal. There was nothing to replace it. I started watching R.

Stalking.

'You'll stay?' I asked.

R's face was scornful. 'For now. But not for ever.'

'What about me?'

'What about you?'

'I don't want you to leave me.'

R smiled. 'We have different things to do with our lives. You're clever. You could go anywhere.'

'I don't want to.'

'No. But you will. If you follow me you'll shrivel and be lost. And you'll end up hating me.'

'You don't want me.'

'Yes. You're my friend.' The hardness was gone from R's face. 'I don't want to hurt you. But I will if we stay together.'

'How?'

'When I get married.'

'I thought you were never going to do that.'

'I will when the time is right. But it won't be about love.' R smiled at me. 'What we did took over my feelings, but that's over now. I want ...'

'What?'

R's look of pity stung me. 'Something you can never give me.'

...

'What did you think at the time?'

'I didn't want to know. You'd have to live in my family to understand ... it was always better not to ask. Loraine hated Kirsten's choice of career. Kirsten couldn't cope with that. Their fight could have been about anything. I certainly never thought it was about the scientist.'

'It must have been, though. Kirsten had just got back from a week in the bush with Sam. You know what it's like when you're tramping with someone, sharing a tent and all that – you talk. About things you wouldn't normally discuss. Sam's convinced she told Kirsten something that led to her death. Kirsten comes home after a week in the bush with Sam and has a major row with your mother. There has to be a connection.'

'Yeah.' Jack glanced behind him and I followed his gaze then stiffened.

I'd avoided a confrontation at Kirsten's memorial service. But somehow I'd known I hadn't really escaped. Mark was crunching his way through autumn leaves, smiling slightly. Jack had no idea who he was. But he'd have had to have been blind to miss the tension. He glanced at Mark, then at me, his expression puzzled.

I started to talk, and Mark lifted a hand. 'Sorry to follow you, Philippa. Justice Latimer said you were in the park. Can we talk?'

'Sure.' I employed my coldest voice. 'This is Jack Browne, Kirsten's brother. And Jack, this is Mark Nolan. He's a reporter. He worked with Kirsten.'

Jack must have recognised the name, but he hid it well, extending a hand to Mark and smiling. 'Hi.'

'What's up, Mark?' I asked.

'I've got something to tell you, that's all. I didn't get a chance to introduce you to Jan Barker at Kirsten's memorial service, but it turns out she might be able to help. She knows the person Kirsten went to see on Otago Peninsula.'

'Who is it?'

Mark lifted a hand. 'It's not that easy. She wants to meet you first. She's dubious about giving away Kirsten's secrets, and quite honestly, I'm not sure she'll tell you. You'll need to use a bit of tact.'

'Something it seems I'm not famous for.' I kicked a drift of leaves and stared at Mark. 'Thanks. Really. This could be important.'

'Yeah.' Mark's tone was flat. 'Jan'll be in the office tomorrow morning – about eight. Can you come in then?'

'Yes.'

'Good. I'll tell her. See you then.' And Mark turned away from us.

'Wait a minute, mate.' Jack shot me an uncertain look as he spoke. 'Philippa and I were just going for a drink. Join us?'

Mark smiled. 'I don't think so. But thanks.'

We stood in the park watching him walk away. Two children raced past him, tugging the strings of a large red kite. Mark didn't even glance at it.

'It's him. Isn't it? Your ex?' Jack put a hand on my arm. 'He's still keen on you Philippa.'

I felt like hitting Jack.

Instead, I practised tact. I smiled.

...

Jack and I slept apart that night. I told him I needed to sleep, but that wasn't true. I also wanted to think.

I didn't think at all, as it turned out. I slept as if I was dead. I might have dreamed but didn't recall anything and woke feeling better than I had in weeks. I could face anything. Even the possibility that my relationship with Jack was getting out of my control.

You'll be seeing shadows in mirrors next, I thought as I walked by the river on my way into town. I felt even more irritated with myself when I approached the newspaper office and felt my heart beating faster. Mark had made a mess of his personal life. He was in no position to judge mine. If I let him worry me, I was a fool.

I gave his name to a security guard and was escorted up an echoing linoleum staircase and through heavy wooden doors into the newsroom. It might have been a coincidence, but I'd never chanced upon a drama in that place yet. You expected to be hit with adrenalin the minute you walked in the door, but as always, the stories didn't seem to be crashing off the wires at Mark's workplace that day. A few reporters were staring at a picture of an oversized beagle on a computer screen, while another group was clustered around a window staring out as if in hope of inspiration.

Mark wasn't at his desk. I sat and stared at the moving boxes on his screen saver, wondering what this lot would do if something happened. There might have been a drama waiting to burst out through the computer system, but things weren't looking hopeful.

Where the hell was Mark? I fiddled with his paper clips, yawned, and pressed a couple of keys on his computer. Nothing happened. I was about to go searching when a woman appeared at my side. She had long brown hair, pulled pack from her face with a black hair band. She wore jeans and the kind of white blouse that was instantly recognisable as expensive - even for someone like me who couldn't tell silk from cotton. Her eyes were blue, accentuated by dark makeup, and her reddened lips highlighted her white face. It didn't occur to me that she might be Jan Barker. She did not match the clapped-out Skoda Mark had pointed out to me after Kirsten's memorial service.

'Philippa?' she greeted me. 'I'm Jan Barker. Mark's had to go off to a fire. He asked me to talk to you.'

'Can I take you somewhere for a coffee, then?'

She hesitated, then smiled. 'Sure. There's a place round the corner that does a good flat white.'

Ten minutes later we were staring at each other across a round wooden table, frothy mugs of coffee in front of us. I sipped, licked foam off my lips, and then stared at the leadlight windows above our table. The need for tact was making me speechless.

Jan propped her elbows on the table, tucked her hands under her chin and looked at me. Her gaze disconcerted me even more.

Behind the expensive clothes and the little-girl hairstyle was a journalist's brain. And it must have been a good one if Kirsten had been her friend.

I shook my head, feeling impatient with myself, then smiled at Jan. 'Mark's told me to be tactful, and it's frozen my mind. So I'm going to ignore his advice and be myself. I'm trying to find out about a friend of Kirsten's who lives on Otago Peninsula.'

Jan laughed. 'You don't need to be tactful with me. I might be able to find out about Kirsten's friend - if you'll tell me why you want to know.'

'Fair enough. It's a long story, but I'll try to keep it brief.'

I'd been expecting this. Jan had been Kirsten's friend. She wouldn't spill her secrets without a damn good reason. I told her how I'd become involved in trying to find out why Kirsten had been killed, though without revealing my relationship with Jack. She nodded a few times but didn't interrupt. I felt as if much I said confirmed what she already knew. When I'd finished I sipped the last of my coffee, forgetting that it would be stone cold, while she steepled her fingers and looked at me. Her face was troubled.

'I wonder if anyone ever dies without making someone feel guilty?' she said after a minute or so. 'I'd known things were wrong for weeks, but I did nothing. Other than the perfunctory "are you okay?" kind of crap question that demands an affirmative answer. You know: we've all got our problems, so don't bore me with yours and I won't bore you with mine. I might have helped her if I'd been willing to listen, but I had a relationship self-destructing at the time and the only thing I wanted to talk about was me.'

'I can relate to that.' I fiddled with my spoon. 'Did Kirsten tell you anything about her new man?'

'Never. I can hardly believe there was one. But there must have been. She was pregnant.'

I stared at her. 'But I thought you knew about the guy who lives on Otago Peninsula?'

'I did. But I didn't realise he was Kirsten's lover. She and I had been out on a story together. She was freelance – you know that

– and I was covering it for my paper. We were late getting home and I asked her in for a drink. She was … I don't know … tense, I guess. Said she didn't have time, then what the hell, why not. Neither of my flatmates was home. I opened a bottle of wine. I was in misery mode. That's why I'd asked her in – couldn't handle being home on my own. So I wailed on about my guy and Kirsten listened, kind of. Then she jumped up and said, "Oh, hell, I need to call someone," grabbed her mobile out of her bag, and took off to the other end of the house. She was back a moment later, swearing. Said her batteries were flat. So I told her to use my phone. Well, you know Mark, right? You know what journalists are like. You can be best friends but you'll let hell freeze over before you'll share a story.'

I smiled. 'I don't think Mark is one of the driven ones, actually. But yeah, I know what you mean.'

'Right. Well, when Kirsten hesitated, I assumed that was why. She wanted to call a contact and she didn't want me listening. So I told her to use the extension in my room. She went in and was gone for ages. And no,' Jan stared at me, 'I didn't pick up the phone at my elbow and listen in. My life was falling apart. Kirsten could have scooped me from there to kingdom come and I wouldn't have cared.'

'Is your life sorted now?' I asked.

She sighed. 'As much as it'll ever be, I guess. I'm not in crisis mode any more, put it that way. Which is more than I could've said for Kirsten that day. She came out of my room looking upset, said she had to go, and took off. Came back two minutes later saying she'd forgotten to transfer the call to her number. Kirsten never made mistakes like that. I really did fail her, Philippa. There were so many signs and I ignored them all. She said it was a toll call to Dunedin and to let me know how much it cost. I forgot all about it. My flatmates … our toll bill's always through the roof and we never remember to write down who made what call. There are always a few not accounted for. But Kirsten didn't forget – arrived here to collect the bill, said she needed to copy it to claim it back on tax expenses.'

'Expenses?'

Jan gave me a strange look. 'Yeah. That's why I assumed she was talking to a source. Anyway, I dug out the bill and gave it to her, asked her to drop it back so my flatmates and I could go through it and try and work out who'd made what calls. Kirsten said she would but she never did.'

'Did you ask for it?'

'Yeah, and she told me she'd lost it. I didn't believe her. But I couldn't understand why she'd lie. I didn't push it. Turned out Emma – my flatmate – had it all on her computer. The bill was being sent to her online as well as through the mail. I've still got it.'

'And it has the Dunedin number on it.' I felt a surge of excitement. 'Can I see it?'

Jan looked unhappy. 'I don't know, Philippa. Kirsten's dead. But the person she called isn't. It was one of her most sacred principles.'

'What do you mean?' I asked, though I knew what was coming.

'Kirsten was more rigorous than most in the way she protected her sources. So how can I betray one of them?' Jan got up and pulled on her jacket. She looked stressed. I said nothing, following her out the door. The day had clouded over and the smell of exhaust fumes on the street seemed overpowering.

'But she wasn't ringing a source,' I said after a minute.

'Maybe. But we don't know that. Not for sure.'

'No. But I have to find out, Jan. If it is just a source, I'm not interested in his story. Just in Kirsten's.'

'Yeah.' She raked a hand through her hair, dislodged the headband, and pulled it off her head, stuffing in the pocket of her jacket. 'Tell you what. I'll ring the number, explain what you're doing and ask if this guy has the tape. Then I'll get back to you.'

'Why not let me ring him? He doesn't know you – it's not like he is your source.'

'He's Kirsten's though.'

'But I'm not a journalist,' I argued. 'I'm not going to do a story on him, whoever he is.'

'No – you're just going to ask him to hand over Kirsten's deepest secrets.'

'You'd be doing the same thing.'

'Look, Philippa – do you want this tape or not? Because it's my way or not at all. Okay?'

It wasn't, but it was going to have to do. I didn't hold the cards and Jan was obviously tougher than she looked.

'Okay,' I said.

...

The phone was ringing when I came in from feeding the hens. Kate was sitting at the table eating toast, making no effort to reach the phone.

I glared at her as I ran past.

'Tim?' I said. 'Sorry. I got your message. I was just about to ring ...'

'Philippa?' The voice was not Tim's. It sounded amused. 'It's Jan Barker.'

My mind lurched from the promise of a day's glacier guiding to Kirsten's lover. The tape ...

'It's sort of okay,' she was saying. 'He's willing to meet you. He'll even come to Franz.'

'Really?' It seemed too accommodating. I was suspicious.

'It's okay,' Jan said. 'I wondered about that too, but the way he told it, he's hanging out for a holiday. He has the tape. But he's not Kirsten's lover. No way.'

'Did he tell you that?'

'No. But he's got about a thousand kids. We're talking a family man here, not a romantic hero. Can you see Kirsten as a stepma?'

I laughed. 'No. But why hasn't he come forward previously? If his relationship with Kirsten is so above board it could be written up in the Woman's Weekly, why's he hiding? Surely he must realise the tape might be important.'

'Because he's a source.' Jan's tone was exasperated. 'So of course he has something to hide.'

'Oh.I see. Look, Jan, I'm really grateful.'

'Don't be. Just give me the story when it's ready to break.'

'What's the guy's name, by the way?' I asked.

There was a pause on the other end of the line, and when Jan spoke her tone was rueful. 'Don't tell any journalist – especially not Mark – but I forgot to ask, didn't I? Hope I'm not getting Alzeimers. Still, I wouldn't worry, Philippa. He knows who you are.'

I shivered, thinking of Kirsten murdered on a rainy track. Loraine Latimer wasn't the only one who was determined to keep the past secret. Only a handful of people knew where the tape was. Jan, me, the man without a name who was coming to see me. And possibly Kirsten's killer.

Chapter 15

'It could be enough. If you'd let it.'

R said nothing.

Days had passed. Weeks even. It's a blur, that downward spiral. We were out on the lake. The last time we'd gone out together we had a canvas-shrouded body lying between us in the bottom of the boat. The water had been black in the moonlight, moving beneath us like a great beast. Today it was a canvas of sapphire edged with silver and white.

'It'll never be enough.' R dipped a hand in the water, avoiding my gaze.

My vision blurred with tears.

'Why didn't you run?' R asked. 'The first time you saw me? You wanted to. I saw it in your eyes.'

'You knew.' I was shocked.

R laughed. 'Of course. Your feelings never leave your face.'

'Stay with me.'

'I can't. I'll bring you nothing but sorrow.'

'No, Robin. I'll only be sad if I lose you. That's why I didn't run. I knew you, don't you see that? Our meeting was meant to happen. If you go now it'll be for nothing.'

'We don't have to forget,' R smiled at me. 'It'll be all the more precious for not being marred by a lifetime of claustrophobia together. I'll look back on you with longing. There. Doesn't that give you a sense of power.'

'It isn't power I want.'

R laughed. The echoes laughed back.

…

It was sunny on the glacier and I turned my face to the sky for a minute savouring the warmth.

The tourist party followed. I cut a new step and ice fragments flew around my head, glittering in the sun. I turned and met the gaze of a man near the back of the line of people. He was small, fair, and radiated enthusiasm as he glanced at the glacier and surrounding mountains. I smiled at him and turned back to my step-cutting.

Back in the village I saw the man again. He was leaning against his car bonnet, looking at a tourist brochure. He grinned at me. 'That was great, going on the glacier. What a brilliant place to spend your days. You'd never get sick of it.'

'You do, actually. When it's raining like hell and the ice is like glass. When the river cuts off the only access track. Then you get a day like today and you forget all the hassles.'

'Are you Philippa Barnes?' he asked.

'Yes. Why?'

'Sorry, should have introduced myself before. But once we got up that valley, I didn't want to talk to anyone. I just wanted to absorb the place. I'm Duncan North.' He paused and smiled. 'You don't know who I am. She forgot to ask my name.'

'You're Kirsten's ...' I didn't know how to finish the sentence. Kirsten's what?

'Kirst's friend. Yes.' He spoke with a lazy drawl, stretching the i in Kirsten's name.

'You've come all the way from Dunedin to see me? I don't know how to thank you.'

'No need. Kirst spoke of you. She told me you were one of her real friends.'

I shook my head. 'I wish that was true. I was no friend to her, not in the end. Friends don't lose touch. I did.'

'Hey, don't think that.' He touched my arm. 'Kirst would've been one hell of a hard person to keep in touch with. It wasn't just down to you.'

I glanced up the road and saw Tom and Angie approaching. 'I was going to suggest we have lunch in the local cafe,' I said, 'but not with those two around.'

He peered at them. 'They look like hard things. Who are they?'

'Franz Josef's answer to MI5. Will you come to my place for lunch? It's out of town a bit.'

'Sure. No problem. Will I follow you in my car?'

'Yes – mine is just over there,' I said, pointing.

Jan had told me this man was one of Kirsten's sources. So my imagination had gone into overdrive, until I was sure the mystery man from the Otago Peninsula was going to be some kind of shell-shocked survivor from whatever horror Kirsten had been investigating when she met him. He'd been stalking my dreams this tall, thin man who slipped through life like a ghost. Then I had felt afraid. Two minutes talking to him and all of that was gone. There was something about him that made me trust him instantly.

One thing was sure, I hadn't been expecting a cheerful man like Duncan. If he was a source he must surely be a marginal one. Someone not intimately connected to whatever horror Kirsten been investigating, just someone who had seen something. But Jan had to be right. He must be a source. There was no way this person could have been Kirsten's lover. Kirsten didn't go for the rustic type.

I swerved into my driveway with more than my usual carelessness, Duncan close behind. Spree came bounding to meet us, planting his front paws on the driver's window of the car. Duncan grinned as he got out of his car. 'Who's this then? Looks like a dog who knows how to enjoy life.'

I laughed. 'He is that.'

Spree bounded over to investigate, landing his front paws on Duncan's shoulders. Duncan scratched his ears. 'He's a giant schnauzer isn't he?'

'Yes. You know the breed?'

'I had one – well, one of my sons still has him – lives with my ex-wife. Your dog has more spark, though.'

'Dodgy breeding,' I said. 'His owner wanted to swap him for a Canadian canoe. We never did get his papers.'

'Give me a good half-breed any day,' Duncan said. 'A bit of rough blood energises them, gives them character. Your fella will go a million miles with an attitude like he's got. Wish my boy could see him. This is what I call a real dog.'

The 'real dog' went gardening while I scratched in the fridge for something resembling lunch. By the time I'd constructed some dubious toasted sandwiches with some ancient cheese, overripe tomatoes, and lots of pepper, Spree was back spraying crumbs of earth in his wake, a bunch of silver beet in his mouth. He gave it to Duncan.

We ate in silence, but there was nothing awkward about it. We were hungry. I left Duncan in the conservatory and went back inside to make coffee. When I returned he had disappeared, though his backpack lay sprawled beside his chair. I waited. He came back, Spree in tow, looking as if he'd lived here all his life. 'What a marvellous view you have. You'd be able to breathe in a place like this.'

'Mostly,' I said and my tone was sharper than I'd meant it to be. He looked quizzical. 'You want to know what I'm doing, of course. I'll try not to make too much of a meal of it.'

Duncan waved a hand. 'There's no hurry, not so far as I'm concerned.' His lazy voice added conviction to this comment and I relaxed.

'I'd been expecting someone different,' I said.

He laughed. 'Yeah, I thought you had.'

'It's just … Kirsten was so secretive about you.'

'Kirst had problems. When you've learned the hard way to trust no one, it's a habit you're never going to break. Not easily, anyway. What are you doing, Philippa?'

I told him. Everything. Starting from the day I'd seen Kirsten at Lake Kaniere. He listened, nodding occasionally, but said nothing.

'So Jane – who's living with my sister and me – is convinced there was something on the tape relating to her sister's disappearance,' I said. 'I guess what I'm hoping to find is some explanation of how a journalistic investigation suddenly turned into something personal for Kirsten.'

Duncan stared at me, the humour gone from his face. What I'd said had got to him. But I didn't know why. He stood up and walked to the conservatory door, facing away from me.

I'd blown it. So I might as well go for broke.

'How did you know Kirsten?' I asked.

'I met her while she was investigating the paedophile story.' He turned round, his face still sombre. 'I knew one of the guys they were investigating. A few innocents got dragged into that net ... Poor sod, he was sad. Not bad. The court case just about finished him. I don't lose my cool often, but I did that time. Kirsten had gone after him, you see. She was so sure, but she was wrong. I told her from the start. But she wasn't hearing a thing I said.' He came back to sit opposite me. 'It was heavy.'

'You speak as if you liked Kirsten though.' I was puzzled.

'Kirst could be wrongheaded – she was that time - but she was brave. I'll never forget her. Now. I'd better be going.'

Yes, I had blown it.

Duncan picked up his pack, but he didn't hoist it onto his shoulder. He was scrabbling inside it. He pulled out a cassette tape and handed it to me. 'Use this safely.'

He was small and cheerful, so I'd missed the pain. It wasn't the sole preserve of the dark haunted types. How could I have been so crass?

'It was you, wasn't it?' I whispered. 'You were Kirsten's lover.'

He looked sad. 'I was.'

'Then why didn't you come forward when she was killed?'

'There was no point. I had no idea what was going on. My loyalty was to Kirsten and she had told me exactly how she felt about her mother. But when Jan rang me I started to think about it all differently. I was concerned about Kirsten's brother. He hadn't done anything wrong and Jan told me the effect it was having on him. I should have gone to the police with this tape much earlier but it felt too late by the time I changed my mind. You seemed a good alternative.'

'But what if I take it to the police? That'll make it worse for you.

He shrugged and his face was bleak. 'I don't care about that any more,' he said.

...

'It's 15 January 2006. I'm Kirsten Browne, a freelance journalist. My life is in danger, so I am setting this record on tape. I'm leaving it with my friend Duncan North. I have hidden my links to him well. He does not know what the tape contains; he knows nothing of this story. I trust him to keep the tape safe. That's all.'

The batteries on my tape recorder were dodgy and Kirsten's voice was a little distorted, but I was in no doubt it was her. I turned off the machine, struggling against a nauseous wave of emotion. I don't know why I felt that way. I had heard nothing so far. Perhaps it was the effect of listening to her voice when I knew her conscious mind was gone. It seemed obscene.

I settled in my chair, turned the recorder on again and listened to Kirsten's description of her meeting with Jane. It was very much as Jane had described it, but with one significant difference. *'Jane thinks her sister is dead but she doesn't know why. I think she went away to have an illegal abortion. A risky business. It's no surprise she died; it's a wonder there weren't many others. So what happened to her body? I'll get to that later.*

'So what do I know? That someone was making a fortune performing illegal abortions in Christchurch, New Zealand's Church of England bastion, thirty years ago. I intend to find this person. Just as I found the names of some of those who had abortions or procured abortions for their lovers.' Kirsten's tone changed as she began listing names. Her voice was impersonal, flat.

'Douglas Adams. Independent candidate for Christchurch East in the last general election. His platform is Christian family values; back in the '70s he procured abortions for two schoolgirls, Beth Hayward

and Joan Williams. Margaret Shay. Chairwoman for Mothers Against Abortion. A frequent protester at the Brinstead Abortion Clinic. She carries a plastic foetus on a wire and waves it at girls going into the clinic for terminations. Margaret Shay had two abortions: one in 1969 when she was aged 14, the other three years later. Helen Grenville, Minister for the Family. Had an abortion when she was 18 in 1970. It was botched and she was accidentally sterilized.'

I flicked the off switch and shut my eyes, remembering Helen's warmth the day I had met her at Jack's. How she'd drawn me out over Kate. Her tears in Loraine Latimer's kitchen the day of Kirsten's memorial service. Her past was part of this scandal. If Kirsten had exposed the abortionist, she would have had to lay raw old sorrows. Helen's. And those of God-alone-knew how many innocent women. No wonder she had been haunted. Kirsten would have been glad to root out the hypocrites. The Douglas Adamses and the Margaret Shays. But how would she have protected the innocent? There was no way Kirsten could have kept control of this investigation. No wonder she'd hidden the tape well and waited. Looking all the while as if she was being chased by demons.

I turned the tape recorder on again. Other names filtered through my consciousness. Mark had been right. There were some pillars of the Establishment here. Not all of them had a public stake in the anti-abortion debate, but no one in a public position wants their past exposed, especially when the things they did were illegal. Any one of these people could have wanted Kirsten dead. I should hand the tapes over to the police.

I started as I recognised a familiar name. *'Man of God, wannabe bishop, Henry Roxborough.'* Kirsten's voice was devoid of emotion. *'Procurer of four abortions for three girls he impregnated between January 1974 and October 1979. Two for Amy Lambert, aged fifteen when she had her first termination. One for Yvonne Mary Reynolds, aged fourteen. And one for Dorothy Susman, aged just thirteen. He was a young vicar at the time; all three girls were in his church choir. I have sworn affidavits for the above – from the women themselves, or from people who knew them. I've investigated them myself and am satisfied the stories are true. I have anecdotal evidence of others, but won't commit them to tape until I'm sure about them.'*

There was a pause, then Kirsten's voice began again.

'I will now record the names and addresses of the people who provided me with this evidence. I do not want the names of these people made public unless it becomes necessary. While I'd love to see Roxborough and others exposed, they would take the innocent with them, and I cannot bear the thought of that.'

She listed the names and addresses, her voice emotionless. Then there was a crackly pause on the tape, and a sigh from Kirsten. *'Now comes the hard part. My father had a bach at Lake Kaniere. And one of the girls died as a result of an abortion. Margaret Sherman. Her body was taken to that bach. Two people were involved. It would have been difficult to wrap and weight a body and dump it in the depths of the lake, but whoever did it knew how to hide a body in water. Margaret has never been found and she never will be. The police won't be able to do a thing about it. The body will be covered in metres of sediment by now. Unfindable.*

I turned off the tape recorder, shocked. Margaret Sherman was Jane's missing sister. This was the connection, then. This was why Kirsten had come to Jane. I thought back to what Jane had told me. Kirsten self-assured and in full journalist mode and the way she had changed later on. How something had got under Kirsten's skin, how she had become vulnerable to something. I got up and paced to the window. Late afternoon sun touched the crowns of the trees with gold and softened the glare of snow on the mountains. I turned the tape recorder on Kirsten's voice pulled me into the past. A past full of pain.

'I shouldn't name the person who told me this,' she said. *'It could place her in danger. Yet I have to, because if I die, she is the only link I have to Margaret Sherman. No. She isn't a link, just a person who was there. Someone who acquired knowledge she never wanted. By chance. Or so she says.'*

There was another pause, and I looked out towards the road, wondering where Kate was. It was time she was home from school.

'Sam Acheson.' Kirsten's voice was quiet. *'Of no fixed abode. She told me. But she wouldn't say how she found out. Or even who the two people were who dumped Margaret's body. Sam wants to protect the innocent. As I do. But I don't need Sam to tell me. I already know. This story will haunt me till I die, be my life short or long. Because it's my history, my heritage.' She laughed but there was no humour in her tone. 'I'll say no more, because now I'm speculating and I said when I began this story that I would not do that. Not on tape.*

'It's funny, isn't it, that new lives can grow out of corruption and death?'

...

The phone sounded louder than usual in the quiet room.

'Philippa?'

'Jack.'

I'd been drinking red wine, but it had done nothing to dispel the torment Kirsten had injected into my evening. I'd been furious with Kate when she returned two hours late from school. She'd been full of some adventure with Sally that had involved wailing at shadows in the glacier valley. I hadn't wanted to know, instead giving Kate a blast about the many ways in which she was ruining my life. I fancied I could smell the acrid smoke of yet another burning bridge long after Kate had stormed off to bed. You could work so long for something, then wreck it in a sentence. My wine was doing nothing to blur the edges.

'What's wrong?' Jack asked.

'How many hours do you have? And what do you want, anyway?'

'Hey, Philippa.' Jack was laughing. I scowled, failing to see anything funny in my latest display of ill temper.

'I was just wondering how you'd got on,' he said after an awkward pause. 'If you'd heard any more about the tape yet?'

'Yes, actually.' I shifted the receiver to my other hand and sighed. 'It's pretty awful, Jack. There are lot of people involved. Including some you know.'

'Helen?' His voice was sharp.

'Yes.'

'Well, it's no surprise. Not after that nasty little tete-a-tete we stumbled into on the day of Kirsten's memorial service. How about His Holiness? Is he involved?'

'Roxborough? Yes, he is. God, Jack, it's a long and horrible story. I hardly know where to start. Look, can your mother hear this?'

'Not unless she has the place bugged. She's working late.'

'So what's it all about, Philippa?'

'What? The tape?' I glanced uneasily at Kate's closed bedroom door, wondering if she was still awake. 'Jack, it's to do with organised abortion, back in the days when it was illegal. I think you should come over and listen to it yourself. I can't come over again. I'm working all this week and probably next too. Then you can take it back to Loraine.'

Jack didn't answer for a moment. 'Yeah, I guess ... The thing is ... Oh, hell, Philippa, I should have said something. Loraine didn't expect you to find the tapes so quickly ...'

'Is it a problem that I did?'

'No, of course not. Ma's always expected the impossible. I told her you'd never agree, and it's too late now.'

'Agree to what, for God's sake?'

'She wanted you to hand the tape over without listening to it.'

'And she expected me to agree to that? I'm not a golden retriever.'

'No. It's not a problem, Philippa. Just let me handle Loraine.'

'There's not a lot of time for delicate handling.' I glanced at Kate's door again, willing myself to speak quietly. 'This isn't something we can hide. I should take this tape straight to the police. By not doing so I'm probably committing an offence. I ...'

'Don't do that, Philippa. Not yet.'

'I'm not going to, and do you know why? It has nothing to do with your mother. I'm keeping quiet till I know more, for Kirsten's sake. She didn't hide this tape to have me blunder into the scene and announce her investigation to the world.'

'Yeah. Look, Philippa. I've been thinking that too. Before you even found the tape I mean. Kirsten went to great lengths to hide it. So what gives me the right to interfere?'

'What are you saying, Jack?'

'Oh, hell. I don't know. Just that I want to back off the whole thing. Don't tell Loraine you've found the tape. Tell her you're busy, that the source won't talk, that you've hit a dead end. Just don't tell her the truth.'

'Why?'

'Because I'm scared it will kill her.'

'Kill Loraine? You are joking aren't you? She's one of the toughest people I've ever met.'

'You don't really know her. Philippa, the more I think of it ...'

'Do you know something you haven't told me, Jack?'

'No. Why?'

'Because you've changed your tune and I don't understand why.'

'I ... Philippa, I can't explain ... It's my family, all right? Can't we just leave things as they are?'

'No. It goes a lot further than your family. No one in your family killed Kirsten. Did they?'

'I hope not.'

'You hope? Surely you know that?'

'No.' There was a long pause and when Jack spoke again his voice was ragged. 'Philippa, I'm coming over. I can't talk to you properly on the phone. See you in about five hours, okay?'

'Wait ...' I was talking to a dial tone.

I replaced the phone, and a slight noise made me glance around. Jane was standing in the kitchen. I hadn't heard her come in, but she must have heard everything. It was obvious from the look on her face.

...

'You've found it?'

A log exploded inside the Rayburn. We both jumped.

'Philippa? You have to tell me.'

I stared across the table, taking in the anguished look on Jane's face.

'I was just talking to Jack,' I said. 'He seems to have decided the tape should be destroyed and forgotten.'

'He doesn't have that right.'

'No. I won't agree to it, you needn't worry. But he's coming over. Now. He'll be here in a few hours.'

Jane stood up, hesitated, and walked to my side of the table. She reached out a hand as if to touch my shoulder, but drew back. 'We should get the tape out of the house,' she said.

'Why? What do you think he'll do?'

'Who knows? But it does involve his family, doesn't it?'

'Yes. It involves them all right.' I rubbed my face in my hands, trying to clear my mind. It didn't work.

'His father?' Jane's voice was intense.

'It must be. There's no one else it can be.'

'Where does my sister come into this?'

I hesitated then said, 'It looks like she was Kirsten's father's lover.

'Philippa, I don't understand this! Why did he kill her?

'He didn't kill her. Her death was an accident. The only thing he's guilty of is hiding her body.'

'Hiding her … What accident?'

'Jane.' I took her hands. 'You knew that. Didn't you? You knew where Margaret was going when she left home that last time.'

'I didn't know. I wondered. But there was nothing to prove it. She never so much as hinted she might be pregnant. She said she'd had a few problems, but they were sorted out. In the past.'

'But you did wonder about an abortion?'

Jane pulled her hands free and went to stand beside the Rayburn, folding her arms tightly across her chest. 'Margie was sick in the mornings, but I was a child, I knew nothing about pregnancy. It's only since I grew up that I remembered. And wondered. I thought it was something else, you see. It was years before I started wondering about her sickness. I told myself she'd run away with him, and I clung to it through everything. At night I'd say to myself, "Stay quiet and Margie will stay happy." Stupid? Yeah, of course. But I came to believe it.'

'So apart from her being sick, there was nothing else to suggest she'd gone off for an abortion?'

'Actually, there was.' Jane came back to the table, perching on the edge of her chair as if she might be about to run. 'A night or two before she went she seemed to be in a daze, like she didn't notice I was in the room. She was muttering to herself. I can't remember her words, but it was something like, "This time it's not an emergency. It's safe." I asked her what she meant and she told me it was nothing. But I kept at her and she told me her lover had nearly died – that his appendix had burst and he needed emergency surgery. It had happened … I don't know, a month or so before. She'd kept me awake half the night while she paced our bedroom floor making bargains with God. Margaret never begged and she didn't make any exceptions for God.'

'She doesn't sound the victim type.'

'She wasn't. She may have been a schoolgirl, but she was the strong one in that relationship. But her lover didn't die. I wish he had. Then I'd still have a sister. Tell me Philippa. Don't soften it. What did he do with her?'

'Someone helped him.' I eased my foot to the floor, wriggling my toes to ward off cramp. 'They took her body to Lake Kaniere, and then when it was dark they rowed her out onto the lake. That's where she's buried.'

Jane was silent.

'They'll never find her now,' she said finally. 'I'll never get her back.'

'Do you want to? She's somewhere beautiful. There are worse places she could be.'

'Yes. I suppose you're right.' Jane leaned back in her chair. Her face was white. I hesitated, then got up and left her alone.

There was nothing I could say.
I couldn't even begin to imagine what it would do to her.
To know where her sister was. Decades too late.

Chapter 16

I didn't suspect anything and R told me nothing.

My imagination's always leapt ahead of me, finding chaos where there's been no cause. Yet this slipped past me.

I wonder what I'd have done, had I known. Would I have forgiven R?

Or was I unhinged enough to try and kill them both?

The thought scares me, yet I must face it. All these years have gone by and I never once wondered. Never once thought to ask what really did happen that day.

I only found out when I saw a look on someone else's face. Someone I didn't know. Someone who should never ... No. I can't say it.

And nothing I did could have changed it.

...

Jane was in need of more help than I could give her.

I was going to have to deal with Jack and when I'd done that I was going to talk to Sam Acheson. She'd told Kirsten some of the story. But she knew more. She had to. And somehow I was going to make her tell me.

But first there was Jack. He'd be here in a few hours and I was going to have to tell him that his father had got a schoolgirl pregnant, and then dumped her body when her abortion killed her.

That was going to be fun.

I still didn't have a clue how this had led to Kirsten's murder. The tape hadn't solved the mystery. Unless Roxborough or one of the others had killed Kirsten to keep their past a secret. I knew I should give the tape to the police so they could investigate that. But not yet.

Jack. What would I say to him? I sat on my bed and turned the cassette over in my hands. I stared at the thin brown tape. It was a frail vehicle for so much pain. I didn't move until I heard his car, then scrambled off my bed and opened the door. He looked thinner and his hair was unkempt, and as he hugged me I noticed the sour smell of sweat.

'Tell me,' he said.

'Perhaps you should listen to the tape first.'

Anger flared, but it was gone quickly, leaving his face drawn and exhausted. 'What does Kirsten say about our family?'

'Almost nothing. There are a lot of other people involved.'

'Well, you grieve for them if you think it's the politically correct thing to do, Philippa. I can't. I don't have room for it.'

He paced around the kitchen. I ignored his anger. I could understand that. What I couldn't understand was the strangeness. Stupid word, but I can't think of any other way of describing the vibes he was giving off.

'Does Loraine know?' I handed him a mug of coffee.

'About the tape? No. She'd be angry you'd listened to it.'

'I don't know what the hell else she expected.'

'Yeah, right. But there's enough trouble without Loraine. I'll deal with that when I have to. It isn't your problem.'

I doubted that, but said nothing. Jack sat at the table. In the same chair Jane had been in. I felt like resting my head on my arms and sleeping. But I couldn't.

'What's my family secret, Philippa?' Jack's voice was light. But it didn't match his tone. Or the look on his face.

'Your mother was right,' I said. 'Your father didn't kill anyone.'

Jack's shoulders tensed and I stared at him, puzzled. I'd expected relief. Not fear.

'What then? What?'

'It was an accident,' I said. 'Even if it was a crime.'

'You're talking in riddles.' Jack jumped to his feet. 'Just tell me, for heaven's sake.'

'I'll tell you when you settle down. Don't look at me as if you'd like to kill me. None of this is my bloody fault.'

He crumpled. 'Sorry, Philippa, I'm really sorry. It's just ... I'm scared.

I should have made allowances for his fear, but I'd been strung up for hours, and now I was angry. It made me a lot more lucid than pity had done.

'Your father got a schoolgirl pregnant.' I told him. 'He arranged an abortion for her. It killed her. So he rowed her body out onto Lake Kaniere and dumped it. The girl's name was Margaret – she was Jane's sister.'

He stared at me for a moment before burying his face in his hands. Then he looked at me, and I stared, unable to believe what I saw. He was relieved. No doubt about it: he looked like someone who'd been living with the knowledge that he was dying of cancer, only to be told he'd been misdiagnosed.

How could it be a relief to discover what I'd just told him about his father? What had he thought I was going to say?

'You think that's okay, do you Jack?' I said, after a long silence. 'That girl wasn't a faceless nobody, you know. Jane's been grieving for her for years without knowing what the hell happened to her. And you look bloody relieved.'

'I'm not.' Jack came over and touched my shoulders. I shrugged away from him, nearly tripping over a chair as I did so. I swore. And not over the chair. As he'd touched me, I'd reacted to him. Despite everything.

'Did Kirsten actually say Dad's name?'

I hesitated. 'No. But that was the implication. You should listen to the tape before I tell you any more. There are a lot of others ...'

'Roxborough for one, am I right?

'Yes. He's one of the worst. He procured four abortions for young girls he got pregnant.'

'And they're going to make the bastard a bishop! How bloody fitting.'

'They won't if this comes out. And it should. The thing is, it'll crucify the innocent.'

'People like Helen? She's involved too, isn't she?'

'Yes. Her abortion was botched. That's why she never had children.'

'Shit.' Jack did another circuit of the kitchen, then turned to look at me. The relief was gone. But I knew I hadn't imagined it.

'What did you think I was going to tell you?'

'I thought Dad must have murdered someone. It was the only thing that made sense. But it was an accident.' It was a reasonable explanation, but I didn't believe him. Intimacy has its uses. If I hadn't been Jack's lover I'd have never picked it: the slight hesitation in his manner which told me he was lying. But I said nothing. There was no point. He wasn't going to tell me.

'Murder or accident, it amounts to the same thing for Jane. Her sister is dead. Thanks to your father.'

Jack winced.

'Margaret Sherman cared about him,' I said. 'When he nearly died she was up all night. Bargaining with God, Jane said. And she won. If she hadn't, she might still be alive. Ironic, don't you think?'

'Dad nearly died? How?'

'His appendix burst.'

'What?' Jack looked amazed and then started to laugh. I stared at him. Suddenly Jane spoke. Neither of us had heard her come into the room, and we jumped. She wasn't looking at me. 'What is it?' she asked Jack. 'What?'

'It wasn't Dad.' Jack stopped laughing as fast as he had started. His voice was quiet. 'That's an operation you never have twice. Dad had his appendix out when I was a child.'

...

'What are you all doing? Philippa?'

Kate stood in the doorway. Her pyjamas were too big for her and were gathered in untidy folds around her body. She yawned and her eyes disappeared into her too-long fringe.

'Philippa?'

'Jack's just arrived. He woke us up and we're going to have a drink and go to bed soon.' It was the best I could manage.

'Why are you here again?' she asked him.

He smiled at her. 'I was missing you all.'

'Yeah? Why?'

'I just was.'

'I don't believe you. Sally was right. You are up to something. And you're not going to tell me.'

I rubbed my face, then raked my fingers through my hair, eyes clenched shut. I prayed that when I opened them they'd be gone. All three of them.

'Kate,' I said. 'Sit down. I'll tell you.'

Jack stared at me, shaking his head. I stared back at him for a moment, then looked at my sister.

'We're trying to find out why Jack's sister was killed. We've found out that Jack's father might have known Jane's sister years ago. That's why Jack wants to talk to Jane. Jane was close to her sister, but when they were children she disappeared. We think Kirsten found out something about it, and that could be why she was killed.'

Kate frowned, turning to Jane. 'Is your sister dead?'

'We think so, yes.'

'What was her name?'

'Margaret.'

'What was she like?'

'She was my big sister. We fought a lot. But she was my best friend.'

'Do you still miss her?'

'Yes,' Jane got up from the kitchen chair she had been perching on, and wandered round the room. 'I still think of her every day. Still wonder what happened and why.'

Kate glared at me. 'Why didn't you tell me?'

'I don't know. I don't bloody know. Stop blaming me for everything Kate. I can't cope with it any more.'

'Philippa …' Jack reached across the table towards me, and I backed away.

'I've had all I can take for one night.' I was amazed how calm and reasonable my voice sounded. 'I'm going to bed. Stay up and talk more if you want to. You too Kate. Do what you want. I just don't care anymore. About anything.'

I walked out of the room, fell into bed and slept.

When I woke the sun was pouring in my window. The phone was ringing. I ran for the hallway. It was Tim, wanting me to take a party onto the glacier.

'Yes,' I said. 'Fantastic.'

…

I stretched and yawned. I had been right up to the second icefall that day. The tourists were young and fit. The glacier had been in perfect condition. We'd had a magic day. I felt physically tired instead of mentally slaughtered. It was much better. I was unreasonably annoyed when Tim told me he wouldn't need me for the next few days, but tried not to show it.

I didn't ask anyone what had happened after I'd gone to bed the night before, and still didn't want to know. Kate had seemed fine by morning, and Jack had slept in the spare room.

Spree came tearing in and crashed out on my feet. I scratched the tangled fur on his head. It was warm and soft. He sniffed my hand, nostrils flaring. 'There's only wine out here, fella, no food,' I told him.

'Margaret's lover had his appendix out.' Jane sipped her wine and stared at the mountains. 'Why would she lie about that?'

No one answered her.

'She told me all about the operation. All about what happens when your appendix bursts. There's no way I got it wrong.'

'I wonder what Sam Acheson knows?' I looked at Jack, wanting him to react in some way.

He shrugged. 'What does it matter? She knew about the abortion. Maybe she knew Margaret too, I don't know. The whole thing was an accident. It's sad, but there's nothing we can do. I think we should leave it.'

I stared at him and he held my gaze. He looked tired but detached.

'I don't understand you,' I said. 'We still don't know who killed Kirsten. Or why. And you want to give up.'

'Well I don't.' Jane was on her feet, pacing. 'Accident or murder, someone covered up my sister's death. Left my family wondering what had happened to her. My parents died not knowing. I could have had a sister now, but I have no one. No one. She glared first at Jack, then at me. 'Don't tell me to give up! I never will.'

Jack looked ashamed. 'Sorry,' he said. 'Sorry. Of course you need to know. I'll help.'

'I need to talk to Sam,' I said. 'I'll go back to the lake and find her.'

'What does she know?' Jack's voice was flat but his body was tense. He wasn't detached at all I realised, while having no idea what he was actually feeling.

'I'll go tomorrow,' I said to Jane. 'After Kate's gone to school. Will you stay with her?'

She hesitated. 'So long as you tell me what you find.'

'Jack won't try and stop me. And I wouldn't be stopped. I promise.'

She nodded.

Jack was staring at the mountains. Most of the pink had leached out of the sunset, leaving bands of grey in the sky. 'What does Sam know?'

'I don't know. But we have to find out, Jack. Imagining is worse.'

'Is it?'

He stood up, put down his wine glass, and walked out the door.

Jane and I sat in silence.

Then Kate came home and we all went inside. We sat watching Coronation Street. Then we had dinner.

I didn't know where Jack was.

And I didn't care.

...

I stormed up the glacier valley. It was raining and there was no one around. Jack and Jane. Sitting there like a pair of ghosts at a Christmas feast thinking about their dead sisters. I'd had enough. All that bloody grief. When my parents were killed I didn't go and park myself in the middle of other people's lives looking for help. Admittedly I'd elevated denial into an art form and that wasn't wildly clever either, but at least I hadn't sat around waiting for someone else to solve my problems. I was tired – bloody tired – of getting grief from everyone around me. I skidded on a loose rock and almost fell into the Waiho River. I swore. After a while my ill temper started to fade. The valley did its usual thing. I'd gone there grumpy and persecuted. I emerged feeling calm and remote.

Then I went home, had a late breakfast, and read the new Minette Walters novel.

Jack arrived but I ignored him.

Jane came in looking as if she was auditioning for Melanie Wilke's death scene in Gone With the Wind. Selfless and brave. I turned a page, unimpressed.

Kate flung herself through the door and stood glaring at me. I glanced up casually then returned to my book.

They didn't impress me.

Hell, detachment was wonderful.

...

Next day I went back to the lake. There was an easterly wind blowing down the lake. The water was choppy and dark. The rimus scratched the car as we turned into the bach driveway. Jack yawned as I switched off the ignition, and smiled at me.

I smiled back.

To be honest, I was just a little tired of being detached.

We didn't speak as we unloaded the car. I slammed my pack down on a chair, sneezing as I was hit by a cloud of dust.

Jack came up behind me and slipped his arms round my waist. I leaned back, grateful for the warmth.

'What do you want to do?' he asked.

'Go for a walk? It might wake me up.'

'You're tired. Philippa, I'm sorry. I'm really sorry.'

'Why?'

'Because I shouldn't have involved you. You've got enough grief without mine.'

'Jack.' I turned to face him. 'What are you scared of?'

'Nothing.' His voice was quiet. 'I was scared. Even if Margaret's death was an accident … If it had been Dad. But it wasn't. And I'm so bloody relieved, but I'm also a bit stuffed.'

I stared at him. I knew there was more.

Jack said nothing. He put his arms around me. I stood tense for a moment, then relaxed. He kissed me. My arms slid up round his neck as his hands slipped under my T-shirt.

'You're so sad,' I whispered.

'Shhh.'

We didn't speak as we walked up the stairs to the honeymoon suite from hell. Dust, a lumpy kapok mattress and filthy windows. Great.

This relationship is over, I told myself, as his fingers slid over my body.

I raised myself on one elbow to tell him. Instead I started to kiss him.

He pushed me onto my back and smiled at me.

I tried to say it but couldn't.

…

I woke to see Jack standing above the mattress with segments of orange in his hand. I sat up and yawned, taking a piece. My throat felt like a vacuum-cleaner bag and the juice cut a line through the dust.

I'd dreamed about Jack and Loraine. It was all a bit vague but it was unsettling. Something Loraine had done … No I couldn't remember. One thing it had brought to the front of my mind was the troubled relationship between mother and son. How Jack had changed from the carefree guy I'd fallen for, into someone tense and edgy. His mother's creature.

Talk about a rampant imagination.

'What are you thinking?' Jack was leaning against the windowsill watching me.

'Trying to remember what I was dreaming about.' I licked my fingers. 'Any more of that orange?'

'Downstairs – I'm actually making breakfast, believe it or not. Then we'll do something. Okay?'

'I'll be down in minute,' I said, settling back into the mattress, trying to find a bit without lumps as Jack clumped off down the stairs.

I kept coming back to Loraine. That it was her past, not her husband's, that was at the bottom of all of this. But it was difficult to see how. Kirsten hadn't named her on the tape. I had to agree with Jack that Kirsten had seemed to think her father was involved. Had she made a mistake? Believed Alex guilty, not having realised the appendix story killed that theory? I didn't know, but found it hard to believe Kirsten had been wrong about something.

There was no way Loraine had murdered her own daughter. Her relationship with Jack was a bit strange but that didn't make her a psycho.

There had always been a problem with the assumption that Alex Browne had been Margaret's lover. It meant that someone else must have murdered Kirsten. It was much more likely to have been the work of the same person.

But whom? According to the tape, there were plenty of possibilities. Had the Reverend Roxborough killed her? It was possible. But there was no suggestion on Kirsten's tape that he had been Margaret's lover. And it was this death, linked as it was to Lake Kaniere, which had probably led to Kirsten's murder.

I scrambled off the mattress and walked naked to the window. It was fine. The easterly was still scything its way down the lake, cutting up the water and shaking the trees. I got dressed absentmindedly. It would be a good day for a walk. I loved being out in an easterly. It was atmospheric.

'We've got to find Sam,' I announced to Jack.

He looked up. He'd been squatting on the floor trying to activate the camp stove. It looked as if the coffee was still a long way off.

'Where will we find her?'

'You could try and sound a bit more keen. Up the far end of the lake. It's a fantastic day for a walk.'

'Do you think she'll talk, with me tagging along?' Jack leaped backwards as a flame burst out of the stove. He was wearing an old white T-shirt with so many rips in it that you could virtually make out his whole muscle structure. Not to mention the way it showed off his tan. He gave me the smile that twisted his top lip. Dead sexy.

For heaven's sake!

'Actually I think it would be a good idea if I went alone,' I said. 'What'll you do?'

He put a couple of slices of bread into the toaster. 'Do some cleaning up round here. Cut a few of those branches back from the windows. I can't say I blame my mother for wanting to sell this place. It hasn't got a lot going for it.'

We sat in the sun with our coffee and toast, swatting sandflies, then I went in and packed my lunch.

I let my mind drift in neutral as I tramped through the bush. It was a fantastic day. The bush crackled in the wind and I felt energised. After a couple of hours I stopped on a shingly beach and ate one of my sandwiches. The lake was sapphire coloured, covered in small choppy waves, the surrounding hills purple. Eight hundred feet of water. It was hard to believe. It was even harder to believe that Margaret Sherman was down there somewhere. What would be left? Would the eels have got to her or would she still be down there, preserved in the mud, waiting for someone to find her? I recalled a Nevada Barr crime novel. The bodies were down on the floor of Lake Superior, preserved to a waxlike substance. Saponified. Would a body in Lake Kaniere be the same? I didn't know. I wondered idly whom I could ask.

I enjoyed the walk, which is just as well as I didn't find anything. Sam's hut was much as I'd last seen it, though this time all I could do was look through the window. The padlock was secure.

I wandered out onto the beach, testing the water with my hand. Cold. I thought of swimming, then thought of eels and shivered, turning back into the bush. The wind had died down and it was a quiet walk home. I started thinking about Kate, and that was depressing. Would she and I ever stop fighting? Start liking each other? I doubted it. I thought of Liam and Susan, and then drove them out of my mind. They'd caused one hell of a lot of grief.

I was absorbed in my own problems by the time I emerged from the track, and jumped when I heard the crunch of a footstep on gravel close by. Simon McKee was standing on the lakeshore. He turned as he heard me.

'Great day,' I said.

'Yes.' He looked at me more closely. 'You're Philippa aren't you?'

I was surprised that he had remembered my name. 'How's Ali?' I asked.

'Busy. Our daughter's here.'

'That sounds good.'

He sighed. 'We haven't seen much of Claire in a long time. She's never much liked it here.'

'Do you?'

Simon looked surprised. Then he smiled and shook his head. 'No not much.' It's too enclosed by mountains and it rains out here a lot more than it does on the coast. The worst thing's the silence.

When you're in a city there's always noise. Life. Here there's nothing. Death without oblivion. It gets to you at times.'

'I guess it could. It's the same in Franz really but I don't notice it really. Would you go back and live in a city?'

'I can't see it. Ali likes it here.' Simon smiled at me, then started to turn back towards his house. 'Call in and see us any time,' he said. 'It's good to see new faces.'

I said I would but could not see it happening. Their place was not welcoming, despite his words.

...

Simon McKee. It could be him. I thought of Jane's description of Margaret and her lover. Margaret had been the strong one, even if she was only a schoolgirl at the time.

It fitted in with what I'd seen of Simon.

Alex Browne hadn't been needy and insecure. He'd been an innovator, a renowned youth worker. You didn't get into that kind of position if you were the kind of person who could be dominated by a schoolgirl.

Simon McKee. It made perfect sense. Kirsten had come to the lake to talk to him about Margaret Sherman and he had killed her.

But had Simon hung out in Christchurch splashing Jack's car headlights with blood and wrecking his sailing boat? Had he then tried to run me off Arthur's Pass? I couldn't see it. What was more, it did not explain Kirsten's torment, her conviction that someone in her family was implicated in Margaret's death.

No, nothing made sense.

I wondered just what Simon knew, remembering the day he'd seemed shocked when I had mentioned Jane Sherman's name.

I sighed with frustration and stood staring out over a darkening lake. After a while I made out a figure in a canoe, coming straight for the beach I was standing on. Sam? No.

A woman jumped out of the canoe and pulled it up onto the shore. She was young with spiky black hair and wore jeans and a black polo-necked jersey. Her face was thin and her cheekbones jutted out sharply. Her bottom lip was pierced with a silver ring and another hung from her left nostril. Her ears were covered in rings, and the mascara which weighted her lashes also made her face look white.

She smiled at me. 'What a magic evening! I just wanted to keep going. You feel a million miles from the real world.'

I agreed, wondering who she was.

'Are you a local?' she asked.

'Not exactly – I'm from Franz Josef Glacier. I'm just staying here for a few nights. What about you?'

'I'm being the good daughter – visiting my parents. I'm Claire McKee.'

'And I'm Philippa Barnes. I was watching you out on the lake wishing that was me.'

Claire laughed. 'Don't. Wish yourself into my shoes, that is. You're welcome to the canoe, though. Just tie it up there when you're finished and hide the paddle over there.' She pointed to a spot where there was a thick cluster of flax bushes.

'Can I really?'

'Of course. I'm off to say goodbye to my parents. I'm a counsellor and I've just dealt with a heavy situation that made me think I should start valuing my own family more. Came home with good intentions and two days later I'm climbing the walls. I can't cope with my parents – they're in a dead marriage and they just bloody stay there making one another miserable. I'm in a great position to pass on advice to others, aren't I?'

'Others are different. It's never the same when it's you.'

She smiled. 'I'm sorry I unloaded that onto you. I don't usually bail up complete strangers. But there's something about you ...'

'There sure is,' I said grimly. 'My family relationships are rather a mess too. I understand what you're saying.'

She looked at me for a moment. 'Let's have a coffee if you're ever in Christchurch. I'm in the yellow pages under the "counsellors" section.'

'Okay. I will.'

'Great. Enjoy the canoe. It's magic out there just now.'

She waved and was gone.

I stared after her, wondering if I had found a new friend.

Then I pulled the canoe back into the water, climbed in and paddled out. The lake was quicksilver, its waters gleaming in the dusk. I paddled slowly, enjoying the very silence that Simon had spoken of so disparagingly. Behind me the trees blackened as it got dark. I stopped eventually, balancing the paddle across the canoe and wrapping my arms round my knees. The canoe turned back to face the shore, rocking in the small waves. I dabbled my hands in the water, enjoying the chill creeping up my fingertips.

It was fantastic to get a bit of space. I'd been so hemmed-in lately. Half the time I didn't even have a bed to myself these days. Not that I'd minded that at the time, I had to admit. No one could get to me here and I was glad of it. I didn't want to go back to Kate, Jack and all the other complications in my life. Right now I could have canoed away from anything, disappeared into the night, to emerge with a new life, a new name. A morepork called and I shivered.

Forget the whole thing, I told myself. Take the tape to the police. Get Jack out of your system. Get on with your life.

Then I thought of Kirsten's troubled face.

No I couldn't give up. I had to follow it to the end. Wherever that was.

I stayed out there for an hour or more, watching the silver water turn black. After a while I noticed that the river sounded louder. I was drifting towards the weir. I dipped my paddle back into the water and turned, gliding back towards the shore. It was hard to tell where I'd come from, and I was staring into blackness, trying to see something familiar when I heard a scream.

High, terrified, and quickly cut off.

Then there was just silence.

No rustle of bushes.

Nothing.

Chapter 17

How didn't I see it?
All these years I've remained silent.
Then I nearly told her.
What would it have done to her?
I don't know.
I'll never know now.
So much death but none of it mine.
None of it was ever mine.
R was right.

...

A canoe drifted close to the shore. A paddle was slung nearby. I pulled both above the waterline, peering into the wall of blackness.

Sam.

It was her canoe. I could feel the thick rope tied to the front that I had noticed when she beached beside me up the other end of the lake.

It was so silent that the scream sounded obscene in its loudness.

I crept forward, ears straining to capture some kind of sign. I heard nothing but the beat of the river.

I tripped over a tree root, stumbled forward, and put out a hand to stop my fall.

I touched something warm and wet.

Blood. I couldn't see a thing, but I could feel it, thick and sticky, seeping into the lines of my hand. I felt something move beside me and crouched down and touched the body on the ground.

'Sam?'

There was no reply.

I glanced over my shoulder but could see nothing. The darkness seemed to have a life of its own – thick and malignant.

I touched the body again, running my fingers lightly across the face and under the nose. She was alive. I felt her breath on my hand. It was warm. For some reason that surprised me.

The blood seemed to be thickest in her hair.

I straightened up and gazed blindly around.

I had to get help.

But first I had to get through that narrow fringe of bush. Sam's attacker could be crouched close by waiting to strike me too.

He won't be able to see, I told myself.

A torch cut the dark near me. Then someone called my name.

I froze.

It was Jack.

I should have been relieved, but I didn't trust him.

He'd wanted me to stop the whole investigation. And he hadn't wanted me to talk to Sam.

'Philippa?'

I couldn't speak.

Then the torchlight caught me in the face and veered over Sam's body.

Jack looked as scared as I did.

Not guilty. Scared.

...

Jack took my hands and pulled me to him. I clung to him. My body was trembling.

'Philippa? You're okay?'

'I'm fine. We've got to stop the bleeding.'

Jack shone his torch over Sam. She was lying curled on one side and I didn't want to move her. The bleeding seemed to come from a wound in the top of her head. 'Give me your T-shirt, Jack – we need to try and stop the bleeding.'

'I'll stay with her' he said a few minutes later. 'We've got to get a doctor. Have you got your phone? My one needs recharging.'

I scrabbled uselessly in my pocket, even though I knew we were outside cellphone coverage..

'I'll go to Ali's – the artist. She lives just round the corner.

I stumbled up the driveway and banged on the door. Simon opened it almost immediately. He was wearing mustard-coloured corduroy pants and a blue fisherman's knit jersey. His hair was messy, as if he had just got out of bed.

'What's wrong?'

'Someone's attacked Sam – she's down by the lake. Ring an ambulance,' I said.

'What the hell's going on?' Ali appeared in the hallway, wrapped in a cream towelling dressing gown.

I told her, watching as Simon picked up the phone and called for an ambulance. She said nothing, just stared at me.

'Is Claire here? I asked.

'Why? What do you want to know that for?' Ali's voice was sharp.

'I met her by the lake earlier. She lent me her canoe. I was just coming back ashore when I heard Sam scream.'

'Oh. I'm sorry for snapping. It's just ... Well, anyway, she's gone. Left an hour or so ago.' Ali's face changed. 'You're not telling me ... Nothing's happened to her, has it?'

'No. It's definitely Sam.'

'I'm going down there,' Ali said.

'Don't, Ali.'

'For hell's sake Simon! This is Sam we're talking about. Sam. I'm worried about her even if you're not.'

He flinched as if she had slapped him, but said nothing.

I left them and ran back down to the lake.

Yes. She was still alive.

Jack and I knelt one on either side of her. I took her hand. 'It's Philippa, Sam. We've called an ambulance. Hold on. You're going to be okay.'

After a while we heard the distant wail of the ambulance siren, and soon the bush was cut with strobes of light. Simon arrived as the ambulance officers loaded Sam onto a stretcher and carried her up the bush track.

Then she was gone.

We were left telling the police what had happened. I didn't think they would ever stop asking questions. It seemed so pointless. They had no idea what was going on. And neither did we. In the end they agreed to come back in the morning and take statements. I don't know about anyone else, but I was pleased to see them go. Thankfully we didn't have to go with them and spend hours at the station being questioned. We mustn't have looked like killers – either of us.

...

'They wouldn't let me go in the bloody ambulance with her.' Ali strode about her living room. Her hair was a black tangle and her face taut and white. She wrung her hands together as she walked.

We all stared at her in silence

'Why the hell would they? You're not family.' Simon's voice was hard.

Ali stared at him but said nothing.

Jack shifted behind me on the couch, obviously uncomfortable.

'We should go home, Philippa. You look shattered. The media will be here again tomorrow. We should get out now.'

'Yeah – you're right.'

Then I started to shake. Once I'd started I couldn't stop. Jack put an arm round me, while Simon hurried to the kitchen for water. Ali watched me, her expression interested. She said nothing.

I took the glass Simon was holding out to me and gulped it down, then lurched to my feet, steadying myself on Jack's arm.

'And I haven't even been drinking,' I said, angling for a laugh. No one responded.

Jack and I walked home in silence.

Once I got inside the bach I started crying, which infuriated me

I was still crying when Jack helped me out of my clothes and got me into bed.

He didn't say anything.

But it felt good to have him there.

...

In the morning we went back to Ali's place. She looked drawn. Simon was nowhere to be seen. We had already seen a police car and a couple of reporters down by the lake.

We drank coffee on the deck, looking down at the lake. The fringe of bush that had seemed full of monsters at night looked insignificant by day. Then the police car turned away from the lake and a minute later reappeared up Ali's driveway. A uniformed police officer got out and started walking towards us. Ali clutched her pendant. I heard her take a sharp breath.

'What's happened?' she greeted him. 'Is she dead?'

'No. Not yet, anyway. I need to talk to you people again , that's all. Starting with the young woman who found her.'

I looked at the policeman, then turned away, feeling disconcerted. He looked macho, with a shaved head and athlete's body, but I felt as if he could read all my secrets – probably just because I was feeling paranoid. His expression was guarded, revealing nothing. 'I'm Detective-Inspector Kelvin Woods,' he said. 'I just want to have an informal talk to you now, but you'll need to come in to the station to make a formal statement this afternoon Are you okay with that?'

'Sure,' I said.

'Is there somewhere we can talk on our own?'

'Simon's study.' Ali's said. 'It's just through here.

'So – let me get this right,' he said when we'd emptied two chairs of clutter and sat down in Simon's study. 'You were out kayaking in the dark on your own?'

'It wasn't dark when I took the canoe out.'

'Ok. So what are you doing here at the lake?'

'Having a holiday with my friend. His family own a bach here.'

'And where was he?'

I shrugged. 'Back at the bach. I'd been out all day, walking. He was doing some work on the section.'

'How long had you been out kayaking?' He got up and walked to the window, bending to peer out at the lake.

'I don't know exactly,' I said. 'An hour, maybe. It seemed to get dark very quickly, and I was having a bit of a hard time working out where to go ashore. Then I heard the scream.'

'Did you hear anything else?'

'No. Not until Jack – my friend – showed up looking for me. I'd found Sam by then. I tripped over her body.'

'You knew it was her? How?'

'I recognised her canoe.'

'So you know Sam Acheson?'

'I'd met her,' I told him. 'I don't really know her.'

I made my decision in an eyeblink. I wasn't going to tell the police anything about what I was doing. I could only hope that Jack would also keep quiet. I was not likely to have the chance to warn him.

The detective came back from the window, sat down, and leaned towards me, elbows on his knees.

'Any idea who attacked her?'

I shook my head.

'How about your … friend? Your friend Jack. He was right there, wasn't he? I find that a little curious.'

'He was looking for me.'

'Then why are you so uptight, Philippa?'

Because I'm lying to you. Because I'm hiding a heap of stuff from you.

I couldn't say that.

'Because I'm worried about Sam,' I said instead. 'Last night was awful. I haven't been able to stop thinking about her. Yes. I am worried. Of course I'm bloody worried.'

Stop gabbling, Philippa, I told myself.

To my surprise the detective seemed to accept this. 'She's in good hands,' he said. 'She'll make it, don't worry about her. Go out there and get your boyfriend to find you some brandy. You look like you could use it.'

'If I start using it at ten in the morning I'll end up with a booze problem,' I snapped.

He laughed.

...

'You didn't tell him, did you?'

I shook my head.

'That's a relief' Jack looked drained. 'Neither did I. Now we have to worry about whether or not we did the right thing.'

'We owe that much to Kirsten,' I squatted by the lakeshore and dabbled my fingers in the water. We'd walked in the opposite direction to the crime scene. From a distance we could see the police moving around, combing the bush and lake margins for clues. I glanced at the sky. It looked like it might be going to rain. The water was grey and lifeless, and the sandflies were biting furiously.

'You think so?' Jack said.

'Yeah, I do. If she'd wanted the police to know about the tape she'd have given it to them herself.'

'I guess you're right. Loraine would've flipped if we'd handed it over to the boys in blue.'

'Yeah.' I stood up and stretched, scratching a million insect bites.

'We should take that tape and drop it into the deepest part of the lake.'

I turned to look at him. He was sitting on the shore, arms wrapped loosely round his knees, staring at me.

'We can't do that.'

'I don't want Loraine to know anything about it.'

'Get real, Jack. She's going to have to find out some time.'

'Not yet. Promise?'

I shrugged. 'Okay, if that's what you want. I don't know what we should do with the bloody thing. In some ways it would've been good to give it to the police.'

'So why didn't you?'

I sat down beside him, wriggling to find a comfortable position in the fine gravel. 'Because of Kirsten. Why else?'

'What if the police charge us?'

'What with?'

'Withholding information.'

I yawned. 'I don't know. I hope Sam's going to be okay. She must know something.'

'Like what?'

'I don't bloody know, Jack! Something that made it worth someone's while to attack her.'

He stood up and paced up and down the beach a couple of times, then flung himself back down beside me. 'It could have been anyone. There are some sick people out there. We shouldn't hang round here either.' We looked across the lake to the crime scene. There was still one police car there but not much other sign of life.

'Well, it's one hell of a coincidence if Sam just happens to have been attacked by a stray psychopath. I need to talk to her,' I said.

'They won't let you near her.'

'Why? She's not under armed guard or anything.'

'Philippa, don't be crazy. Anything we do, the police'll be onto us. We need to keep right out of it.'

'That would suit you, wouldn't it?' I snapped. 'Don't you care about what happened to your sister?'

'Of course I bloody well do. You don't understand …'

'Understand what?'

He didn't answer. But he looked tortured.

…

Sam looked tiny in her white hospital bed. Her head was bandaged and all the life seemed to have leached out of her face. I thought she was asleep, but as I approached, her eyes opened.

'What do you want?' she whispered.

'I just wanted to see how you were.'

'I'm fine. They say I'm going to be fine.' Her smile lacked humour; her voice lacked relief.

'What happened, Sam?' I glanced down the corridor. An old man was swaying towards me on crutches. He wore a grubby grey dressing gown. He passed us without a blink of interest. I shivered.

'I don't know,' Sam said. 'The police keep asking me that. And I don't know what happened. I can't remember a thing.

I recalled the morning's headlines: 'Vicious lakeside attack – scientist in serious condition'. The story had been interesting. Sam had been bashed with a rock and, given the darkness, her assailant's aim hadn't been good. The police said it looked like an unpremeditated attack. There had been no sexual assault. Probably because of the arrival of 'another canoeist'. Me. The story wasn't pretty. Or comforting for those of us who enjoyed time out alone in the wilderness. The story had gone on to make the inevitable link with Kirsten's unsolved murder in the same area.

I glanced at Sam. She had propped herself up in her bed and was staring at me. 'You found me. Didn't you?'

'Yes. What is it that you know, Sam?'

She shook her head. 'I can't tell you. It's dangerous. A curse. If I tell you, you'll suffer too. Just like Kirsten … Thank you for helping me. Now go away and pretend you don't know me.'

'You told Kirsten?'

'Yes. And she was killed. That's why I was attacked. They'll get me eventually … I won't tell another living soul. I can't let more people die.' Sam's voice was raised and I looked nervously over my shoulder, expecting to be ordered out of the ward by some officious uniform. There was no one in sight.

Sam shut her eyes and turned her face away from me.

I left. There was no point in staying. I recognised absolute determination when I saw it.

The killer need have no concerns about Sam Acheson. I doubted if she would have told her story under torture.

Chapter 18

What's the point of it all?
Why do we love people?
Why does love turn into a whip to be used against you?
Why are people so bloody cruel?

...

Life seemed bad enough when I walked out of the hospital that day.

And it was about to get a whole heap worse.

Even now, I can't understand how I could have been so careless.

Jack and I had a tense lunch in town, then went our separate ways. He had things to think about, he told me. He'd be in touch. In the meantime he wanted me to drop the whole thing. I didn't argue with him. But I had no intention of going home and taking up mountain biking. Or growing runner beans.

I shopped for groceries, flinging things into my trolley that we couldn't afford. Why shouldn't we have nice cheeses and deli meats occasionally? I was bloody tired of living like a student. I drove home with the windows wound down, enjoying the fresh air. After a while I started to feel better. By the time I pulled up outside the house I felt almost cheerful.

No, I hadn't anticipated a thing.

Spree was out to it on the conservatory sofa, but woke with a start when I slammed the door. There was fresh bread cooling on a rack on the kitchen bench. I glanced at my watch. Three o'clock.

Kate would be home soon. I carried my groceries in from the car, swerving to avoid Spree's questing nose.

I did not notice the envelope at first, and when I did I was puzzled but not alarmed. As I opened it, two letters fell out. One was addressed to Kate.

That was when I started to feel cold.

I tore into the living room, flung open my desk, then rocked back on my heels with a curse.

The tape was gone.

I scrabbled wildly through my heaps of paperwork. There was nothing there. I walked down the corridor to Jane's bedroom. All her possessions had gone.

I sucked in a great draught of air as I stood in the doorway. Then I turned back to the kitchen and picked up my letter. Spree's front paws appeared on the table. 'Down boy,' I said absently. He ignored me.

'Forgive me, Philippa,' Jane had written. *'I can't trust Jack to do the right thing with the tape. He wants it destroyed. And he is determined. There are things about him … well, be careful how much you trust him. I've waited for thirty years to find out what happened to Margie and I still don't know it all. I can't just sit and wait for someone else to find the truth. Or hide it. I have to act myself. I didn't when she disappeared and I've never been able to forgive myself for that. I want justice for her even if it comes very late. I intend to find her killer. Yes, killer. I can't accept that what happened to her was an accident. Abortion was illegal then. And unsafe. He must have known that. She died and he didn't have the guts to accept his guilt. He left her family to live without knowing. I can't forgive him. And I will find him. Kate will be hurt that I left without saying goodbye. I hope this letter helps her. And that you'll let me see her again when this is over.*

Jane.

And that was that.

I stared at the table for a minute or two, scratching Spree's head, then leaned back against the wall, shutting my eyes as Kate crashed across the threshold.

'Jane's left us the bread maker,' I said.

In hindsight it was not a wonderful way of breaking the news.

...

'I hate you Philippa. You made her go.'

'Just read the letter, Kate. This isn't my fault.'

'You're jealous of her. That's what Sally thinks.' My sister faced me across the kitchen. Her hair hung in untidy hanks on either side of her face. She was flushed, somewhere between rage and tears.

'I'm not,' I said. 'Maybe at first. But I'd got to like her. She was good for you.'

'Oh, please!' Kate's chair crashed on its back as she sprang and me, flailing with both fists.

I ducked, then grabbed her wrists. She wriggled like an eel, spinning out of my grasp. She grabbed a cup from the bench and hurled it against the wall. I flinched as it smashed. Kate glared at me, then burst out crying, 'I hate you! I hate you!'

'Funny, I'd have never guessed. Get a grip, Kate. You'll see Jane again.'

'Why's she gone, then?'

'She wants to find out what happened to her sister. She needs to do it herself. And she can't do it from Franz Josef.'

My voice lacked conviction, and I didn't know how to do it better. Kate had lost her parents. She was too fragile to cope with another abandonment. And I was too tired to cope with any more fallout. I slumped down in my chair, propped my elbows on the table and buried my face in my hands.

Remembering.

Kate running out of the school that day.

A daffodil lying on the concrete where someone had dropped it.

White-faced silence.

What will happen to the child?

Tom, our brother. Staying away. Staying sane.

Our parents. Dead and unmarked.

This is a joke. This is a bloody joke.

Kate dropping letters in their coffins.

Me. Hating them.

Yes.

I still did.

No, I couldn't handle any more. I'd run out of answers. I'd never had them, not really.

'Why did Jane's sister disappear?'

I looked up at Kate and shook my head. 'I don't really know. It looks like she had an abortion. It was illegal then, and couldn't be done in a hospital where it would have been safe. Margaret died.'

'Abortion is murder.'

'Why do you say that?'

'Sally told me.'

'If I were you, Kate, I wouldn't listen to everything Sally said. She doesn't know everything.'

My sister nodded. 'So it's okay? Abortion?'

'Sometimes. And it's always the choice of the woman who's pregnant. Not some bloody man who doesn't know what it's like to have their body taken over.'

'But what if the man's the father?'

I got up and paced. I didn't need this.

'It gets more complicated, for sure,' I said. 'But it doesn't really change anything. He still isn't the one who's pregnant. Your body, your choice. That's what I think. Religious people don't agree. They say it's murder.'

Kate looked anxious. 'Mum didn't want me. So why didn't she have an abortion?'

'Susan did want you, Kate. I was there. I remember it. And once you were born, it was like you were the world's first perfect baby.'

'She never made me feel perfect.'

'You're not on your own with that. You know, Kate, one thing I've come to realise? Susan could never show her feelings. She wasn't warm, but that doesn't mean she didn't care about us.'

Kate got up and pushed a crumpled piece of paper across the table to me. 'You can read it if you like. It's Jane's letter to me. I don't want the bloody thing.'

And she stumped off to her room.

...

I got up from the table and wove an uneven path to the door, pulled on my gumboots and wandered outside. I glanced up at the swirl of red in the sky, walked out to the chook house and scattered wheat, my mind a blur.

I leaned against a fencepost and thought about nothing for a while. Then I went back inside and picked up Jane's letter to Kate.

I have to go away for a while I hope I can see you again one day. Thank you for sharing your home with me. It's been a very special time. I hate leaving without saying goodbye, but I have to. It's to do with my sister Margaret. I was your age when I lost her. Now I have the chance to find out what happened to her. You understand that, don't you? Philippa will tell you more. She cares about you a lot, Kate. And she doesn't know I'm going, either. None of this is her fault. Don't be angry with her. Be angry with me. I'm not saying goodbye. I'll see you again soon. Until then, I'll think about you every day.

Your friend, Jane

I sighed. It wasn't a bad piece of damage control, but it wasn't going to be enough.

Jane's departure had devastated Kate. She'd had been furious an hour ago. Now she was calm.

But it wasn't over. I'd been there before.

Even now I find it hard to think about the bloodletting that went on between Kate and me over the next few days.

She only stopped talking when she was exhausted. Her anger seemed to have a life of its own. It's not just me, I told myself. She's unloading two betrayals onto me because I'm here: our parents' deaths and Jane's departure.

It wasn't personal. It wasn't me she hated.

Yeah, right.

My sister had a bitter tongue and so did I.

She's a child, I told myself as she screamed at me. You're the adult. Don't react. Let it all run over you.

Like a ten-ton truck. Very therapeutic.

She told me I was cold.

'I was there for you wasn't I?' I yelled. 'No one else was.'

'But not because you care,' Kate retorted. 'You don't care about anyone. You were too selfish to marry Mark.'

'I'd have been selfish if I had. I'd have made him miserable.'

'You sure would. It's unnatural not to want children.'

I spun round from the sink and glared at my sister. 'And who the hell put that pious little thought into your head?'

'Aunty Jo.' Susan's disapproving sister.

'Go and live with her then.'

'All right. I will.'

I turned back to the salad I was making. 'You'll be back in a week.'

Kate launched herself at me, grabbed my arm, and sank her teeth into my wrist. I slapped her face.

She burst into tears. I stood and looked at her.

It went on for days, the bitter rows, the yelling. I don't know what scared me more – Kate's hatred or my anger.

It took me far too long to realise that I couldn't deal with this on my own. Kate needed help and so did I.

I was thrashing round in bed trying to turn my mind off and go to sleep when I thought of her. The woman who'd lent me her canoe. Ali's daughter.

...

I didn't want to make another phone call, so I just went up the village and talked to Tim. He was cleaning the boots; the guides' office was closed. I helped him for a while in silence the tang of boot cleaner mingling with the smell of silt from the glacier valley as it made contact with the dirt on the boots.

'Kate and I are having some problems,' I said in the end. 'I'm not coping with things.'

Tim put a boot down on the wooden bench between us and looked at me or a minute. 'You've had a rough time lately. I still can't believe that you were at Lake Kaniere when one friend was murdered and another person you knew was attacked. Anyone would be upset – you should cut yourself a little slack. You know, I've never said this to you before, Philippa, but I really admire what you've done for your sister. It's a hell of a situation – for both of you.'

'Thanks, Tim, but the thing is I've run out of answers. Kate seems to hate me and she's driving me crazy. You'd think things would be getting better by now, but they're not.'

'Have you thought of talking to someone?'

I picked up another boot and scrubbed vigourously for a minute. 'Yeah. I have actually. I met a counsellor just by chance recently. I wouldn't mind taking Kate to talk to her.'

'If it's time off you need Philippa, that's fine. This is more important than work.'

My eyes filled with tears as I thanked him. He looked embarrassed.

...

'Okay, Kate, you and I are going walking in the park. It's not up there with Franz Josef Glacier but it's a good place to talk.'

'Why are you wearing all those rings in your face?' Kate asked.

Claire McKee looked thoughtful. 'I like jewellery. I got my first piercing – through my nose – just to annoy my mother. Now I get them because I like them.'

'Don't they hurt?'

'The one through my lip did. And the eyebrow one. The ones through my nose weren't so bad.'

Claire's consulting rooms were in the back of a white weatherboard house at the end of a long tree-lined driveway. It didn't look like the kind of place to find someone as startling as Claire. Kate had been mutinous as she followed me up the driveway. Her expression turned to wide-eyed amazement when she saw Claire. She'd been expecting a teacher figure but Claire looked more like a street kid in her faded jeans and black polo-necked jersey.

'I've never seen anyone with rings like that. No one wears them in Franz.'

Claire grinned at her. 'The most boring woman in the village might have her navel pierced, for all you know. We've taken over rings from the guys and lots else besides.'

'Guys?'

'Of course. Pirates started the body-piercing trend. They wore their gold under their skin so no one could steal it.'

'Really?'

I could see the way Kate's thoughts were heading. Another thing to tell Sally Stuart. I could only hope she'd stick to pirates and restrain herself from telling Sally that she and I were having counselling.

'What time should I pick Kate up?' I asked Claire.

'Why don't we meet in the gardens café in an hour?'

Kate gave me a grim look. 'Why does she have to come?'

'Because she's your sister. Sisters fight but they're bloody fools if they lose one another.'

'Have you got a sister?' Kate asked.

'Yeah. I fight like hell with her and love her to death. She hates my rings.'

Kate laughed. She looked at me as I left but didn't respond to my wave.

...

'She's deep, isn't she?' Claire sipped a glass of red wine and looked at me across the café table.

I'd left Kate with my old flatmate Deb. They'd been immersed in making biscuits when I left and seemed happy. Deb was the eternal student. She was doing a PhD on some obscure facet of English literature, totally unconcerned about the limited job prospects it would offer. She always appeared vague but her dreamy manner hid a sharp perception. She'd picked up the vibes between Kate and me the minute we'd landed on her doorstep. Admittedly that was hardly surprising, but more impressively, she'd known what to do with Kate. She'd had little contact with children, yet she soon had her talking and laughing.

I'd suggested to Claire earlier that we could meet for dinner. The food was great. I was working my way though chicken parmesan while Claire ate a vegetarian lasagne.

'I'm not a fanatic,' she said, 'but I only eat meat a few days a week. I think it's a reaction to all the red meat that Mum shoved into us when we were kids.'

She didn't look as if she ate much of anything. She was waif-thin.

'We got that too,' I said. 'Chops for breakfast, can you believe?'

Claire shuddered. 'I'd rather not.'

'Kate,' I said. 'Yeah she is deep. Thanks for talking to her. I really appreciate it.'

'It was no problem. I like her. But I am worried about her.' Claire lifted her hand and leaned towards me. 'Don't be alarmed. It's fixable, I'm sure.'

'There's been so much wrong in Kate's life. It's hardly surprising if she's not dealing with it.'

'Actually, I think she is dealing with it. Most of the time, anyway.' Claire frowned and propped her chin on her hands. 'She's … I don't know … mature, in some ways. She's been very hurt by your parents – especially your mother – but I think she's working it through in her own way.'

I took a large gulp of wine. 'And you got all of this out of her in an hour?'

Claire smiled at me. 'Not exactly. I'm theorising a bit about the reason for her anger. But I think I'm right.'

'It makes more sense than some of the things I've been thinking.'

'You're too involved. I think you've been wonderful to your sister. And that she values it more than you think.'

'She defected to Jane in a minute.'

'No. She replaced your mother with Jane. She wanted both of you.'

'She lost Jane and I'm still around, so I get all the grief. Hell, I understand that. But I'm not sure how much more of it I can take.'

'You need a break from her, that's for sure.'

I sighed. 'I wish. But I can't see it. Especially now Jane's gone.'

Our coffee arrived. I'd have preferred more wine. I glanced across the room. Young lovers at one table. A toxic couple at another. Eating grimly and silently. Nothing left to say.

So why didn't they just get out? Other people's lives always seemed easily solvable.

'Kate's sorry,' Claire said. 'I think things will be better when you go home. How did your parents' deaths affect you, Philippa?'

I put my cup back into its saucer as my thoughts scrambled.

'I was fucking angry,' I said after a few minutes. 'Susan and I had a huge row just before they left on that last climbing trip. I told her she wasn't there for Kate. She told me she didn't have to be, as long as I was there. That Kate loved me better than her, anyway. I've never told anyone this before, but I lost it. I slapped her across the face. We never made it up. Two days later she was dead.'

'So – no more chances.' Claire leaned back in her chair, rubbing the back of her neck. She looked at me. 'That's heavy, Philippa. But you know something? She might have deserved that slap.'

I shook my head. 'I doubt it. But by God it was satisfying.'

'Mothers and daughters. There's so much pain in that relationship.'

I was silent. She wasn't talking about Susan and me.

Claire finished her coffee. I gathered the last of the froth onto my spoon and licked it clean.

'You're right,' I said. 'It lays you right open, lowers your emotional threshold - and for what? I'll never, ever go there. I couldn't bear it.'

'Couldn't you?' Claire looked interested. 'Funny thing is, I feel the opposite. Despite the difficult relationship I had with my mother, I still want my own child. I tell myself I won't make the mistakes she did – and I'm sure I won't. But I'll probably make others that are every bit as bad.'

'Why don't you get on with your mother?'

'You've met her, haven't you?'

'Yes. After Kirsten Browne's murder. Kirsten was an old friend of mine. But I'd heard of Ali before that. I bought one of her paintings.'

'She's a good artist – but she's not so great at family stuff.'

'In what way?'

'I can't forgive what she did to my father. Always comparing him to Michael. My uncle. Her precious brother.'

Michael. I remembered the faded studio photograph I'd seen at Ali's house.

'How do you get on with Michael?' I was curious all of a sudden.

'I never knew him,' Claire's voice was flat. 'He walked out of everyone's life thirty years ago apparently, and he never came back.'

Chapter 19

For years I thought I'd go and see her.

To tell her how it had happened.

But it was too big and I wasn't brave enough. It wouldn't have changed anything, and it would hardly have made her feel better.

People talk of the importance of closure, but I think it's far better to have hope.

Not to know there's none

...

He had disappeared thirty years ago. Just like Margaret Sherman. A coincidence? Maybe, but I wanted to know more.

Deborah's house was well lit up when I got back that night. Spree was looking right at home, sprawled on the sofa. I heard laughter in the kitchen and found Kate and Deborah surrounded by enough utensils to cater for a funeral lunch.

'We've been baking,' Deb informed me superflously. There was a streak of flour on her cheek and various others on her jeans and blue blouse. Kate was bright-eyed and tired. But she smiled at me and handed me a gingerbread man. I looked at the creation in amazement. He wore a harlequin suit. The black-and-white icing diamonds were precise and even. His face was half black and half white and the expression on his face whimsical. It was hard to believe that a few well-placed lines of icing could produce such character.

'This is way too clever to eat,' I said.

'There are more.' Kate looked pleased. 'But that one's best.'

And she'd given it to me. I felt warm – for all of two seconds.

'Mark's here.' Deb told me looking vaguely around. 'Well he was, anyway. I don't know where he's got to.'

'He's in the shower,' Kate said.

'What's he doing here?' I asked.

Deb looked at me. 'He just turned up – he often calls in for a coffee.'

How many people just turned up and helped themselves to showers? I didn't say it, but I'm sure Deb knew what I was thinking. I tried to control the sudden surge of jealousy. You don't want him, I reminded myself. He and Deb could be made for one another.

Deborah rinsed a basin under the sink and turned towards me, brushing her hair back from her face. 'Mark doesn't usually stay to shower, Philippa – don't get the wrong idea. He wanted to see you, actually.'

I opened my mouth to respond, but shut it again as Mark appeared. His dark hair was wet and he wore an ancient Coast to Coast T-shirt and an equally scruffy pair of Levis. He smiled at me.

I smiled back. Mark was like an old pair of slippers - familiar and comfortable. Bloody annoying at times, but at least I understood the way his mind worked. Unlike Jack who I didn't understand at all.

As I thought of Jack I remembered the lost tape. I wasn't looking forward to telling him about that.

'What's wrong?' Mark asked.

I sighed. 'How long have you got?'

'You don't need to worry about me, Philippa,' Kate said, licking black icing off a huge spoon. 'I'm okay now. Claire's cool.'

'Claire?' Mark looked at me.

'A woman Kate and I saw today. A counsellor, actually.'

Mark looked surprised but he said nothing. He glanced from Kate to me, obviously wondering what new crisis had broken.

Deborah handed him a mug of coffee. I noticed the smile that passed between them and tried to ignore the prick of jealousy. Deborah looked at me and gave a small shake of the head. I wasn't sure what she was trying to say.

Stop it, I told myself. You're being over-sensitive and pathetic. These people are your friends.

We sat around the table amid the clutter of baking paraphernalia and talked for the next couple of hours. Nothing deep and meaningful, and we had plenty of laughs. So often the things that aren't planned that end up being the most fun. It turned into the best evening I'd had in ages.

Kate broke it up with a succession of yawns, and Mark looked at his watch and got to his feet.

'There's something I need to ask you,' I said to him. 'Can I come into the office tomorrow? I want to look at some old newspaper files.'

He opened his mouth to ask why, then shrugged. 'Okay. Morning would be best.'

'Great,' I said.

'Bye, Mark,' Kate and Deb called to his retreating back.

'You know something, Philippa,' Kate said when he had disappeared, 'Jack seems fun, but he's not. Mark seems serious, but he's fun.' She looked at me for a second, then stood up and yawned. 'Night.'

Deborah laughed. After a moment I joined in.

...

'You don't want much, do you?'

I glared at Mark. Last night we hadn't annoyed one another once. I should have known that wouldn't last.

'Surely something like that would have had fairly major news coverage?' I replied defensively.

'But you don't even know the guy's name.'

'His first name was Michael.'

'That's a big help.' Mark turned back towards his computer screen.

'I'm not bloody well asking you to help. Just let me into the newspaper archive. I'm quite happy to search myself.'

The newsroom chose that moment to go silent. A blonde woman at a nearby terminal looked up and smiled at me. It looked like empathy. Maybe Mark annoyed her too.

Mark sighed, dragging himself to his feet as if it was all too much. 'Okay. But don't say I didn't warn you. Why don't you ring this Claire and get a few more details?'

'I can't. She'd want to know why.'

An hour later I was beginning to see Mark's point. The papers weren't indexed and a muscle above my left eye was throbbing from the effort of scanning microfilm. I hadn't found a thing.

A day later I was no further ahead.

'I've got plenty of time,' I informed Mark when he came in to see how I was getting on.

'Where's Kate?' he asked.

'With Deb.'

'You're imposing on her, Philippa.'

I sat back, closed my eyes and massaged my temples. 'Yes – I know.'

He shook his head and walked away.

Ten minutes later I found it.

I let out a long breath.

The article was short and I almost scrolled past it. The words "missing doctor" caught my flagging attention. My mind flashed back to the faded studio photograph in Ali's house as I remembered her words. 'He's a doctor – a healer,' she had said.

I stopped the film and began to read:

Christchurch Police are investigating the disappearance of Dr Michael Lawrence, whose car was found abandoned at Sumner beach on Friday. The missing doctor is considered a leader in his profession, bound for a brilliant future in gynaecology. He had been working long hours and was thought to be going away for a short holiday, but it now seems unlikely that he ever left Christchurch. Dr. Lawrence was understood to be tired and depressed, and concerns are held for his safety.

The following days saw the story escalate. Search-and-rescue teams scanned the hills and coast for traces of the missing doctor, while police made house-to-house enquiries. It was apparent that they had no leads. I was surprised that there was no comment from Ali, or indeed any other members of his family. The story stumbled on for a while, but with nothing to feed it, it eventually died. Michael Lawrence's disappearance was obviously being treated as a suicide by the police. There was no hint of any suspicious circumstances.

He had disappeared at the end of July 1979. According to his niece, Claire McKee, he hadn't been seen since. Yet Ali still talked of him as if he was alive.

He could have killed himself.

Or it could have been something else.

At last there was a link between Ali McKee and the case Kirsten was investigating.

Michael Lawrence had disappeared about six months after Margaret Sherman went missing. He was a doctor, a gynaecologist.

The abortionist?

If so, maybe someone had killed him.

...

Later that night I took Spree for a walk on the beach. It was almost dark, but I felt safe. Spree might be harmless but he's huge, with a bark to match. We cut through a small park on the way back to Deb's house. I saw something move by the trees, and Spree growled. I froze. Nothing happened. Don't be so paranoid, I told myself, it was probably just the wind. And Spree didn't bark. All the same, I was glad to get back to Deb's house.

As I lay in bed, I wondered. Jack didn't know I was here ... I sat up. Why the hell was I thinking like that? How had he managed to creep into my mind like a threatening shadow?

He wanted me to stop asking questions about his sister's murder. But that didn't make him the killer. And if he was, why would he have asked me to investigate in the first place? No. It was time to stop my runaway imagination.Jack didn't know Deborah. He didn't know I was still investigating. He didn't know what I'd found out about Michael Lawrence, and it would mean nothing to him anyway.

Settle down, I told myself. But I lay awake for hours, worrying.

...

'So what's the story, Philippa?' Deborah moved her legs slightly. Heathcliff, her black cat, looked up from her lap and glared.

What story?' I ruffled Spree's ears. He shook his head and sneezed. I wiped my face absently.

'Well, you're a thousand miles awayI leaned my head against the verandah post and looked at the sky. We sipped our coffee in silence, listening to the clear notes of a bellbird somewhere in Deb's garden. Its song rose in pitch, then stopped. A high note falling into nothing.

I remembered the slap of waves on the canoe, a dark circle of forest on the shore and Sam's scream.

Deb was looking at me, her expression concerned. I felt irritated and fond of her in one hit. Friendship is a complex business.

I sighed. 'It's a long story.'

Deborah stood up, dislodging Heathcliff, and came and sat near me on the verandah step. 'I never did like Kirsten Browne,' she said. 'Don't wreck yourself over her, Philippa. She wouldn't have done it for you.'

'Why didn't you like her?'

'She was just so bloody arrogant. People are welcome to try and change the world. But they have no right to expect it of everyone else.'

'That bothered you?' I was surprised. I'd always envied Deb's quiet self-assurance.

She shrugged. 'Kirsten got under my skin somehow. I guess it's the quality that made her a good journalist. But it's not comfortable in a friend.'

I smiled. 'I always thought she felt we were a bunch of no-hopers. But it didn't worry me. Strange really, considering I was pretty insecure back then.'

'I couldn't believe it when Mark told me you'd got together with Kirsten's brother. You don't like to make life easy for yourself!'

'You're probably right. Lust leads to grief. Every bloody time.'

'I'll take your word for it.' Deborah stood up and stretched. 'You do know that you're driving Mark mad with jealousy?'

'I doubt it. And anyway, what right has he got to be jealous? After what he did to me.'

Deborah laughed. 'When does right arbitrate your feelings? Jealousy just is.'

'You and Mark should get together.' I'd intended it as a joke, but the words had an edge.

Deb did not answer, but she did sit down and look at me.

'What?' I was irritated.

'Nothing. Philippa, where are you going with Jack Browne?'

'Nowhere. I don't even trust the guy.'

She nodded.

Things were getting dangerous. I'd be telling her everything soon. 'Where's Kate?' I asked in a futile attempt at evasion.

'Out to it. She was up till after midnight, don't forget.'

'Okay, I'll tell you. If you promise not to mention any of this to Mark.'

'Of course I won't.' Deborah stroked Heathcliff and he began a loud stuttering purr.

It was a relief to talk about it. Of the dive out of emotional control with Jack. Of the war inside my head. Of the way I kept thrashing it round, deciding to end it, then falling into it again. Shutting my eyes so he couldn't see the doubts. The things he wasn't telling me.

'So what do you think is worrying him?'

'I don't know,' I said. 'I don't think he'll ever tell me.'

'Could he have killed Kirsten? And attacked Sam?'

I winced. 'He was there. Both times. But if it was him, why did he ask me to help him find the killer?'

Deborah hesitated. 'He could have been using you, Philippa. He might have known about the tape and thought you could find it. And you did.'

'But it didn't threaten him. It was about an abortion scam that was going on before he was born.'

'It threatened Helen Grenville. His godmother. I got up and paced back and forth on the verandah.

'Mmmm. And Kirsten named a lot of people. The names meant nothing to me, but they could have to him. But it's a pretty elaborate way to go about things, surely? And if it was so important, he wouldn't have let that tape out of his sight. But he drifted off and left it to Jane to help herself to. And don't forget he was attacked – well, his boat was. And someone put blood all over his car headlights.'

'Yes,' Deb said, 'but he could have done all that himself.'

I thought about him going out running that night. He'd had the opportunity.

'Loraine would have had to have been in on it too. She was the one who said she heard a prowler.'

'He knows his mother,' Deb wrapped her arms round her knees. 'Maybe he knew she'd interrupt you in bed. Hearing a prowler's a pretty good reason to charge into your son's bedroom.'

'You think he calculated that?'

Deb shrugged. 'Maybe I read too many crime novels. But yes, I think it's possible.'

'He backed her up. Said he'd heard something too.'

'Did you?

I shook my head. 'I was too busy being embarrassed at her catching me in bed with her son.'

Deb laughed. After a moment I joined in.

'So what do you think happened?' she asked.

'Who knows? It looked like Alex Browne was Margaret Sherman's lover. But he wasn't.'

'Philippa, Mark told me someone tried to run you off the road on Arthurs Pass. When you were driving Jack's car.'

'I wish he'd learn to keep his bloody mouth shut. Yes, that did happen. But I don't believe it was Jack.'

'Then why are you angry?'

'Hell, Deb, why don't you get out of academia and join the police force? You'd make a damn good interrogator.'

She smiled. 'Come on Philippa. Tell me.'

I glared at her. 'If you must know, I did wonder if it was him. But what motive did he have? I'd found out nothing. Anyway, I had a good look at Loraine's car when I came back. Whoever hit me must have got a few dents and scratches – Jack's car sure did. But hers was fine.'

'He could have hired a car.'

'And taken it back with its front bumper bashed in?'

Deborah smiled. 'I guess not. So are you going to see him?'

'Jack? Yes, I have to. I need to tell him about the tape.'

'Why don't you just ring him?'

'Because that would be hiding, Deborah.'

She shook her head, but she didn't argue. It might have been better if she had.

...

'Does the name Michael Lawrence mean anything to you?"

Jack stared at me. 'No. Should it?'

I stretched my legs out into the sun. It did not warm me. A dry oak leaf, caught by the breeze, whirled into the conservatory. I looked at Jack and shrugged. 'I think that's the name of the abortionist. He's Ali McKee's brother.'

'So it was her ...'

'What?'

Jack leaned forward in his chair and looked at me. 'What's the problem? Why are you so bloody uptight?'

I said nothing.

Jack moved closer. He put a hand on my knee. I didn't move a muscle, but I felt like screaming.

'Why should it be Ali?' I asked instead.

Jack frowned. 'If Kirsten was about to expose Ali's brother as an illegal abortionist it would have ruined him.'

'He's ruined anyway, from what I've heard. He's been missing for 30 years.

Jack stared at me. He looked totally bewildered.

'Then what? Do you think someone killed him? Because he was doing abortions?'

'You have to admit it's a possibility. I wonder if Ali knew what her precious brother was up to?'

'She's bloody horrible, that woman.' Jack's voice was quiet, but there was a ton of feeling in it.

'She's not that bad.' I was puzzled. Jack had hardly ever spoken to Ali.

'I can't explain it,' he said, 'but there was something about her that gave me the creeps.'

'Yeah?' I didn't really believe him. Not about anything. It was really over between Jack and me. The chemistry was gone. The realisation left me feeling empty.

'Sam Acheson's involved,' I said after an awkward pause. 'She has to be. Something she knows caused Kirsten's death.'

'She could be one of the women who had an abortion.'

'Why didn't Kirsten name her on the tape, then? Jack, I've got something bad to tell you. I've lost it.'

'You've what?'

'Jane took it. We should never have let it out of our sight,' I said.

'So you found it. And didn't tell me. We had an agreement, Philippa.'

I spun round.Loraine Latimer stood behind me. It was like déjà vu, except she looked a lot less friendly than last time.

Jack put his head in his hands and groaned. When he looked at his mother his eyes were cold.

She stared at him, then turned to me. 'You let Jane Sherman take it? How could you be so careless?'

I shook my head. Her quiet tone was more frightening than anger would have been.

Jack gave a harsh laugh. 'Well there's one thing certain, Ma, you can't do a thing about it. Even you would be hard pressed to explain to the police why you asked Philippa to find the tape before they did.'

Loraine stepped into the conservatory and sat down. 'If you can't think of something useful to say, be quiet, Jonathan. I need to think about this.'

'I've got no idea where Jane went, and no way of finding her,' I said, 'but you might be able to think of a way.'

Loraine smiled. 'Not off the top of my head, I'm afraid. I underestimated you, Philippa. I didn't expect you to find the tape so quickly. You listened to it?'

'Yes.'

'And?'

'Kirsten had uncovered an abortion scam.'

'In which the revolting Reverend Roxborough had a starring role. I'd think again before I let him into my bed if I were you, Ma.'

I flinched. Loraine merely looked amused.

'I know how to look after myself, Jonathan.' She turned to me. 'Who else was involved?'

'I can't remember them all. There were a lot of names.' I started to list the ones I remembered.

'And Helen,' Jack interrupted staring at his mother. 'And Margaret Sherman. Jane's sister.'

'What does the woman hope to achieve?' Loraine was impatient. 'She's not going to bring her sister back.'

'No. But she needs to know what happened to her. Surely you can understand that?'

'I can understand it,' said Loraine. 'I don't have to like it, though. Well, there really isn't much we can do. At least this should prove to you that your father was not a killer, Jonathan.'

Jack said nothing.

'There is one thing we can do,' I said.

Loraine raised her eyebrows. 'Oh?'

'We could try and find out more about Michael Lawrence.'

Her reaction was extraordinary. Her smile didn't slip but the colour drained out of her face. Something blazed in her eyes, then was gone, leaving them cold.

Cold? Or scared?

I'd have been less surprised if she'd stripped naked and started to dance.

Chapter 20

The problem with all of this is the grief it has sown. Not mine. Not R's. But that of so many others. I liked Kirsten Browne. I trusted her. She was blunt and I like that. Clever and full of integrity. I know I told her far too much that day. The knowledge led to her death. But it's even worse than that.

The way I told the story was cruel.

Insensitive.

And wrong.

...

Jack didn't know what was going on. So he wasn't involved. It was as if a clamp had been released from around my brain. The relief was enormous.

You're over him, I reminded myself. So why does it matter?

'So you know him?' Jack asked his mother.

She shook her head. The fear was gone and the control was back. But she had lost it, even if only momentarily. Somehow I didn't think such a thing had happened to Loraine Latimer in years.

'Ma?' Jack's voice was impatient.

She sighed. 'I knew him years ago. When I was a girl. But I haven't seen him since.'

'So why are you frightened?'

'Don't be so stupid, Jonathan. I'm not. He killed my daughter. Didn't he?'

'It'd be a bit difficult, Ma ...'

'He was the one who had the most to lose,' Loraine interrupted. 'Michael Lawrence. Yes. It fits. He was hungry. Ambitious. And poor. He did abortions to get himself through medical school. How bloody ironic.'

'You sound like you knew him well.' Jack's voice was ironic.

She ignored his tone. 'I did, yes. He wanted to marry me.'

'So why didn't you?'

'Because, my dear boy, I was selfish. Michael could give me nothing. Except love. Such as it was …'

'And maybe you couldn't have controlled this guy, Ma. Not like poor Dad.'

Loraine smiled. 'You're probably right. I often wondered what happened to Michael Lawrence. Somehow I thought I'd hear from him one day, but I never did. He's probably living quietly in some mansion, set up for life. Far away from those who knew him when he was a scruffy boy from the wrong side of town.'

'And then Kirsten found him.' Jack did a reckless circuit of the conservatory before sitting down and staring at his mother. 'Is that what you think?'

Loraine frowned. 'Yes.'

'And if that's what did happen, how will you feel? Responsible?'

'Why should I?'

Jack shook his head. 'Just an idea. Were you engaged to him?'

Loraine looked at him for a moment. She smiled. 'No, as it happens. I turned him down from the start. He said he loved me, but his real hunger was for my money.'

'He didn't kill Kirsten, Ma.'

Loraine watched her son.

'He can't have.' Jack stared at her. Both of them had forgotten that I was there. 'Michael Lawrence has been missing for thirty years. You know that. You must do. Half the country's police were out looking for him.'

'Yes.'

'Well he's dead, isn't he?'

'Of course he isn't,' Loraine snapped. 'Die and leave behind all that lovely money? Not Michael. He wanted a new life long before it became necessary. He had a sister who was smothering him with love he didn't want. He always intended to get away from her, just as soon as he could. He planned it well, abandoned his car near a well-known suicide spot, and moved on to his new life.'

'So why did he go there to kill Kirsten? To Lake Kaniere?' I asked.

Loraine looked at me. 'What do you mean?'

'Well, he surely wouldn't have wanted to risk running into his sister.'

'Is she there? My God. You don't mean… Alison? Her name was Alison Lawrence. Ali McKee. Michael's sister found Kirsten's body! I knew the woman was familiar but I didn't know why.'

'So if you're right, surely Michael would have found somewhere safer than Lake Kaniere to kill Kirsten,' Jack said.

She waved a hand impatiently. 'Why should he have known where Alison was?'

'And why would he go there? He wasn't one of the paparazzi. You're not going to suggest that he's established a new life as Prince William's private doctor, are you, Ma?'

Loraine didn't answer. She looked ill. Jack could have been a terrier tied up and barking three blocks away for all the impact he had.

'Robin,' she whispered. 'That's what he called himself when he wanted to be a different person.' She looked at me. There was sorrow in her expression, and something else. Something I didn't understand.

It was only as I was driving back to Deborah's that my thoughts cleared.

Loraine Latimer knew everything.

She knew who had killed Kirsten. And she knew why.

…

'Seems to me that Simon McKee's your man,' Deborah said, opening a bottle of red wine.

I stirred the stacks of books and newspapers on the table, trying to make room for my glass. 'What man?'

'Margaret Sherman's lover. His personality sounds right. He's the right age. He was there when Kirsten was murdered; he's guilty of something. What more do you want?'

'A direct link to Kirsten's family. It's the only thing that makes sense.' I sipped my wine and wandered over to the window. Kate and Spree were tearing round the lawn together.

'Loraine Latimer sounds like one hard woman,' Deborah said.

'She's a woman with secrets, that's for sure. Trouble is, I don't know how many of them are hers. I can't see her protecting her ex-husband. But today it seemed like she knew who'd killed Kirsten – and why. I got the feeling she's going to do nothing about it. And I can't imagine why.'

'To protect her reputation? No high-profile judge wants to be involved in a scandal.'

'But even if it involves her husband – he's dead and they were separated anyway.' I frowned. 'She's cool enough to handle that.'

'Perhaps it is about her. If Kirsten found out something terrible about her mother it would explain why she was so upset.'

'I thought from the start that Loraine was involved. But there's one big problem with that. I can't believe she'd have killed her own daughter ...'

'Mmmm.' Deborah sipped her wine.

I sat for a moment thinking. Then I gasped.

Deborah looked at me. 'What?'

I think I've realised something important. It's been there all the time and I haven't bloody seen it. Kirsten lied.'

'About what?'

I said nothing, remembering Jack's unhappiness. It had seemed so destructive. So deep. And I still hadn't realised.

'I need to talk to someone who'll know. Someone who could have told me before – only I didn't know the question to ask.' I sat down and pressed my fingers against my face, then caught my chin in my hands . 'How would you like a few days' holiday, Deb? There's someone in Dunedin I want to see.'

...

Spree went into a dog home. It was more like a hotel, with the large tree-lined exercise paddock, luxurious cages with underfloor heating, and soft rugs and sheepskins spilling out of large beds. He was not pleased.

Deb, Kate and I drove south, along straight roads, through small country towns, until five hours later we caught out first glimpse of the sea, its blue water cut by whitecaps.

I felt my spirits begin to rise. Yes. It was going to work out.

'You haven't told Jack?' Deb asked.

I glanced into the back seat where Kate sprawled, apparently asleep.

'No. I haven't told anyone. Except you.'

She raised her eyebrows. 'That's a little scary.'

'You could have stayed home with a book.'

She laughed. 'No, you're right. It'll do me good to have a bit of action in my life for a change.'

'There shouldn't be any problems.' I overtook a campervan lumbering along at about 50 kilometres an hour. 'Duncan North doesn't know Kirsten's family. And he doesn't want to.'

'So what are we actually going all this way for?'

'I'll tell you later.'

Actually we didn't do much talking at all once we'd driven over the last hill and down into the valley full of houses that heralded the entrance to Dunedin. Shadows were falling from the encircling hills, enfolding the city in evening. We paused for a takeaway dinner, sitting on a park bench high above a winding street of houses. Then we joined the evening traffic, swirling along the narrow peninsula road, smelling rotting seaweed and watching black shags perched on rocks, wings outspread. We took a turn up a steep road to a castle with a sad history. The owner had shot himself years before, driven to suicide by a family scandal. He had imported Italian glass and other treasures from all over the world to build his castle. But in the end none of it mattered.

These days the castle was one of the city's tourist attractions, and outhouses in the grounds had been turned into motels. I left Kate and Deborah in front of the television and went to find Duncan North.

...

'Yes she did lie. She had to.' Duncan North leaned his elbows on the gate and looked out over the sea. He wore ancient black corduroys, gumboots and a grey homespun jersey. His face was unshaven, his eyes tired.

A black-and-white dog licked his hand. He patted the dog and it grinned at him.

Trees sculpted by the salt wind leaned toward the white weatherboard house. It looked cold and uninviting, dark in the evening shadows.

I shivered. 'Why?'

He smiled, but there was no humour in it. 'Don't you know?'

'I think I'm starting to. But I'd like you to tell it the way you saw it.'

Somewhere a dog barked and a child laughed. Duncan North stared toward the sound. 'She was afraid for him. She wanted to help him. But she knew she could do nothing. It was too late for that.'

'How did it happen?'

He shrugged. 'Loraine Latimer wanted power above all else. And she got it. Kirst disliked her mother. But when she found out what she'd done, she was devastated. Funny, isn't it?'

'You can't explain your own feelings. Let alone anyone else's.'

Duncan scratched his dog's ears. 'That's certainly true.'

'So Alex Browne ...'

'Was an innocent man – and a decent one. When he found out about Loraine he left her. But he didn't betray her. He should have.' Duncan's voice was harsh. 'I loved Kirsten and she loved me. For a while it was perfect, but then things changed. I didn't know why – she'd never tell me. She'd just say that her family would get her in the end. And she was right. They did.'

'What did Kirsten tell you about her brother – about Jack?'

'That he was his mother's creature. "He acts like he's in control," she used to say, "Loraine doesn't care. It's the rope she allows him, that's all."'

'How did she establish such a hold over him?'

'You probably can guess. By making him dependent on her for, one thing. The guy never holds down jobs, never has any money. But it's more than that. It's the emotional dependency – that's what scared Kirst.'

I swallowed. 'Is it sexual?'

'She didn't think so, no, but I did wonder that myself.'

'Even if it was just the suggestion – the possibility?'

He looked at me properly for the first time. 'Then you saw something?'

'They try to make each other jealous.' My voice was flat, stripped of emotion.

'Kirst used to say how dangerous it was. That she'd tried to help Jack, but she couldn't reach him.'

I sighed. 'Yeah, it's so obvious. God know why it's taken me so long to see it.'

Duncan put his hand on my shoulder. 'You love him, that's why.'

I shook my head. 'It was never good enough to deserve that word. Jack was using me to try and escape. I … well, I was using him too. I'd been hurt by someone and I've got a hell of a lot of pride. So love – no. Not like Kirsten felt about you. I think she really did love you. I'm so sorry.'

He looked at me and smiled. 'Thanks.'

'Kirsten told Jack she'd found out something about her father. But of course it was really about her mother. The question is, what was it?

'Kirst didn't want to tell me,' Duncan said, 'and I didn't want to know.'

Chapter 21

The best way to lie is to tell the truth.
About every detail but one.

...

Weeks ago I'd eavesdropped on Loraine Latimer's phone conversation. I hadn't understood it then, and I didn't now. What had she said? That she knew exactly what someone had done. And she could not take much more.

Something banged. I jumped and spun around. It's just a door slamming, idiot, I told myself, there's no one here.

I was at Loraine Latimer's house again. She was in court. Jack was at the dentist. I'd dropped him off myself, lied about my plans, and hurried back to the house. I knew where he hid the key and how to de-activate the burglar alarm.

Jack no longer wanted my help. Kirsten was dead. Nothing was going to help her.

None of this was rational. But I had to know. Call it guilt, hurt pride: I don't know. One of them might have been right.

I had to know.

Even if it kills you? Like it did Kirsten? The voice mocked somewhere in the back of my brain. I tried to ignore it.

I searched Loraine's study. Nothing.

Her desk was locked and I didn't have the nerve to break in. Not till I'd exhausted all other possibilities, anyway.

Jack's room was the proverbial bombsite. Clothes were strewn over the floor. A T-shirt hung on the door handle. A stack of CDs teetered in an uneven stack on the floor. The bed was unmade, the sheets grubby.

I opened his bedside drawer, grimacing at the three packets of condoms inside. Either he had more hope than me for our relationship or he had other plans. The second option seemed more likely. I scrabbled through his drawers, hating myself. He searched your desk, I reminded myself. It did not make me feel any better. And I found nothing.

Loraine Latimer's room was untidy too. That surprised me. She was so immaculate; I would have expected her room to be ordered, tasteful and cold. Instead there was confusion. Clothes were strewn on the floor. Books and papers crowded her bedside table, threatening to fall off the edge. Her bed was unmade, the duvet thrown back to reveal pale blue linen sheets. Pillows spilled onto the floor. A lipstick-smeared glass and empty coffee mug sat among a slew of make-up on her dressing table.

The walls were bare but for one charcoal painting.

It was of a young man. He was lying on a riverbank, leaning on one elbow. His shoulders were broad, his body muscular. The muscle tone belied the languid pose. It was as if he was about to spring to his feet. His lips were curved in a half-smile. He was staring straight at me.

I stared back, feeling uncomfortable. No one would ever look voyeuristically at this painting. Its subject would never let you. It was as if he could see into the room and into my mind.

I looked away.

A tumble of clothes – blouses, a green silk jersey and a charcoal jacket were thrown over the back of a chair. A silver photograph frame lay face down on the dressing table next to the coffee mug.

I picked it up.

Loraine Latimer. Young, her expression ironic, long black hair falling round her angular face like a curtain. The wedding veil was incongruous, white and frothy, garlanded in small white flowers.

Just like the flowers that had been found on Kirsten's body.

Killing her had not been enough.

Kirsten's killer had wanted Loraine Latimer to know who had killed her daughter.

Whoever it was knew she could do nothing.

Because he – or she – knew what Loraine had done.

...

I couldn't get Simon McKee out of my head. What if Deborah was right? Simon was needy and unhappy. Ali had a hold over him. Maybe it was just a control thing, with her strong personality dominating his weaker one, but what if it was more than that? What if she had found out that her husband had made an underage girl pregnant? That she'd had an abortion and died? And that her beloved brother Michael had performed the abortion? You'd think she would have been beside herself with rage against both Michael and her husband.

Maybe she had killed her brother. But surely Simon would have been the real focus of her anger, and he was still alive. Maybe she had chosen the punishment of life for him. It would explain why the poor man disliked Lake Kaniere. Having to look at it every day, knowing that down there somewhere was his lover's body. Had Ali brought him there on purpose to make him suffer? He would have found it hard to object. She had knowledge that could have put him in prison.

I sighed. I wondered if Loraine had known Simon. Or had Michael Lawrence kept all his friends in separate compartments? I'd think about that later.

But first, I had to go back to the place where this whole thing had started. With Margaret Sherman's death thirty years before. And Michael Lawrence's disappearance.

Yes ...

I recalled Loraine's face the day she found that I'd lost the tape. I felt cold thinking of it.

I was starting to understand. Michael Lawrence. Perhaps it had really started with him. Thirty years … could anyone worship someone for that long? With nothing to feed on? No sane person could. Things change. People move on, whether they want to or not. A person would have to be mad to keep an obsession alive for so long.

What had Loraine said? That he called himself Robin when he wanted to be someone else. Her tone had been amused – or maybe ironic.

I was sitting on the banks of the Avon River. The surrounding city had once been a flax swamp; now it was tamed into an English-inspired city. Willow trees and grass had replaced the flax. The curtains of green stirred in the breeze.

The easterly wind. I liked it. Its freshness restored, just as the hot nor'wester choked the soul.

Loraine was clever. She'd bent Jack's beliefs to her will. Hell, she'd nearly done it to me too.

But what had she done? And what did Sam know?

Plenty more than Kirsten had put on tape, that was for sure. The family stuff she hadn't been able to talk about. And something that had made someone kill her.

Sam was right. It was better not to know.

It was a threat that had not gone away. Instead it had slowly gained momentum. Over all these years.

I got up and stretched. It was time to go and collect Kate. Then we'd go back to the place it had all started. Lake Kaniere.

…

Kate was cross. She'd expected an ecstatic reception from Spree, but he had other things on his mind. He'd just managed to get himself into the kitchen where many bowls of food were waiting to be delivered to the canine boarders. He couldn't believe his luck. And he didn't know which one to choose, so he lost precious seconds before the kennel owner caught him.

She brought him out into the sunlight, laughing and indulgent. Spree was not pleased.

It was obvious from the dejected droop of his shoulders that if he could chose between lots of dinners or Kate and me, the dinners would win each time.

'Sorry old chap,' I scratched his head. 'No food for you till we get home. And that's hours away.'

'And it's not even home,' Kate informed him. 'Philippa's taking us to that dump by the lake.'

Spree sighed, glancing wistfully at the kitchen.

I paid his board, collected his rugs and toys, and we headed for the Coast.

Kate was tired and Spree soon crashed out completely on the back seat so it was a quiet trip.

It was pitch black when we pulled up at Jack's bach. I could hear waves scratching the gravel on the lakeshore as I unloaded the car. Spree came to life and tore off up the road. I shrugged. Yelling would be useless. He'd be back soon for his dinner.

Kate woke up, grumbling.

We snapped at each other as we carried the our things inside, but none of it had the usual edge. We were too tired.

Spree erupted inside. We fed him then crawled up the stairs to bed.

I would have expected to lie awake thinking, but I was asleep within seconds.

...

I saw Simon standing by the lake next day, so I asked him. And he told me.

The lake was energised by the wind scything down from the mountains.

'What did you expect Kirsten to do?' I asked him.

'I'd been guilty for so long – I thought she could make it better.'

'You should never have expected that. It was your responsibility, not hers!' I was surprised at my sudden burst of anger. And it was not going to help me find out what I wanted to know. I cursed myself, waiting for him to walk away.

He didn't. 'You're right,' he said, 'but I was so unhappy …'

'You really loved her. Didn't you?'

Simon stood up and stared up the lake towards the mountains. 'I thought it was a way of being close to her. She would have hated the silence here, just as I did. I thought I could share it with her. I used to look into the water sometimes, but I could never reach her.'

'Does Ali know?'

'No!' Simon looked appalled.

'How can you be so sure?'

He sighed. 'I suppose I can't – not entirely. But I never told her.'

'Did Kirsten?'

'I'm sure she didn't.'

'What was Michael Lawrence like?'

'Michael? He was a lot of things. Ambitious. Clever. Charismatic. And amoral.'

'You were his friend.' I stared down at the water.

'It wasn't really a friendship. He despised me. And yet I couldn't resist him. He was sure of himself and I wasn't. I was proud he'd chosen me to be his friend.' Simon paused and looked at me for a moment. 'You're so sure. You won't understand …'

'Try me – I'm not that bloody sure.'

'I wanted his friendship. So I let him control me. He made me feel good about myself, but then he let me see, little by little, just how much he despised me. I came to depend on him. And then he left.'

'And Ali?'

'She doesn't understand anything. She recognises no emotions but her own – and they're pretty damned sick. She's spent her life idolising her brother and he didn't return her feelings – not at all. I'm lucky compared to her. I know what real love is. I had Margaret … Ali had no one.'

'So what happened to Michael?'

Simon picked at a smear of white paint on one of the jetty boards. 'He left. I've no idea where he went. But it was all planned, every last detail. And do you know why? He wanted a new life where no one knew him as the poor son of a drunken father. But more than that, he wanted to get away from her. His sister. My wife.'

'Have you never wondered where he went.'

'When a person who knows your greatest weakness vanishes, you neither wonder nor care. You just pray to God they'll never come back. I'd forgotten him …'

'Until Kirsten came back?'

'I didn't kill her.' Simon stood up again and paced back and forth on the jetty. I have two deaths on my conscience. Margaret's. And our child's. I loved her. I should have married her, not forced her to have an abortion.'

'I don't think it was you who made that decision,' I said. 'I think it was Margaret. She was the strong one. She died and you married another strong woman.'

'You're probably right.' His voice was flat.

'Kirsten had found out about Margaret, and that's why she came here to see you. But there's a lot more to it than that.'

'Like what?' Simon looked puzzled.

'Where does Loraine Latimer fit into all this?'

'I don't know what you mean.' His voice was defensive.

I pressed him a bit further. 'Do you know who Robin is, Simon?'

He winced, then leaned forward and touched his arm. 'Leave it,' he said. 'Leave it and walk away. While you still can.'

…

So what did I have? I walked round the Kahikatea Track, deep in thought. There was little sound but for the rattle of the creek.

I had one seriously messed-up man who'd had two good reasons to kill Michael Lawrence. Because Michael had botched Margaret's abortion and caused her death. And because he had some emotional hold over Simon that he'd been too weak to walk away from.

Kirsten had found out and confronted him. So he killed her too, and Ali helped cover what he'd done, despising him even more than she had before.

But would she help him? Especially if she finally found out the truth: that Simon despised her brother; that he still loved a girl who had died thirty years ago.

I shivered, blinking in the filtered green light on the track. What a horrible marriage. Ali had brought to it an obsession with a brother who had disappeared; Simon had no love to give her. Yet they'd stayed together, had children, and then come to a lake in the middle of a rainforest to live. And they'd never talked about the things that really mattered until Kirsten had come knocking on their door.

The next day Kirsten was dead – murdered here, on this track.

I shook my head in frustration. He couldn't have done it. I was still missing whole chunks of the story.

I walked out of the bush and back to the bach. Kate had not emerged from her sleeping bag, but Spree came running out to meet me, his eyes bright. I made coffee and took it outside.

I was finding it hard to believe that Ali might have killed Kirsten to help Simon.

Robin … Robin was important. And Sam. She knew something bad. Something that had poisoned her life and allowed her to slide into alcoholism. She might have seen Ali or Simon kill Kirsten. Then one of them had attacked her to stop her telling. But she wasn't at the lake when Kirsten was killed. And anyway, I didn't believe that theory.

No. I didn't have much to base this on. Call it a gut feeling, but I knew her connection was not a casual one. It was right there at the heart of the mystery.

Kirsten had lied.

And so had Loraine.

I gasped as the puzzle formed into one clear picture in my mind.

Yes. It explained everything.

Would Sam tell me now? Or would it be too cruel to ask?

Loraine wouldn't tell me. And I had no proof.

Chapter 22

'It's over. You know that.'

'So what do you want me to do?'

'Leave. Before I do. Because it's going to be harder for you.'

'Robin...'

R turned away from me to look out the window. It was dirty and cracked. I can remember the lines, even now. Like the veins in a leaf.

'Do you hate me?' I asked.

'For what?' R's shoulders were tense.

'For what we did. If I hadn't picked up the hammer, would you have?'

'I don't know. But that's not why I'm leaving. We did it for a reason, and I'm not about to ruin my life with guilt.'

'Even if you loved ...'

'Shhh!' R whirled across the room and grabbed me by the shoulders. I winced as fingers dug into my flesh. R's eyes ... Why hadn't I seen it? Love. The word meant nothing.

Suddenly I was angry. It boiled up inside me in a fetid wave, but as the words washed out there was no relief. 'You've never loved anyone but yourself. You never will. You'll spend your life grasping new sensation and throwing them aside when you've sucked them dry. People mean nothing.'

'They do, actually. Else how would I have grown angry enough to kill someone?'

I could not speak.

R smiled. 'Whereas you've never found anyone to love. So you hang on the edges of other people's passion. You're pathetic.'

'Why do you hate me?'
'I don't. I just don't care.'

...

I walked back to the bach, Spree sailing along far in front of me.

I opened the door. Kate slept on. I made coffee. I still didn't want to ask Sam. Loraine certainly wouldn't tell, and I had no proof.

I felt sick. This story was all about manipulation. And abuse of others. I poured bran flakes into an enamel plate, sniffed the yoghurt and then added a few heaped spoonfuls to the bran.

'This place is the pits.' Kate stood in the doorway, dressed in an oversized blue T-shirt. The flesh round one of her eyes was swollen and red.

'What's wrong with your eye?'

She scowled. 'Mosquitoes. All bloody night. While you slept.'

'I didn't actually.'

'Where've you been?'

'For a walk. It was beautiful an hour ago. Sunny.'

'You shouldn't have left me.'

'You were out to it.'

'Spree.' Kate ran to the door. 'Where is he?'

'He was here a minute ago. Spree! Spree!' I yelled.

Eee. Eeee. The echo sounded across the lake. It probably startled the ducks. But it didn't attract the attention of our errant schnauzer.

Kate hurtled past me, down through the tunnel of trees and onto the road, wailing his name. Nothing happened for about five minutes, when there was a stir in the thick shrubbery and he appeared, looking as if he was ready for a fancy dress party. He was like a moving forest, garlanded with strands of rimu, while a scaly green fern frond hung over one eye.

We spent the next ten minutes reclaiming Spree from rainforest, and when we'd finished we were laughing together. Friends again. I didn't bother wondering for how long.

'What do you want to do today?' I asked.

'Go shopping.'

It was an attractive option when you lived in a village where the only things to buy were tourist souvenirs and overpriced fruit. Kate and I browsed in Hokitika's bookshops and I bought us each a sweatshirt, trying not to think of my overburdened credit card. We walked on the beach while Spree chased seagulls, then we bought fish and chips and ate them on the shore.

It was oppressive, driving back to the lake. The sky seemed darker as we left the seacoast behind and headed into the bush. Kate shivered and I glanced at her.

'We are going home tomorrow?'

'Yeah.' I didn't want to argue.

'We should have gone today.'

'It's called a holiday.'

Kate stared at me. 'It isn't. You're up to something.'

I yawned. 'Not tonight, I'm not.'

'He's not coming here is he?'

'Who? Jack? No, he isn't. It's just you and me.'

'Huh.'

We drove the rest of the way in silence. Even Spree was subdued, pegged out on the back seat instead of thrusting his nose out the window as he usually did. In his case it was simple tiredness brought on by a great seagull chase and sea air, but I could have done with a bit of exuberance from him to lighten the mood. I turned into the bush tunnel, scraping the side of the car on a rimu branch. I swore. Kate scrambled out and hauled open the garage door and I drove in, wrinkling my nose against the sour smell inside.

'What do you want to do now?' I asked Kate.

'Read.'

'I might go for a walk.'

'Okay.'

I gave Kate a dubious look. I hadn't expected co-operation, but perhaps my mind was too suspicious. She had Spree and the latest Harry Potter book. She'd be safe on her own for half an hour. It was still light outside.

'Lock the door behind me and don't open it for anyone,' I said.

Kate looked alarmed. 'Why? What's going to happen?'

'Nothing. I'm just being extra careful.'

It was a relief to get out of that gloomy bach. I walked beside the lake and scrambled down onto the shore, perching on a flat rock while flax blades tickled the back of my neck.

I couldn't explain to Kate why I'd wanted to stay here another day, because I did not understand it myself. But I'd been reluctant to leave. Now I couldn't imagine why.

The waves whispered among grey stones. A mass of grey and crimson cloud obliterated the mountains. The lake was pale blue, shot with copper from the sky.

I ran a blade of flax across my lips, savouring its smooth chill.

Someone was walking towards me. I stared in amazement. It was Jane.

She looked at me, and for a moment I thought she was going to run.

'It's okay,' I said. 'I understand.'

Emotion surged in her face and was gone. Behind her the rimu trees were gold, splashed with the last of the sunlight.

'I couldn't take it to the police.' She crunched along the shore towards me, and hesitated, then sat down, sieving gravel through her fingers.

'I never thought you would,' I said. 'It wouldn't help.'

'I listened to it.'

'And?'

Jane looked at me. 'It's hard to believe, isn't it?'

'So what did you do with it?'

'I came back here to say goodbye to her. I borrowed a canoe and rowed to the middle of the lake. I dropped the tape in … But nothing seems real.'

'You should talk to Simon. He loved her too.'

'Who?' Jane's voice was listless. She crouched by the water, touching it with her fingers, and pressing them to her eyes.

'Margaret's lover. He lives here.'

She spun towards me. 'No! How could he?'

'He didn't get to choose. You were right about him, Jane. He is weak. And punished beyond anything I can imagine. Living here all these years. In a place of nightmares.'

'He's lived here? Knowing that Margaret's body is in the lake? I don't understand how he could.'

I shivered. 'Neither do I.'

'Where's Kate?'

'Here. We're staying at Kirsten's bach. Kate's there with Spree. She's fine.'

'Has she forgiven me?'

'It's me she has the problem with. Not you.'

'I didn't help her.'

Mount Tuhua rose steeply at the edge of the lake. One of its bushy shoulders was tinted red. I looked at it. I couldn't look at Jane. 'You did help her.' My voice seemed steady, calm. 'Then you took it all away. She's getting used to that from life. I wouldn't worry about it.'

'You're angry with me.'

'No, Jane.' I scooped a handful of lake gravel in my right hand. It was cold and heavy. 'I haven't got the energy to be angry with you. It happened. We dealt with it. Who the hell cares?'

'I do.'

Something in her quiet response stung me and I turned to look at her. 'Ignore me,' I said. I'm so bloody tired my head's getting out of control.'

'You know everything. Don't you?'

'I'm guessing large chunks of it. But yes, I think I do.'

'How long are you going to stay here?'

'Till tomorrow. I promised Kate we wouldn't stay any longer.'

'I'll take her home if you want to stay.'

'Don't you want to know what this is all about?'

'Yes. But you're not ready to tell me.'

'And you're prepared to wait this time? There's nothing to find in my house.'

She flinched. 'I'll never do anything like that again. That's not why ... I just want to try and make things right with Kate.'

'Where are you staying?'

'In my tent.'

'Come round in the morning,' I said. 'If Kate wants to go home with you it's fine by me.'

Jane stood up and reached out a hand as if to touch me, then stepped back. 'Thank you,' she said. I said nothing, just sat on a rock watching her walk away.

I should have felt better. But I didn't.

...

Kate was cool when Jane arrived at breakfast time next day. Neither had much to say, so I found myself in the role of peacemaker. It irritated me. It's not something I'm good at. I inadvertently solved the problem by snapping at Kate over some triviality, instantly turning Jane into the preferred option.

They left about an hour later, Spree's nose sticking out the back window of Jane's car. I was too strung-out to feel relieved.

No breeze stirred in the clearing. The rimu trees looked as if they'd been there forever and I felt as if I would too if I didn't do something radical. I'm not sure why I was so determined to stay. It wasn't as if I had any reason to believe there was any point. This lake had kept its secrets for a long time. It wasn't about to reveal them to me. I was wasting my time.

But I stayed.

I walked. That helped a bit. I drove to town for more food, and when I returned the cloud had blown away from the lake, which was now energised by an easterly wind. Waves smashed onto the shore, the tree crowns stirred against a blue sky, and a bellbird sang.

I prepared a salad and cut thick slices of bread to go with it, uncorked a bottle of red wine and poured myself a generous glass. I leaned back in a battered brown armchair and sipped. After a while I felt my mind relaxing. I drifted for a while, thinking about nothing, but the questions were there, edging their way into my consciousness. I poured another glass of wine.

Had Jack killed Kirsten to prevent her revealing the truth about their mother? Did Loraine have that much power over him? He'd been tortured, frightened, sad. Trapped.

He'd been attacked, but he could have set those things up himself. Just as he could have followed me that night and tried to push me off the road on Arthur's Pass.

Oh, yes, it was possible. Jack had been there when Kirsten was killed. When Sam was attacked. But he hadn't known about Sam. Not until I started asking questions.

I reached for the wine bottle, then hesitated. I'd already had two large glasses, and the glow had gone. A walk would serve me better. It wasn't dark and the trees, energised by the easterly, tossed all around me. I walked for an hour, maybe more, enjoying the atmosphere, refusing to think. It was dark when I returned to the bach and I stood outside for a while, reluctant to go back in.

If Jack had killed his sister, he'd be capable of killing me too. But did he understand what he was protecting Loraine from? I didn't think so.

Jack was capable of anger. Well, weren't we all, but something about his had scared me.

I shivered. I knew I would never forget him. But it was over. Even though I knew he would come here. That's why I was hanging around. Why hadn't I acknowledged that until now?

He would tell me this time. Everything.

...

He didn't come that night. Or the next. I slept well, which surprised me. During the days I walked or borrowed Ali's canoe and explored the lake.

On the third night I knew he was coming. Don't ask me how. At midnight I went outside and stood in the tunnel of bush. It was dark, a place shielded from the moon. A morepork cried. I heard the car engine long before I saw its lights.

Jack didn't seem surprised to see me. He touched my shoulders and we stood together for several minutes. Saying nothing. I felt his breath on my cheek, but it was too dark to see his face.

I wasn't frightened any more. Despite everything I'd thought, I knew he would not hurt me. Whatever else he'd done.

'Philippa? Are you okay?'

'Yes. You?'

He shivered. 'No.'

'You haven't told her?'

'Loraine? Told her what?'

'That you know.'

'I don't know. Not everything. Do you?'

'I think so. But we'll never prove it.'

He moved closer. 'Why are you so sad, Philippa? It's more than all that. It's us, isn't it?'

'Mmmm.'

'It's over. Isn't it?'

'Yes.'

He said nothing and I reached up and touched his face. It was wet. Suddenly I was crying. We held each other and sobbed. My throat was raw, but there was no sense of release. I doubted there was for him either.

We went inside. The lamp was flickering, casting shadows onto the wall. I felt Jack move behind me, but I didn't turn round.

I knew what was going to happen and I wasn't going to fight it. Tonight I was going to do what I wanted. To hell with common sense.

Afterwards I turned, trying not to react to the sadness in his eyes.

It would never be that good again. Not with anyone. Not ever.

...

'She lived here once. Hard to believe, isn't it?' Jack handed me a mug of coffee.

'Who?'

'Loraine.'

Suddenly I was wide-awake. 'What did you say?'

'Loraine lived here. With Sam Acheson.' Jack's voice was flat. 'For a winter the year before she married Dad. She told me she needed time away from her life and was desperate enough to come here.'

Another piece of the puzzle clicked into place. 'So she lied about Robin,' I said.

Jack stared at me. 'What do you mean?'

I clambered out of the tangle of sleeping bags and dressed. Jack made no move to touch me, and I was glad.

'Your mother killed someone. And Sam helped her. Robin was an insurance.'

'Philippa, I don't know what the hell you're talking about.'

'I'm guessing.' I lifted a hand. 'There have been so many lies.'

'Just let me get this right. You're suggesting that Loraine killed Kirsten? Or was it Sam? Jesus Christ! They killed no one. Don't you understand anything? They were lesbians. In a time when that was not an option. That was their so-called crime. That's why Dad left. Because Sam never did. She was always there, on the edges of Loraine's life. She wrecked my parents' marriage.'

'How?'

'By being so bloody needy. By coming back all the time. That's what the fight was about.'

'What fight?'

'You know.' He paced around the room, and when he turned his face was angry. 'The fight I heard between Loraine and Kirsten. Sam told Kirsten about her relationship with our mother. And Kirsten came back and confronted her with it.'

'Jack, do you really think Kirsten would have cared about your mother having a lesbian relationship when she was young?'

'Did you know her well enough to know she wouldn't? She would have been angry – for Dad's sake.'

'I'm sorry.' I lifted a hand. 'You could be right. But it doesn't explain why Kirsten was killed. And it doesn't explain the attacks on you. I don't believe Sam Acheson was responsible for either. Do you?'

He shrugged. 'Not really.'

'Are you sure about Sam and Loraine?'

'What? That they were lesbians? Yeah. Loraine told me.' Jack glanced around the dusty kitchen, then walked over to the huge coal range and ran his fingers over the long-cold surface. 'Do you think she'd have spent two minutes in a place like this without some reason?'

I watched him for a few minutes. Something was different about Jack. Something had gone. But what?

'What did Loraine tell you?' I asked.

'She'd been drinking. It was last night. That's why I came here. I had to get away. She was lit. High. No one does that like Loraine. She started quizzing me about you, but I wouldn't tell her anything.'

Was that it? I wondered. Was he finally going to break free from her? No, my cynical mind screamed. Never. The ties are built of steel.

Jack paced over to the sink, turning on one of the taps. The ancient plumbing groaned as he held out a glass, which eventually filled with clear water. He drank then gave me a distant smile. 'Loraine just looked at me and said: "You're so young and so worldly, my son, yet you've yet to discover the true power of sex. It's a drug. Especially in some of its more unusual forms." I didn't say anything. So she poured another whisky and told me. How she'd seduced Sam. How she'd moved on. How Sam had never recovered. For the first time I really saw her – my mother – a seriously sick human being. It's not something the average person has to face every day.'

I thought of Sam and how damaged she was. Was that why? Could one failed relationship wreak such damage? Even given Loraine's powers of manipulation? I didn't know. But I was sure of one thing. 'You've got to get away from her, Jack. She's bad for you.'

'I know. But knowing and doing - there's such a gulf between the two.' Jack looked at me and smiled. 'But I will do it. You could help me.'

'I can't.' I hated myself but it had to be said. 'It won't work if you can't do it on your own.'

'I don't know if I can.'

'Kirsten did.' I sat by him at the table and took his hands. They were cold.

'Loraine never tried to own Kirsten. And she didn't love her – not like she loves me.'

'It's not love, Jack. Loraine loves no one. She's sick. And she hasn't told you the whole story. She's just told you enough to make you jealous. She's saying, "Look at me, look how fascinating I am, look at how people want me." But she's not telling you everything.'

'Isn't it enough?' Jack pulled his hands free. 'Sam's hanging about, she knows something about Loraine that'll wreck her career if it comes out. Christchurch is a conservative city. Maybe if it comes out that a high court judge is a lesbian, she won't make it onto the New Year's Honours list. Loraine wants to be a Dame.'

'So you're saying ...'

'That she tried to kill Sam. Yeah. And that she wanted to destroy the tape, because she was sure Sam's story was on it.'

'Maybe. But I don't believe she killed Kirsten. Do you?'

He hesitated. 'Of course not.'

'So who did?'

'I don't know. Maybe the police are right. It could have been one of her sources. It was probably someone connected to that abortion scam. The most likely person is Michael Lawrence. He did those abortions. If this comes out, he'll be ruined.'

God. Jack didn't have a clue.

'Michael is missing – he has been for years,' I said, after the silence between us became oppressive.

Behind us someone laughed.

We whirled around.

Loraine Latimer stood in the doorway.

. . .

'This place should be bulldozed.' Loraine perched on the edge of an armchair, looking as if she didn't want to trust her blue linen suit to its dusty depths. She smiled.

Jack and I said nothing.

'Aren't you going to ask me why I'm here?' She stared at her son. He didn't respond, and she shrugged. But she couldn't hide the flicker of anger. I tried to beat down the surge of hope. Perhaps he would break free of her after all.

'I thought I might recapture something.' Loraine's voice was quiet. 'But it's gone.'

'You're cruel,' Jack said.

'And you're a fool, Jonathan. I knew what I wanted and I went out and got it. You buy your own luck, even if you don't always like the price you have to pay.'

'Sam paid the price. Not you.'

'Sam?' Loraine smiled then she leaned forward and stared at her son. 'She was an adult, Jonathan. It wasn't just down to me.'

'Why did you do it, Loraine? You had Michael Lawrence. Why didn't you leave Sam alone?'

'Michael betrayed me. Sam just happened. It wasn't calculated. Relationships are never simple. I really did love her, you know. As far as I could.'

Jack went and stood by the window. 'Why did you leave her then?'

'She'd have ruined my career, but who knows?' Loraine leaned back in her chair and ran her fingers through her hair. 'Maybe I could have lived with that. If she'd been honest about what she really felt.'

Jack glared at her. 'Sam turned you down, didn't she? That's the thing you can't forgive. Was that why you tried to kill her?'

Loraine was across the room in an instant, grabbing her son by the arms and shaking him. 'You bloody fool. You weak-minded bloody fool. You understand nothing. Nothing!'

'So tell me,' Jack shook himself free of his mother's grasp.

Jack was in control of this. Not Loraine. I looked at them, feeling hope despite everything. Perhaps ... no. I didn't believe in fairy tales.

'It's ironic, really. There's only one person I ever wanted. And he's...'

'He's what Loraine?'

'He's dead. And your bloody mother killed him.' Ali McKee stood in the doorway. She was aiming a hunting rifle at Jack's head.

Chapter 23

I saw Alison McKee every day when I first came back to the lake. She was friendly. I could tell she was unhappy, but she didn't confide in me. When I met her husband I thought I understood. He was weak, self-absorbed and indifferent to her. I wondered why she stayed with him. She was so bright, so glittering, so strong.

When I found out the truth I felt terrible.

I had done it.

Ruined the life of someone who had never hurt me.

I'd lacked the imagination to see past the cardboard villain who'd betrayed R.

I'd seen nothing but my own needs.

...

'How does it feel - Robin?'

Ali had lowered the rifle. But there was no doubt in my mind that she could shoot Jack just like that if she wanted to.

'I don't know what you're talking about.'

I had to hand it to Loraine. She was cool. Even if her face was white. Without taking her eyes off Ali, she crossed the room to stand by her son.

'I want you to tell me.' Ali's springy dark hair was pulled back in a tight ponytail, tautening the skin on her cheeks. She looked ill.

'I can tell you whatever you want to hear,' Loraine said. 'No court in the country is going to convict a high court judge who's being held at gunpoint by a mad woman.'

'You killed my brother.'

Loraine laughed. 'Michael's fine. It was you he wanted to get away from, not me.'

'You bloody liar.'

'You'll prove nothing. You've killed Kirsten to feed your madness. You threatened Jonathan with those stupid games – mystery calls, blood on his car. And me. Philippa too, I dare say – because she's foolish enough to be here. Keep killing if you have to, Alison. Michael will never come back to you.'

Ali raised the gun against Jack. 'Michael will never come back. He can't, can he? He's in the bottom of this lake. Where you put him.'

'Michael betrayed me.' Loraine had not reacted to the gun, and now her voice was measured, relaxed.

'How?' Ali snapped.

Loraine stared at her for a moment, her expression contemptuous. She shrugged. 'This all started with you, Alison. Michael was beautiful, talented, intelligent. You weren't. You thought that if you had him, then you would be. You were clever. He told me about it after we'd made love one night. About all the ways you tried to make him depend on you. But it didn't work, did it Alison? He was too strong for you.'

'You're sick.'

Loraine smiled. 'Not me, my dear.'

'I loved him.' Ali's arm was shaking and she lowered the rifle.

'You stupid woman. You don't know what love is.'

'And you do?'

'Oh yes. I loved your brother. And he loved me. Never doubt that.'

'Then what about Sam?'

'Sam?' Loraine lowered herself onto a chair. 'You'll probably find it hard to believe, but I loved Sam too.'

'You don't keep the people you love though, do you? You move on to the next victim. Now it's your son.'

Loraine smiled. 'That's a different kind of love. You have children of your own – I thought you'd have known that. But then they're girls, aren't they Alison?'

'This has nothing to do with children. It's about being mad. And manipulative. I'd say you only know one thing about love: how to use it to get the things you want.'

'And what do you know about love? Your passions have been one-sided and unwanted. I pity you, Alison. I pitied you thirty years ago, and I pity you now. You loved Michael but he never loved you.'

'I could kill you,' Ali snarled.

Jack and I flinched, but Loraine did not react.

'So do it,' her voice was calm. 'With a rusty old gun that probably hasn't fired a shot since the war. In front of two witnesses. Or will you shoot us all? Evidence is easier to collect from a house than a rain-lashed bush track. You got away with my daughter's murder but you won't get away with this.'

'Who says I want to get away with it?' Ali had lowered the gun but her posture was tense, ready. 'I want justice.'

Loraine laughed. 'You'll never get it. You don't in a court of law, and you won't in a hut in the bush. The system is about winning and losing. About ego. Not about justice.'

'Why did you kill him?' Ali was screaming.

In the brief silence that followed I heard a branch rustle against the window, the sound of Jack's breathing.

'Because he betrayed me,' Loraine said. 'Or so I thought. I was angry, hurt. I can't explain it. Everything was white hot – the good times, then the bad. And then there was Sam.'

'You blame her for Michael's murder?' Ali asked.

Loraine sighed. 'I blame both of us. One way to explain it is to call it a folie a deux. Separately we'd have been harmless. Together we were dangerous.'

'You planned it?'

'Oh, yes.' Loraine moved away from her son and sat down on the edge of a dusty armchair. She stared at Ali for a moment, her face expressionless. 'It was a monstrous fantasy – but then it all came true. She wouldn't have done it without me. And I wouldn't have done it without her. He came to see me … Sam was jealous. She took to him with a hammer.'

'And you did nothing?'

'No! I helped her. He was hard to kill.'

'You evil bitch.'

'But love excuses everything – doesn't it, Alison? You're just as bad. You've stalked my son for months. You tried to kill him on Arthur's Pass – even though it was poor Philippa who was driving his car that night! You tried to kill Sam because you were scared she'd talk about Michael. You did kill my daughter. Covered her with flowers so I'd get the point. That was a terrible thing that you did. Kirsten had nothing to do with it. She had integrity. She wanted to find the truth, and do you know something? If she had, she'd have come down on your side.'

'I know that now, but it's too late!'

Loraine stared at her.

'I knew he was dead,' Ali whispered. 'The things you say are cruel. But they're true. He didn't want me. But his spirit was mine. I knew when he wasn't there any more. I knew he was dead, but I didn't know why. Not until the day your daughter walked into my house with her notebook and her questions. I killed her, but not because of you. The flowers came later: call them a postscript.'

'So why did you kill her?' Loraine asked.

'Because I loved my brother, why do you think? My Robin. You took everything from him, even the name I gave him when we were children. But do you think I was going to stand by and watch him being torn to bits? He was dead but he was my brother and I was proud of him. I wasn't going to see him feed the news story of your daughter's life. Watch him being exposed as a profiteering abortionist. That's why I had to kill her. To stop her.'

'And the flowers.'

'I wanted you to know that Michael had been avenged. He loved those flowers. You knew that.'

'How did you know that I'd killed him?'

Ali laughed. 'Sam told Kirsten and Kirsten told me. She thought I'd be grateful for her honesty. She was a crusader, but she didn't know a lot about human nature.'

'She cared about people, though, Ali.' I hadn't planned to say it but I could not keep quiet any longer. 'She was special.'

Loraine shot me an amused look, then turned back to Ali. 'She was more special than you ever knew,' she said.

'What do you mean?'

'Sam was out when Michael arrived that day. We'd talked of killing him. I hated him. Then I saw him again, and I wanted him so much. God, but he was beautiful …'

'No. No.'

'Yes, Alison. Right here in this room.'

'No! I don't believe you. How could you kill him? After that?'

Loraine smiled. 'Sam thought it was about betrayal and she was right. But the real betrayal happened after we'd written the script.'

'What do you mean?' Ali lowered the gun for what seemed like the hundredth time. 'Well?' she spat.

'Margaret Sherman meant nothing to him. She was Simon's lover, just as Michael had told me. But Michael was away a lot. He had the opportunity. Then when he told me he'd performed an abortion I didn't believe that he'd have taken such a risk for Simon. He wasn't the kind of man to risk himself for a friend. The only thing that made sense was that it was that he was the one who'd got her pregnant. What I didn't know was that he was doing lots of abortions – for money.'

'So you killed him because of this?' Ali's face was scornful.

'Of course not. Don't you understand anything? I'd come to the lake to get over him, but I hadn't – not really. Meanwhile your brother had moved on to someone else. Another rich girl. That's what he'd come to tell me. But he still couldn't resist me. He told me after we'd made love. Just before Sam came back.' Loraine paused for a moment. 'Poor Sam. She misinterpreted everything. Michael was no threat to her. He was going to leave me. If Sam had known that, she wouldn't have been so desperate. She struck the first blows.'

'Because you misled her.'

'She was right about one thing,' Loraine said. 'Something had changed while she was out that afternoon. Something major. You know what it was, don't you Alison? I can see it in your face.'

'No!'

'Yes. You worshipped your brother. Held onto a dream for thirty years. Then when you had the chance of something real, you killed it. Killed her. My daughter. And Michael's. Kirsten was your brother's child.'

'I don't believe it.'

'You won't be able to stop yourself, Alison. Just like I couldn't stop myself wanting him that day – right here, in this very bach. Think about it Alison and you'll know it's true. Afterwards he sat up in bed smoking, telling me about this young girl with money back home in Christchurch. How he wanted us both. Well I don't share with anyone. He should have known that!'

Suddenly Loraine looked completely mad. Her eyes glittered as she stared at Ali. 'It was hard getting him over the side of the boat. We'd covered him in an old tarpaulin but it tore loose and I saw his face as he went under. It was like he was looking at me in the torchlight. You know what I thought, Alison?'

I stared from her to Ali's enraged face. Didn't she see what she was doing? Ali was a killer with a rifle and Loraine was taunting her as if she was harmless.

Loraine smiled at Ali. 'I thought of the marriage ceremony he was never going to have with his rich girl. I thought of the words as I watched him disappear. It is a beautiful lake, some would say, but I see it more as a body of murk and eel-infested water.

'Do you take this man?
Lake, take my love!
With my body I worship.
Lake, destroy this body.
The lake can have you!

Loraine laughed.

Ali lifted the rifle and this time she fired.

My eardrums felt as if they'd cracked and I watched mesmerised as the spray of red flew around the room. I heard the thud as Jack's body hit the floor, then thrashed at our feet. I didn't think it was ever going to stop. Loraine threw herself on top of her son and grasped his arms, trying to stop his tortured writhing.

I screamed and screamed.

Chapter 24

God, but I'm sorry.
And how useless that is …

…

The rest of the night was a blur. All I can remember are jagged pictures.

Loraine punching the buttons of her cell phone. Swearing when she couldn't get a signal. Yelling at me to phone for an ambulance.

Me running through the bush to Ali's house - it was the only place to go – then screaming for Simon to phone an ambulance and the police.

Sirens.

Then silence.

Jack.

Jack was dead. I'd known that from the moment Ali shot him, and I felt nothing. Just this dreadful space where my emotion should have been.

'You need to grieve,' someone told me. But how do you grieve when you can't bloody feel? First my parents. Then Kirsten. Now Jack. It all seemed unbelievable some days. On other days I felt guilt – that somehow all the deaths were because of me. If I hadn't been so damn curious …

I wandered around in a daze. I answered endless questions from the police. Then the fog started to clear and I told them the whole story, right from the start. I didn't notice the way they were looking at me.

It took me days to realise what should have been obvious. They thought what I'd seen had pushed me over the edge. Their victim support woman got me referred to a psychiatrist.

'This all started with Loraine Latimer,' I told him. 'She killed Ali's brother. His body's in Lake Kaniere.'

'You've had a severe trauma,' he replied.

I argued and finally yelled at him, but it was no use. No one believed me. Ali had been arrested with the proverbial smoking gun. Loraine hadn't.

I went to stay with Deborah. She listened to me and believed me – but she was the only one who did.

'Trouble is, you have no proof,' she said.

'There was the tape.' I leaned back against a verandah post and gazed at the sky. 'But bloody Jane destroyed it.'

'And Duncan North never listened to it, so he doesn't know what was on it.'

A few days later Loraine came to see me. She bought me flowers and spoke softly to me. Like humouring a prisoner she was softening up for a killer sentence, I thought crossly.

She looked strained and sad. She'd lost her son, but not her freedom. 'What can they prove?' she asked me. 'You're the only one who heard what I said that night. The police have nothing on me – and you know something, Philippa? They don't want to find anything on me either.'

'You're forgetting Ali.'

Loraine smiled. 'Ali won't say a word. Think about it.'

I stared at her. 'If she takes you down, she takes her brother's reputation too.'

'Not only that. Killing me would end my pain. She wants me alive to savour it. She'll plead guilty, so there won't be a trial,' Loraine told me. 'Judges attract hatred. She's just someone I hurt through my career on the bench. That's what it'll look like.'

'So you'll get away with it.'

'Prison, yes. I'll get away with Michael's murder. And so will Sam. Does that make you feel better, Philippa?'

I shook my head, but not at her question. This was a woman who had seen her son shot dead but she was still functioning and in control, still her same ironic self. But then she redeemed herself, just a little.

'The only thing I have to live with is the loss of both my son and my daughter. My children for her brother. That's my punishment. It's a worse one than I've ever handed down in my entire career, Philippa.'

Loraine got to her feet and walked to the door. She made to go through it, then turned and looked at me for a moment. Then she smiled and walked out of my life.

...

'Is it true?'

'What?'

'That Kirsten was really Michael's daughter?'

'Yes.' I looked at the burn on the edge of the café table, then at the chocolate froth on Mark's cappuccino.

'So who was Robin?'

'It was what they called each other. Michael – and then Loraine. That's why Loraine used the name. As insurance. Robin was a killer – of whom, it wasn't clear. Michael had disappeared. So he could have been Robin. The bad guy. Disappeared, not dead.

Mark shook his head. 'I can't get my head around it.'

'Neither can I.' I shut my eyes.

Jack writhing at my feet. It had gone on for so long.

'What'll happen to them?'

'Who?'

'Loraine and Ali?' Mark's voice was patient.

'Ali will go to prison. Loraine will go back to being a judge.' I started to laugh but the sounds coming out of my throat were more like sobs.

'Philippa, what are you going to do?'

'Go home. Back to being a glacier guide.'

'How do you feel about that?'

'Good. Neutral. I don't really feel anything.'

'Is Jane going to stay with you and Kate?'

'I don't know,' I said. 'I can't see why she'd want to hang around. It's not her fault, but I've never liked the woman and I bloody hate the things she'd remind me of. I want to forget all this and move on.'

'You don't need me to say this, I don't suppose,' Mark said. 'But I'm your friend, Philippa. I really care about you.'

'I know you do.' I could feel my eyes brimming with tears.

'And Jack?'

'Jack's dead. I'm alive. That's all there is.'

...

Actually, it wasn't.

Not quite.

There was something else. One last way in which I might obtain the proof I needed. I hadn't scored well so far. I'd had some hard proof and I'd lost it. Kirsten's tape was at the bottom of Lake Kaniere.

But so was something else.

Michael Lawrence's murdered body.

It had been there for decades but that didn't mean it would have vanished. It was a glacier lake. A deep one. There was a chance it was still down there.

I stopped off in Hokitika on the way home. I knew a man there who was a keen fisherman, a bit of a character.

I found him in his back yard sewing up a whitebait net. He was sitting on an upturned bucket, a transistor radio blaring at his side. He wore a multi-patched jersey that had once been dark blue, but now sported various clashing colours. His eyes were bright, but his body was ruined. He had the heavy beer gut of the hard drinker and when he got to his feet to greet me his movements were stiff.

'Is it you, Philippa Barnes?'

'Yes. How are you, Dan?'

'Much the same. Had me fiftieth wedding anniversary at the weekend.'

'I don't know how people do it,' I said. 'How does any couple stay together for so long?'

'Nowhere else to bloody go,' he grunted.

I laughed.

'You had lunch, girl?'

'No…'

'Come on in, I'll make us a brew. Molly's away in Christchurch with our Julie. Husband's left her. No loss, to my mind, but she's upset, course she is.'

I followed him inside murmuring something non-committal. There was little sign of the fisherman's personality in this neat kitchen. His life was in his back yard, and I'd have preferred to stay out there. I watched him potter around by the stove and accepted a plateful of stew when I'd have much rather had a coffee. It was surprisingly good. I hadn't realised how hungry I was.

'Now, girl,' Dan said. 'You didn't call in just to pass the time of day. What are you after?'

I choked on my last mouthful, then grinned at him.

'I know, I know, I've been a slack visitor.'

He thumped my shoulder. 'Only kidding. You've had your troubles.'

'They don't seem to be quite over,' I sighed. 'If you dumped a body in Lake Kaniere would it still be there in fifty years.'

'Looking to immortalise your Aunty Jo are you?' he chuckled. 'I wouldn't worry if I was you. No one'll thank you for it.'

I laughed. I'd forgotten that he knew the most unlovable of Susan's sisters.

'No. I'm not thinking of murdering anyone. It's something that happened a long time ago.'

I gave him a brief outline of what I'd told the police. I have to say, he was a much more appreciative audience.

'You don't seem surprised,' I said, when I'd finished.

He sighed. 'Nothing much surprises me any more. But you've got some big problems here. One, you don't know where they dumped this chap. Two, the lake's so bloody deep you'd never get a diver to the bottom. Wouldn't see anything down there, either. It's bloody murky.'

'I was wondering if the eels would have eaten him. Do they go down that deep.'

'Go down? They never bloody well come up. They live down there and they're monsters. They can't come to the surface, can't handle the changing pressure. Like what divers get but in reverse. Catch one of those in your net and they'll pull it right down with them.'

'They sound like monsters.'

'Huh. I like that. Anyway, girl, you ever been fishing for eels? You toss a freshly killed body down to them and they'll be there in minutes – never mind years. And never mind any wrappings either. They can smell blood from 40 watery miles.'

I sighed. 'I read somewhere that eels only eat fresh meat and they can't easily eat a big thing like a human body.'

Dan snorted. 'You ever seen them go for a sheep's head? Nothing wrong with their teeth if you ask me.'

'So there's no way I can prove this.'

'Leave it, Philippa Barnes, that's my advice. What'll you gain? Prison for the judge, but one hell of a lot of suffering for innocent people. How about those poor girls who had abortions? You didn't do that for nothing back then.'

'You're right Dan,' I said. 'Think I'll go back to the glacier. That's something I can deal with.'

'You think?'

I laughed. There didn't seem to be anything else to say.

...

I walked in white silence.

The icy grass crunched. My bare feet burned but I walked on, out into the paddock, then turned to face the mountains, luxuriating in the cold sunlit air.

Spree burst onto the scene, breaking apart the silence, and I caught his mood and capered with him, not pausing until I was panting.

A small, disapproving figure watched from the doorway. I laughed and waved. My sister didn't respond. She was burning toast when I walked in the kitchen door, and her shoulders were stiff.

'You've probably got the menopause,' she remarked.

'I'm decades too young for that!'

'Some people get it early.'

I don't think it has quite that effect.' I laughed.

'Why are you so happy?' Kate dug a margarine-covered knife into the honey, a habit that never failed to annoy me.

'I just like winter. It's a brilliant day out there.'

'So you go dancing in the frost. And you thought Mum and Dad were crazy.'

'At least I haven't fallen off a mountain.'

Kate thumped the fridge shut and eyed me over the rim of a glass of milk. She said nothing, and I shrugged and put coffee in the plunger pot and scrabbled in the pantry for my cereal. Kate passed me the yoghurt and we sat together, eating our breakfast.

It felt strangely companionable, but I didn't want to risk anything so I remained silent. Jane had gone the week before. She had left Franz Josef altogether. I didn't know where she was going. Kate didn't seem worried, which suited me just fine.

'When are we going to Castle Rocks?' she asked.

'Any time,' I said. 'Whenever Tim's free.'

'Why does he have to come?'

'Because if I'm taking you and Sally, I need another adult along. It wouldn't be safe otherwise. We could go this weekend.' I got up and peered out the window. It looked as if it would never rain again, but I knew how deceptive that was.

'You're not going to end up going out with Tim are you?' Kate sounded like a tired adult, worn out with the stupidity of youth.

I shook my head. 'I'm not going out with anyone. Ever.'

'Oh yeah?'

'Kate, he's my boss. And my friend. I'm not going to wreck all that for a fling.'

She looked as if she was about to argue, then shrugged and began assembling her lunch for school. After she'd gone, I wandered round the house, aimless yet strangely happy.

I'd got myself back over the last few months. It wasn't a lot to celebrate, but I could survive without surrounding myself with people. I wasn't back to liking my own company. But I could live with it.

The next morning was frigid. Sun illuminated the ice and snow high above us, but it did not reach down into the cold grey valley. Sally and Kate, buried in wool and fibrepile, tramped along in silence. Tim strode along beside me, his ice axe tucked under his arm. I shivered as the chilled air bit though my layers of clothing and touched my body.

On the glacier a pinnacle collapsed in a shower of sparkling ice.

Jack and I had had a summer together. That was all. A relationship given no depth by changing seasons. Unrounded. Unreal. No. It had been real. Else why was there so much bloody pain? I had worried about feeling nothing when it happened, but that hadn't lasted for long.

I'd dreamed of him again last night. It was always the same dream. He was standing by the sea looking at me. I tried to walk towards him but I couldn't move. He smiled, and then became angry. I couldn't respond to any of it. So he turned and walked away.

Tim was looking at me and I dragged my thoughts back to the present as we walked up to the glacier, attached crampons to our boots, then crunched our way up the terminal face. We didn't hurry and I felt the tension leave me as I gazed into blue crevasses and listened to the faint sound of water flowing beneath the ice.

Eventually we reached the bottom of the steep and jagged Defiance Ridge.

'We're not going up there are we?' Kate asked.

Even Sally looked subdued.

No one spoke much as we began the climb, but after a while Kate began to complain. I tried to ignore her as I stretched my legs upwards, flexing my knees to ward off cramp. My pack lurched on my back like a dead body.

'Now I remember why I haven't been up here for years. It's a climb through hell,' I said as we paused for a chocolate break.

'You got that right.' Sally eased her pack off her back 'How much longer?'

I sighed. 'Another hour. Maybe more.'

'Well that's bloody marvellous.' Kate glared at me.

'You're the one who wanted to come here,' I reminded her.

'You didn't tell me how hard it would be.'

'Life is hard,' I snapped.

'Don't I bloody know it.'

Tim coughed.

'Don't worry,' Sally said. 'They fight all the time.'

I laughed and hoisted my pack onto my back. My shoulders flinched, but there was nowhere for them to go.

We climbed. I got my second wind and started to feel happy again. Kate seemed better too. Sally toiled in silence. Tim strolled. There was no other word for it.

We scrambled over the last of the stones and onto the sloping alpine pasture that clothed the ridge. The leaves and tussocks not buried in snow were glazed in ice.

'There's the hut,' Kate yelled.

'Cool,' said Sally.

The door creaked as Tim opened it, and Kate wrinkled her nose as she looked at the spartan bunks and rough wooden table in the centre of the room. I fired up the gas cooker and we cooked up pork chops and a rich steamed pudding.

We sat around reading for a while after that.

'Philippa? Can we go out?' Kate looked at me, her expression a curious mix of defiance and entreaty.

'Okay.' I scrabbled for my boots and pulled on my fibre pile jacket. Sally and Tim were in their sleeping bags. They made no move to join us.

Kate took my hand as we stepped out of the door, into a freezing sunset. I gasped as the cold air sliced into my body, then gazed at the pink light slipping down from the mountains, washing across the snow till it reached our feet.

I gripped my sister's hand and we stood in silence for a moment. Then she tugged me on, up towards the snowy ramparts of the Castle Rocks.

I didn't know what Kate was doing, but I knew it was important. I felt strangely peaceful. As if I'd been waiting for this for a long time; as if things were going to come out right. The pink light had faded, but its glow remained.

We looked through the turret-like rocks down onto the glacier.

Kate looked at me, and I saw that her eyes were full of tears.

'What is it?' I whispered.

She swallowed and turned away, pulling something from her pocket. Then she began to climb again, close to the edge. I wanted to scream at her to come back, and my heart hammered as I watched her small body move against the darkening sky, but it was as if my voice had frozen. She turned and beckoned, and I climbed up behind her. The ground fell away from our toes, a sheer cascade of rock vanishing into darkness.

Kate opened the packet and I gasped as I recognised the glossy dark lock of hair.

'You and Kate are close. That means a lot to me.'

I saw Susan again as she'd been that last morning, her long hair falling down her back in a single plait. Strangely reluctant to leave, or so it had seemed.

I looked at my sister and saw her lips tremble as she took an untidy tangle of fair hair from the packet.

I saw Liam running his fingers through his hair as he enthused about something wildly impractical.

Kate had cut the hair the day of their funeral.

Now she lifted her hand, slowly opening her fingers. We watched in silence as the wind took the strands of hair and mixed them, before whirling them away towards the glacier.

We stood close, huddling against the cold.

'Now they'll be free again,' my sister said.

Susan had been killed when Kate was so young. Yet somehow Kate had known her spirit.

'I'm sorry,' I whispered. 'I should never have buried them. We should have brought their ashes here, but I hated them for dying. So I took them to a dreary graveyard out of sight of the mountains.'

'Do you still hate them?'

'No. It's all gone.'

'Philippa? I'm sorry. I've been horrible to you.'

'I haven't been great either.'

A gust of wind hit us and we retreated from the edge. I cast a last look downwards. 'Stay free,' I whispered into the night air. I imagined our parents' spirits out there. It made the rock and snow seem warm.

Kate cried then and I held her, gazing down towards the hut.

It was strange to step inside into warmth and light. I felt as if we'd come back from another world.

'Sorted, are you?' Sally looked up from her book. 'You two have wanted your heads banged together for years.'

...

Sam left Lake Kaniere, telling no one where she had gone. One day a small parcel arrived in the mail. It was a worn school exercise book. I opened it slowly and started to read: I've come back, though I said I never would ... I fell into her dark story and when I closed the book I thought I understood how it had all happened.

...

A week or two later Loraine Latimer was in the headlines.

Dame Loraine Latimer had lost her children, but she'd achieved her dream.

She was a torch bearer for women and the New Zealand justice system, the newspapers said. Her unfailing integrity, her commitment to truth was a challenge for others to aspire to. Dame Loraine was said to be thrilled at the honour. She planned a small celebration at her home with her friends. Well, she had no family left.

A week later she hanged herself.

...

On a clear day the glacier lives. It creaks and groans with its own relentless flow, like an animal moving through its underground liar. Blue light glows in the surface hollows. Ice bridges break or turn into tunnels and caves. Ice is just water. The waters of the lake swallowed the bodies of Margaret and Michael, and the glacier could do the same. A slide into any of the dark crevasses that cut the ice could be fatal.

A party of my clients are leaning dangerously over a convoluted hole to glimpse sunlight filtering through cracks in the ice. They talk and their voices are awed. I've heard it all before, but suddenly it feels amazingly good just to be alive. The sun strikes crystals in front of me and I watch the patterns changing. I think of my parents without pain. They live on in us - and they always will.

Author's Note

There are only two factual characters in Assigned to Murder - the rugged environment of Westland and Spree (aka Pete) the giant schnauzer.But it has only been possible to make the other characters breathe by taking sparks, impressions and inspiration from real life and turning them into fiction. The people who live in these pages, though imaginary, have become very real to me - and I hope they will to you, the reader, as well.

Glacier Murder

Trish McCormack

Philippa Barnes mystery 2.

Available in print and ebook editions

What do you do when you need to escape from your life? Vivien Revell didn't intend to die. She was conflicted and scared but she was also creative and clever. She should have got away but years later Philippa Barnes discovers her mangled body in a crevasse on the Franz Josef Glacier. It looks like an accident but Vivien's friend Julia is convinced she was murdered and persuades Philippa to investigate. It soon becomes clear that someone is determined to keep Vivien's story hidden. A brutal murder brings a large police team to the village and as connections are made with the past more lives are threatened. In a case where empathy is dangerous Philippa discovers greater depths than she ever imagined in human relationships

Cold Hard Murder

Trish McCormack

Philippa Barnes mystery 3

Available in print and ebook editions

The darkness felt tangible. Like it was pressing against my blind eyes … We were going to die here. Slowly, slowly.

Two people struggle on a ledge high above the surge pool at Punakaiki's Pancake Rocks. One falls to their death, beginning a sequence of violence as Department of Conservation ranger Matt Grey announces plans for a commercial tourism venture bitterly opposed by the local community. More people die, and it seems their murders are motivated by something more personal than a threat to the integrity of the national park. But the trail is as cold and twisted as some of the park's most labyrinthine caves. Philippa Barnes is asked to do some unofficial sleuthing, which is not welcomed by the police. She delves into the lives of some strong-willed individuals, many of whom have secrets, uncovering a dark story that resonates with events in her own life. But caught in a desperate struggle deep underground, has she run out of time to stop a determined killer?

More about Philippa and her world

Find out the latest on Trish's writing on her Facebook page
Assigned to Murder – Trish McCormack – Community
www.trishmccormack.com